BALL BOY

Copyright © 2021 by Paul Shirley

Cover art by Scott Shaffer
www.asyouwishpro.com

Fourth Bar Books
1932 S Shenandoah #2
Los Angeles, CA 90034

ISBN-13: 9780578800356

Printed in the United States of America

First Edition

14 13 12 11 10 / 10 9 8 7 6 5 4 3 2 1

BALL boy

by Paul Shirley

Also by Paul Shirley

Can I Keep My Jersey?
Stories I Tell On Dates

"That's just the way it is. You need a mythology."

- Cleopatra "Patra" Patterson

"I'm not just going to assume that some outsider should be an insider. You know what I'm saying?"

- Bobby Murphy

"Basketball, whose grace comes not beneath a helmet, but in full view of one's fellow man."

- Desmond Rutherford

For Jim, Tim, Mark, Dan, and Yehuda

BALL

boy

A Novel

PAUL SHIRLEY

CHAPTER

1

The sun was relentless. A siren whined in the distance. A traffic copter whapped overhead.

In other words, it was a Friday like a lot of Fridays in the low-slung Los Angeles suburb of Reseda. With one important difference. On *this* Friday, Gray Taylor was going to make his move. He would be charming and romantic and Stefanie Espinosa would probably want to kiss him.

But first he had to get to her.

Gray was accomplishing the task of getting to Stefanie Espinosa on a skateboard that looked like it was being controlled by someone who didn't like him very much. His skinny arms were flailing. His black hair was a mess. And the board itself was veering dangerously close to the edge of the faded crosswalk on Ventura Boulevard.

"Watch it!"

This came from the driver of a silver Camry that screeched to a stop just in front of the crosswalk.

"Sorry, Mr. Benitez," said Gray.

"Are you one of mine?"

"Yessir! It's me, Gray! Third hour!"

Mr. Benitez's fingers tapped the edge of the Camry's window. "Be careful on that thing, Gray."

The light turned green. Mr. Benitez hit the gas. And Gray slapped the board back onto the pavement, letting go of the snub. He had more important things to think about.

Stefanie Espinosa.

Del Taco.

The message in his backpack.

And this time, in this crosswalk, Gray caught a line. His knees were bent and he was strong. His feet were centered and he was balanced. His arms were out but not too far out and he was doing it, he was skating! Or he was, until an empty Flamin' Hot Cheetos bag fluttered across the pavement and tangled with one of his front wheels, sending him to the pavement like a man falling off a ladder.

Randy, the vagrant who was always on this corner, peered over the blue raspberry Slurpee he was nursing. "Damn chief, you alright?"

Gray looked down at his hands, where bits of the street were now embedded.

You can go down. But get right back up.

That was something Gray's dad had said, back when he'd been around to say things.

"I'm fine," said Gray. "But thanks, Randy."

"The hell? You know my name?"

Gray's blue eyes flamed like they did when he was annoyed or agitated. But he stopped himself from what he wanted to say, which was that *of course* he knew Randy's name. He'd seen him every day, twice a day, for the past three months.

"See you, Randy," said Gray. Under his breath, he added, "Maybe."

And then Gray was back on the board, his eyes on the Del Taco where he knew Stefanie Espinosa went after school on Fridays.

Two years before this, in seventh grade, Gray had held Stefanie's hand. It had been terrifying and exhilarating and quite possibly the best moment of his life—such a great moment that he'd forgotten to savor it, assuming it would happen again. But it hadn't happened again. They'd lost each other in the big Reseda high school, mixed like nuts in a bowl. Then Gray's mom made her pronouncement: if she couldn't get a job they had a month left in Reseda. Then the month became three weeks and Gray was still reassuring himself. His mom would find something. Then it was two weeks and that was still 14 whole days—14 opportunities to do something about Stefanie. Then it was one week. And now, a weekend. That's why the sign was in his backpack, folded neatly into quarters so it would fit inside a navy Mead folder he'd nabbed from a supply closet.

SATURDAY
NOON
BELLWETHER
MEET ME THERE?

Bellwether being a coffee shop on Ventura that doubled as a bar at night. Neither Gray nor Stefanie was old enough for the drinks the place served after six. But that was part of the charm.

They could get cappuccinos or lattes and pretend they were old enough to saddle up to a bar. And maybe that would lead to Stefanie holding his hand again. And maybe there'd be that kiss. And maybe if Gray had to move it wouldn't be for long and he and Stefanie would send each other messages and that would actually bring them closer and when he got back they would be a real thing. Or maybe he wouldn't have to leave at all. His mom could be pretty charming and when he got home maybe she'd have good news for a change.

Then Gray was rolling over a crease in the asphalt and into the Del Taco parking lot and it was time to forget about his mother and jobs and what would happen when he got home. Stefanie was in her window seat, her straight brown hair framed by the red trim, and Gray had one concern and one concern only: getting the sign out of his bag and charming Stefanie Espinosa.

He jumped off the board and unzipped his backpack, happy the zipper didn't catch like it sometimes did. He yanked the sign from the folder. Quarters, halves, and now unfurled completely, like a flag in battle. He lifted the sign, extending his arms like he'd practiced.

And now Stefanie Espinosa wasn't just *looking* his way. Stefanie was *pointing* his way. It was working, just like he'd planned! Because, yeah, he could have DMed her or Snapped her or even WhatsApped her. But Stefanie Espinosa got plenty of those. That's why this had been such a good idea.

Except, what was this?

A head was popping in front of Stefanie.

Eyes were following her finger.

An arm was snaking her shoulder.

Gray felt the humiliation wash over him like a bucket of mop water. The head, the eyes, the arm: these belonged to Chuy McMuffin, one of those kids who was two years ahead of everyone else in both wisdom and testosterone.

Now Chuy was tapping Stefanie's shoulder and pointing at Gray, both of them laughing.

Gray heard a voice behind him.

"Hey man, you can't do that!"

Still holding his sign, Gray turned to find the voice, confused. He was being humiliated but he wasn't doing anything *wrong*.

Gray was right. It wouldn't have made much sense for the man to be yelling at him—there's no law against 14-year-olds making grand romantic gestures in fast-food parking lots.

And sure enough, the man *wasn't* yelling at Gray. He was yelling at Randy the Vagrant, because Randy the Vagrant was at the nearest corner of Ventura Boulevard, peeing into the street.

Gray spun back to the Del Taco as the truth dawned on him.

Stefanie and Chuy were looking at Randy.

Pointing at Randy.

Laughing at Randy.

They hadn't even seen him.

The apartment looked like most of the apartments in this section of Reseda. It was neither old nor new, neither white nor tan, and while there was a swimming pool in the concrete courtyard, it wasn't big enough for anyone to use.

Gray propped his skateboard against the wall next to the front door and slung his backpack onto the low couch they'd found at Goodwill. The backpack tipped over and Gray's sign—now crumpled at the corners—peeked out.

Gray righted the backpack, stuffing the sign further into the pouch. He'd considered flinging it into the Dumpster behind the Del Taco after he'd fled the scene—all those civilians gathered to watch a homeless man pee in the street. But as he'd skated away he'd realized that this wasn't all bad. There might be a next Friday.

"Hon, is that you?"

Nicole Taylor was in one of the metal chairs that sandwiched the table on the patio in back of the apartment. She was leaning over a mug, her hands in her lap. She seemed shorter than the five-foot-ten-inch catalog model she'd once been.

As Gray slid into the metal chair across from her, she asked how the ride home had gone.

Gray flashed the palms of his hands, which still contained several pieces of asphalt.

"Gray! What happened?"

"Pothole," said Gray.

"You could have broken your wrist!"

"But I didn't," said Gray. He flexed one of his skinny arms. "Young. Strong."

His mom grinned and this grin gave Gray hope. Maybe it *had* worked out at the tiny pharmacy her friend Esther had discovered in Van Nuys. Gray congratulated himself for not tossing the sign.

But then Nicole Taylor's green eyes started blinking and she was wiping at one of those eyes. She rocked in her chair. It squawked against the concrete.

"I thought this one was different," she said. "Esther said they wouldn't care."

"So that's it," said Gray.

"Unless."

"Unless what?"

"Unless I call your dad."

Gray stood and slid open the patio door. It squealed as its wheels navigated the dusty track. This squeal followed Gray to the cupboard where his mother kept her tea. That cupboard: he jerked it open.

Sharply. Curtly. Those were the sorts of words they were learning in Mr. Benitez's class.

Gray took the bright orange kettle from the dish drainer where his mother had left it, thinking back to the Target trip when she'd found it.

"Look how pretty!" she'd said, pulling it out of the box.

Gray had shared a look with his father and his father had smiled in his small, furtive way and even though Gray was only 8 back then, in that moment he'd learned something about being a man—that it didn't matter that it seemed silly whether the kettle was orange or black or silver or made of solid gold. What mattered was that *she* liked it.

Gray fired a burner and put the orange kettle on to boil.

Impotent.

That was another word they'd learned in Mr. Benitez's class. It was a word that had inspired a round of tittering laughter from the back of the room.

Mr. Benitez had planned on this. "Au contraire," he'd said. "It's not just that."

Mr. Benitez had gone on to explain that the origin of the word was its Latin root: *potentum*—powerful, strong, having an influence. *Im*potent meant only that you felt like you had no power, no strength, no influence. That you were not living up to your *potential*.

Gray took a tea bag from the bin. Chamomile, because it was the afternoon. He draped it over a fresh mug and tapped his fingers on the counter, like Mr. Benitez on the car window.

After a month of trying, his mom hadn't been able to get a job with her degree in pharmaceutical tech. According to what everyone said (except Esther, apparently) it was impossible in LA unless you were a full-fledged pharmacist. So now they would have to move to the far-off state of Kansas, where she was from and where her parents had a place waiting for them.

Unless.

Unless she called Fausto, after three years, five bouts of back-sliding, a half-dozen haircuts, and a dozen Instagram posts *about* those haircuts.

Gray poured the boiling water over the teabag as the vision came to him. It was like a movie. He had to go to the living room, grab his skateboard, let the door bang shut behind him, and take off down Ventura to the Ralphs parking lot that was opposite the Del Taco. He'd buy a Mountain Dew and sit behind the Dumpster and listen to the workers complain about customers. Later, he'd do some more sitting, under a bridge, brooding. He'd find (and try) a cigarette. He'd meet some older kids and they'd take him to a party in Woodland Hills and they'd crash that party and he'd get drunk for the first time and he'd kiss someone not named Stefanie Espinosa. And throughout, he'd be wearing a blacked-out Dodgers hat. Which he would turn around backward.

In the process, he'd teach his mother a lesson, which was that just because things weren't going well for *her* didn't mean

GRAY

You can just uproot me, *Mom!*

But Gray wasn't very good on his skateboard. And he didn't have a blacked-out Dodgers hat. More important: Gray was tired of being the kid everyone looked past. He was tired of being impotent.

So he picked up the mug.

He yanked open the sliding door.

He set the tea in front of his mother.

He said, "I'm ready."

On Saturday, there was a U-Haul to rent and big boxes to pack. Although not as many as might have been expected because once Nicole Taylor had recovered from her rejection by the proprietors of Crescent Heights Compounding, she'd decreed that they were packing light, moving fast, changing everything. She'd seen a show on Netflix about this. And she used the battle cry from that show as she pushed Gray—reminding him over and over to leave it behind if "it doesn't spark joy!"

By Sunday afternoon they were packed and ready. A pause in the proceedings found them standing in the patch of yellow grass in front of the apartment building.

"Mom," said Gray. "The car."

"Oh my," said Nicole Taylor.

"Does it spark joy?"

Nicole Taylor spun her blond hair into a messy bun as she gazed at the car in question: her 12-year-old Honda Civic, red in some places and—thanks to the merciless Southern California sun—yellowish-orange in most places.

"It does not."

So Nicole Taylor drove the Civic to a used car lot (of which there were many in this part of Los Angeles County) and sold it for more than it was worth. Then they got into the U-Haul and they were off, out to the 101 and then to the 134 and then to the 210 and for a while, it felt to Gray like maybe they were taking a rare trip to Pasadena. But soon they were passing Pasadena and they were passing Ontario and they were passing Rancho Cucamonga and Victorville and then they were in the desert, yellow lights fading behind them and the dark sky expanding above them.

"Mom," said Gray, as the Mojave night turned blackish-blue. "What's your town's name again?"

"You mean *our* town."

"Right. That."

"Beaudelaire," said Nicole Taylor.

"Bo-duh-*lair*," said Gray.

Nicole Taylor glanced at her son, then back to the highway. A sign announcing that Las Vegas was 212 miles away flashed green in the U-Haul's headlights.

"I don't get it," she said.

"It's our new headquarters. Bat cave. Lair. Bo-duh-*lair*."

Nicole Taylor reached across the seat, running a hand through Gray's hair.

Gray closed his eyes, selling his mother on the charade that he was slipping into sleep. He didn't need to worry her. He could do plenty of that himself. Because what had he gotten himself into? When they got to Beaude*laire* he would have to start all over. New friends, new school, in the middle of the semester, in *Kansas*.

He'd been to Kansas twice to see his grandparents. And there was nothing wrong with the place. It was just so quiet. And there weren't any Stefanie Espinosas there. Or Espinosas of any kind. Or anybody like an Espinosa. Did they even allow people like him in Kansas? He'd seen the videos about walls and brown people and white people.

Gray cracked an eyelid, gazing at his mother in the light of the highway. At least she looked like she looked: tall, blonde, green eyes. Probably, they wouldn't even be able to tell where his dad was from.

Probably.

Nicole Taylor leaned into the space between the U-Haul's long dashboard and its tall windshield, wiping at the condensation that had frozen there.

"Sure you don't want me to come with you?"

"Yeah, Mom," said Gray. "On my first day at a new school in a new town in a new state, I want to show up with my mom holding my hand."

"Sorry, jeez. I wasn't planning on holding your *hand*."

Gray rubbed *his* hands on his pants—a pair of hound-stooth-patterned slacks his mom had found at a store that sold clothes previously used in television productions. He'd never worn them back in Reseda.

Then, before he could second-guess the confidence he'd been mustering for the past three days, Gray got out of the U-Haul. He shut the oversized door and marched up a sidewalk sprinkled with frozen acorns to the stone monolith that was Beaudelaire High School. It looked like something out of a movie about castles. The walls were made of limestone blocks. The windows were tall and narrow. And the oak doors waiting for Gray were ten feet tall, like they were protecting a king, his knights, and the townspeople.

Gray took one last look at the gray U-Haul. Its near side was emblazoned with an advertisement for the state of West Virginia. It seemed like a miracle that West Virginia wasn't one of the states they'd driven through on the three-day trip that had featured nights in Cedar City and Denver.

An icy pellet skittered off Gray's cheek.

His hand went to his face as his eyes went to the sky. This wasn't snow—they'd seen snow in the mountains. It was called "sleet."

Gray took hold of the iron handle embedded in the tall wooden door nearest him. He curled his hand around the handle, imagining it was attached to a sword sticking out of a stone. Because that's what Gray had decided as the western half of the United States had unspooled in front of the U-Haul. This was going to be an epic quest involving rebirth and rediscovery. And maybe some dragon-killing, of the metaphorical kind.

But then, before Gray could pull his sword from the stone, the *other* tall wooden door swung open, revealing a silver-haired man in a blue blazer and tan chinos.

"Well now, who do we have here?"

Gray looked at his own hand. Then at the iron handle it was attached to. Then at the man.

"I'm Gray Taylor."

"Well, Graytaylor, you going to stand there in the cold?"

Principal Peter Patterson let go of his door. Gray put out

his arm and the force of the ten-foot door spun him into Beaudelaire High School like one of the tumbleweeds that had blown across the highway in eastern Colorado.

Gray caught his footing on the tile floor in time to catch sight of a different man—a man leaving the hallway he'd tumbled into. This man was wearing a bright blue windbreaker. He moved like a penguin, his hips dipping up and down.

"That's Coach Bickle," said the principal, following Gray's eyes. "Drilling down on some details. Pep rally at the end of the period. That's why I was in the hallway. Then I heard you at the door and thought, *Who could that be, in the middle of second period?* I don't open the door for every person who comes to it. That would be absurd, for the principal. Say, never mind *me*. What are *you* doing here?"

"I think I'm supposed to go to school here," said Gray. "We got an email?"

"That's outstanding news!" said Peter Patterson. "Let's get you inside to see Mrs. Rutherford."

Gray followed Principal Patterson through his office (messy desk, high-backed chair, wall covered in diplomas) and into the school's main office: thin carpet and white metal desks and the smell of old coffee and the principal speaking in his almost-shout.

"Mrs. Rutherford, have I got a surprise for you!"

"No surprise," came a voice from behind a monitor. "This must be Gray Tor-"

"Taylor!"

Gray clapped a hand over his mouth. It had come out louder than he'd planned. Technically, his name *was* Gray Torres because Torres was Fausto's last name. But he'd been going by Taylor for three years now.

The school's secretary, Mrs. Rutherford, rose from behind the monitor. She was wearing a tan dress that looked like it had been sewn on.

"Mr. Patterson," she said. "I think we have this under control."

The principal bowed. "It's been delightful to make your acquaintance, Gray *Taylor*. But Mrs. Rutherford, before I skedaddle, what's his first class today?"

Mrs. Rutherford bent to the monitor, her movements catlike thanks to the yoga studio where she was a regular.

"Physical Science," she said.

"I think you'll be impressed by the instructor," said Mr. Patterson. "Now, for tomorrow, the day starts at 8:15, not 9:30."

Mr. Patterson's eyebrows went up once, twice, and then he was gone, leaving Gray alone with Ramona Rutherford.

"Thanks," said Gray.

"For what?" said Mrs. Rutherford with a sly grin. Her printer jerked into action. "His wife. That's the teacher he's talking about."

"His wife is a teacher here?"

"Where are you coming from, Mr. Taylor?"

"Reseda, California," said Gray. "LA, basically."

"Probably a few hundred in your class?"

"Eight," said Gray. "Hundred, I mean."

Mrs. Rutherford tapped at a few keys. When she was done, she turned her desktop's screen so Gray could see it. One of her long, pink nails pointed at the cursor. It was blinking under the 7 in the number 37.

She deleted the 7 and changed it to an 8.

"That's how many in your class. You're going to meet students whose parents are teachers. Teachers who are married to each other. Teachers who are married to, well-"

She smiled.

"-coaches."

Then Mrs. Rutherford recovered her earlier poise. She glanced at the clock above her desk, digital red numbers on a black field.

"You need to get a move on."

"Yes ma'am," said Gray. "Sorry about being late. Time change. And our only car is the moving truck but my mom couldn't return it until...nevermind."

Gray folded his schedule and slid it into the back pocket of his houndstooth slacks. He started for the door he'd come through—the one that went back through the principal's office.

"Huh-uh," said Mrs. Rutherford, pointing at the door to the deserted commons area that could be seen through the office's front window. "Students at Beaudelaire High School use that one."

Gray smiled.

Mrs. Rutherford folded her arms, her pink nails flashing. "What?"

"It's dumb," said Gray.

"Out with it," said Mrs. Rutherford.

What was the point of starting over if you couldn't be someone else?

That was something Gray's mom had said at least a dozen times in the past three days. The first time, she'd been coming out of one of the truck stops that marked the path from California to Kansas like bread crumbs: Love's and Flying Js and oversized Conocos. The bathrooms were always in the back. The lights were always too bright. And the fresh fruit by the register was hardly fresh and barely fruit. In the parking lot of that particular truck stop (a Flying J) his mom had thrown her arms out, thrown her head back, shouted that it was good to be alive. It was the happiest Gray had seen her in, well, maybe ever. She hadn't even made him take a picture for her Instagram.

"It was a fitting end to the scene," said Gray.

"You could just go," said Mrs. Rutherford. "Then the scene would be over."

"I will. But before I do, can I ask you something?"

"Of course," said Mrs. Rutherford.

"I'm new here, right? And I'm trying to have things be different this time around. But I have to be honest. I don't know how to actually *do* it."

One of Ramona Rutherford's hands went to her chin. Then one of her fingers went up.

"I have just the thing."

———————————

Gray peered through the window into the classroom that was the domain of Trina Patterson (PhD). A periodic table dominated the back wall, all black squares and colorful letters. Beneath the massive canvas poster, pairs of students sat at tall granite tables facing the front of the room, their conditions varying between nearly and fully asleep. And whether they were sleepy or not, Gray couldn't imagine a graceful entry. They were all going to be looking at him, no matter what he did.

He glanced down the hallway he'd come from. It wouldn't be hard to jog home, go back to bed, and try again tomorrow.

Thwack.

Gray was surprised by the intensity of the rubber band's impact with his wrist. The secretary, Mrs. Rutherford, had pulled the bright blue band out of the file cabinet next to her desk. And just like she'd promised, the band "snapped" him out it—out of his usual worries and fears.

Gray raised a hand to knock on the door. But before he could follow through, one of the sleepy students spied him. Her name was Mitzy Tundin and she was wearing a sweatshirt with a grinning cartoon cat on its front.

When Mitzy saw Gray standing on the other side of the cross-hatched window cut into the classroom door, she slid out of her desk and opened the door with a flourish.

"You seem new. Are you new?"

Without waiting for an answer, Mitzy snatched the schedule Gray was holding. After a glance at it, she looked up at Gray's eyes and then down at Gray's body, assessing him like he was a painting.

"Nice eyes. Good cheekbones. A little skinny. Hair's not bad, although you could use a trim-a-lim. Those pants might get you in trouble."

Mitzy spun into the classroom.

"MAY I HAVE YOUR ATTENTION, PLEASE? Everyone, this is Gray. Gray-"

Mitzy held out a hand like the class was a *Price Is Right* Showcase.

"-this is Everyone."

Gray flashed a wave to the roomful of students as Dr. Trina Patterson started toward him from the chalkboard at the front of the classroom. She tented her hands in front of a face framed by graying hair that was six inches too long.

"Thank you, Mitzy, for that generous welcome. It's a wonder to meet you, Gray. Is there anything you'd like to share with the class?"

"I'm hoping he can share something about them pants."

This from a sophomore named Bobby Murphy, whose red hair was spilling out the back of a sweat-stained John Deere hat. Bobby was taking Physical Science for the second time.

Gray glanced down at his pants.

What was the point of starting over…

"My mom got them," he said. "We just moved here, her and me. And the pants, they're from this place that sells clothes when the actors are done with them. They were in a movie?"

There was a beat. Then Mitzy Tundin began clapping, hoping she was leading a round of applause. But she was the round of applause.

"What do you say we get you settled?" said Dr. Patterson. She motioned to an empty stool in the back of the room. "I think there's a seat there next to Elmer."

"Careful you don't split a seam in them tight-ass movie pants."

One of Dr. Patterson's hands went to one of her hips. "Bobbeeeeeee!"

"Just looking out for the kid's pants," said Bobby Murphy with a shrug.

Gray knew the best move was probably to hustle across the room and punch Bobby in the nose. That's probably what his dad would've done; he'd always been more Cobra Kai and less Daniel Larusso. But Gray also knew his 68 inches of height and 108 pounds of body mass were not sufficient to do any punching, especially when it came to Bobby Murphy, whose red hair was accompanied by the beginnings of a red mustache. So Gray slunk to the back of the room and plunked down on a stool next to his new tablemate, whose name was Elmer Niehaus and who had shoulders like a lumberjack and tightly trimmed hair the color of unbuttered popcorn.

Elmer ripped a sheet of paper out of his notebook and wrote something on it. He slid the paper across the slate table to a spot in front of Gray. But Gray had had enough interactions with scary fellow students.

He ignored the paper and kept his eyes on Dr. Patterson, who was clicking to the next slide in the presentation she'd used all 19 years she'd taught at Beaudelaire High School.

"And this," she said. "Is the precious Sumatran rain forest, which is being destroyed at a pace of, I think, 2,000 acres each day?"

Elmer tapped the paper with his pen.

This time, Gray risked a look.

> *Great start*

And

>   *;)*

Before Gray could make sense of what the winky face meant—was it also a jab?—a bell jangled and Dr. Patterson was clasping her hands again.

"Make sure you bring those National Park letters tomorrow!"

Elmer gathered his things and Gray was going to let him go. But then he pulled on the rubber band and felt the satisfying burn against his skin.

"Wait," said Gray. "Where are we going?"

"Gym," said Elmer. "Pep rally."

In the hallway, Mitzy Tundin was leaning against one of the blue lockers that lined that hallway. She rolled up the sleeves of the oversized cat sweatshirt and tucked her hair behind an ear. It was long and blond on top, buzzed short and dark on the sides.

"Sorry about Bobby Murphy," she said. "He's just uptight about the game."

"Yeah," said Elmer. "That's it."

Ahead of them, a crush of students flowed into the hallway like streams meeting a river. Every so often a bright blue BEAR-CATS jersey bobbed up out of the crowd and Gray was granted a topic safer than whatever was bothering Bobby Murphy.

"What's a bearcat?"

"Her department," said Elmer.

Mitzy stopped in the middle of the hallway. With students streaming past her, she dropped to a knee and pulled back on an invisible string.

"We used to be the Bowmen. But, like, twenty years ago, people decided that was offensive. Cowboys, Indians, that sort of thing."

"Couldn't it have been referring to knights and dragons?" asked Gray.

Mitzy shot her invisible arrow past Gray, at Elmer. "See?"

Elmer pulled the fake arrow out of his chest and fake-snapped it in two.

"So," said Gray. "Now your mascot is a non-animal animal. And on game day they wear their non-animal animal jerseys."

He turned to Elmer.

"Where's yours?"

Elmer Niehaus had once been the star athlete at Beaude-laire Middle School. So starlike that the head coach at Beaudelaire *College* had already begun scrambling up a recruiting pitch when Elmer was in eighth grade. But during a fall football game against Perry Middle School, Elmer had folded over awkwardly after an 18-yard run, tearing his meniscus. The result: Elmer's mother, a professor at Beaudelaire College, had begged her only son to focus on school until his body was ready for the wear and tear that sports inevitably brought. Consequently, six-foot-four-inch, two-hundred-and-ten-pound Elmer Niehaus had sworn off sports.

Which is why, after Gray said what he said about the football jersey Elmer wasn't wearing, Elmer calmly and methodically lifted Gray, rotated him, and squished him into the blue lockers that lined the hallway of Beaudelaire High School.

"Want to try that again?" asked Elmer, his face neither menacing nor not.

"Elmer! He didn't know!"

Mitzy Tundin was rapping on Elmer's shoulder blades.

Elmer looked from Gray to Mitzy, from Mitzy back to Gray. He released Gray's armpits and Gray slid to the tile floor while a different commotion broke out at the end of the hallway, where the river of students was flowing into the commons area.

One of those students stopped Bobby Murphy with an arm across Murphy's chest. This student was also wearing a blue BEAR-CATS jersey. He had shiny black hair that spiked out in every direction as if he'd started the day attached to an electrical outlet.

"Damn," said Bartholomew Karp. "Just like the old days! What's the call, Murph?"

Bobby Murphy pulled the green John Deere hat off his head and used it to chop his other arm like a referee.

Bartholomew Karp cupped his hands around his mouth and said, "I've got a personal foul on number…69."

Then something on the other side of Gray's crumpled body caught Bartholomew Karp's attention. He collared Bobby Murphy and the twosome disappeared around the corner.

"Can I help you dears with something?"

Trina Patterson was locking the door to her classroom. Or trying to. Her ring of keys was tangled in the billowing sleeves of her dress.

Mitzy's voice echoed down the hallway.

"I think we're OK, Dr. Patterson!"

By now the hallway was nearly empty, so it didn't take long for Trina Patterson to scoot over to the threesome. Elmer was scraping his fingers through his short blond hair. Mitzy had her hands on her hips, looking up at Elmer. And Gray was scrambling to his feet from the bottom of the lockers.

Trina Patterson brought her hands to her nose.

"Elmer, was there another incident?" she asked.

Elmer's head swiveled between the teacher and Gray, who was still on the tile floor.

Mitzy mouthed a "Sorry" and somersaulted her eyeballs toward Elmer's back in a way Gray recognized. There'd been a time in his life when he'd caught his mother using this look behind his father's back, like when he cursed at a fellow driver, flirted with a waitress, or forgot to come home on a Friday night.

It was this look from Mitzy that made Gray say what he said next. If nothing else, he needed allies. Even if those allies could pick you up and smash you into a locker. Or especially if they could.

"This lummox doesn't know what jet lag is," Gray said to the teacher. "So I was trying to explain that this-"

Gray let his body go slack.

"-is what it feels like."

Dr. Patterson dropped her arms, the sleeves of her dress covering her hands. "You came in an airplane?"

"We drove," said Gray. "But it's basically the same."

Dr. Patterson rocked back on her flats. "Is that true, Elmer Niehaus? Or did you maybe lose that composure again?"

"Yeah," said Elmer. "That's about right."

Dr. Patterson said, "I think *Mister* Patterson might have the cure for both of you. A little pep! To the gymnasium we go!"

She scampered past the group, waving them after her like she was playing Mary Poppins.

Gray stuck a hand up toward Elmer, waggling his fingers.

"I owe you one," said Elmer, yanking Gray to his feet.

Gray could tell that Elmer wasn't the sort of person who just said something like that. So, as the three of them followed Trina Patterson down the hallway toward the gym, he allowed himself to enjoy the warmth in his chest. Sure, the locker-slam hadn't been *ideal*. But the rubber band had worked! He'd been quick! And clever! And now he had not one, but two friends. And one of those new friends was going to be on his side, if and when he needed him in a week or a month or a year.

Or, as it turned out, in five minutes.

CHAPTER 4

At the far end of the brick tunnel that led to the gym, Desmond Rutherford was waving students into the stands for the pep rally. Rutherford was tall and rangy but the motions he was making to guide the jostling students were tight and economical: a point of his long fingers here, a nod of his goateed chin there.

Behind him, the gym's ancient sodium-vapor bulbs bathed the scene in yellowish light, haloing Rutherford's puffy thicket of silver hair as he made a show of unnecessarily rising to his toes so he could see Gray over Elmer and Mitzy. "And who might this be?"

Mitzy fluttered her hands toward Gray. "May I present: the new kid."

"Kid comma New," said Rutherford. "That your full name?"

"No sir," said Gray.

"Sir! Must not be from around here."

"He's from California," said Mitzy. "I mean: he's from California, *sir*."

"I could get used to this," said Rutherford. "You play any ball, California?"

"I'm kind of small for foot-"

"Not football, California. Basketball, whose grace comes not beneath a helmet, but in full view of one's fellow man. That's my department. Well, that and PE. And the occasional chaperone job. Although not as many of those these days, come to think of it. I should probably ask Ramona about that. Maybe at dinner tonight. I wonder what she's mak-"

"Let's go up there!"

Back at the brick tunnel's entrance, the spiky-haired Bartholomew Karp was stuck behind a clot of students.

"Cool your jets, Karp. I'm up here introducing myself." Rutherford returned to Gray. "Now, as I was saying-"

"Yo, check it!"

This time, Bartholomew Karp's voice cut through the crowded tunnel like a chainsaw.

"We've won more games in *one* season than he's won in *two*!"

There was silence in the tunnel, everyone wondering how the coach would respond. Gray was among those wondering. The coach seemed like the sort of person you wanted more of in the world. It didn't hurt that he looked like Morgan Freeman. It was hard not to root for Morgan Freeman.

But the coach only rubbed his silver goatee, lost in the thoughts of a man who's just been cut down to size by a teenager. Especially because Bartholomew Karp's calculations had been generous. Beaudelaire's football team had already won 11 games during the season in question. In the past two seasons Coach Desmond Rutherford's basketball teams had won a total of eight games.

"He's just scared."

The words came out before Gray had time to think. He'd lifted them from one of his mother's pep talks after a run-in with Chuy McMuffin. Fortunately, he'd only whispered the words.

*Un*fortunately, a truth about confined, brick-lined spaces is that sound travels very easily within them. The whisper made it to Bartholomew Karp like he was four inches away and Bartholomew began pushing through the crowded tunnel, his hair all the more electrified and his eyes flickering as he swam past the last person between them.

"You think I'm scared? Of what, you?"

Gray was ready to panic, apologize, capitulate. Yes, the basketball coach seemed like the sort of person you wanted more of in the world. But had he really needed to *say* something? Especially on his first day?

Then Gray remembered the rubber band. He snapped it and an entirely different thought hit him. The damage was done. Now it was a matter of *not* chickening out—holding strong, doing what he wouldn't have done back in Reseda.

"Yeah," said Gray. "It was me. But I didn't necessarily say you were scared of me. I mean, look at you. And look at me. There's no reason for you to be scared of me."

"Look at this genius," said Bartholomew. "So, genius, who are you?"

Gray felt a jostle at his shoulder. He wondered if it was the basketball coach—Rutherford—coming to his rescue. The rescue would be welcome. The form, not so much. He didn't need coaches and teachers intervening on his behalf. That's how you got kids like Chuy McMuffin calling you their bitch biscuit.

"His name's Gray."

Elmer. It was Elmer.

"And he's your new buddy?"

"Could be," said Elmer.

"Sounds about right," said Bartholomew. "You can teach him how to knit. Or whatever it is your mom makes you do."

"Dude," said Mitzy. "He's told you this one hundred times. It's cooking. They *cook* together."

"Whatever," said Bartholomew. "Tell your new buddy here I've got my eye on him."

"Sure thing," said Elmer.

Then Elmer caught Gray's eyes and jerked his head toward the stairs and Gray was happy to comply, grabbing the concrete banister and following Mitzy past Coach Rutherford into the bleachers. When he was four steps up he glanced into the passageway. Bartholomew Karp was making a half-hearted lunge at Elmer's back, like one of the *cholos* Gray thought he'd left back home. The same jerky movement, the same pent-up rage. But instead of a white T-shirt and khaki shorts, a blue football jersey and khaki pants.

"If everyone could take their seats, we'll get this party started."

The voice boomed through the gym. The principal, Mr. Patterson, was standing behind a microphone that was four inches too short for him. He tapped his watch, waiting for stragglers to find seats. Gray was one of those stragglers. He scurried past knees and ankles and plopped onto an empty wooden bleacher next to Mitzy.

Elmer dropped into the space beside Gray, his weight shaking the ancient wood.

"Didn't take you long to call in that favor," said Elmer.

"Is he always like that?" asked Gray.

"He's riding high, " said Elmer.

On the court, Mr. Patterson leaned into the microphone, snapping open a piece of paper from his back pocket.

"Before we get to the fun stuff, a little business. Mr. Hoffman would have me remind you that the Forensic club's talent show is this Friday, which happens to be the same night as the presentation of Miss, I mean, *Senorita*, Contreras's Spanish skits."

The principal glanced at the row of teachers.

"Maybe you two could, uh, *hablar* on the ol' *calendario*?"

He paused for a laugh that didn't come. He looked back at the page with a sniff.

"And as you will recall, the meeting about our district's *vital* bond issue is this Thursday at seven. Tell your parents if they don't already know."

Mr. Patterson folded the paper into quarters and slipped it into the back pocket of his chinos.

"That's enough logistics. Let's get to the reason we're all here today: your Beaudelaire Bearcats, who head out this afternoon to face Ridley County in the state semifinals. To take it from here, let's hear it for a man you all know and love. Normally we call him Mr. Bickle. But today we're calling him Mr. Davidson."

Peter Patterson leaned into the microphone.

"*Harley* Davidson, that is."

With a bow, Mr. Patterson stuck out his hand and one hundred and sixty-two sets of eyes followed that hand while one hundred and sixty-two sets of ears took note of a sound coming from the gym's rear doors, which were normally only used as an emergency exit.

From the perspective of all those eyes and ears, the doors appeared to fly open on their own. The truth, though, was that the football coach, Harris Bickle, had stationed two of his favorite football players at the doors. On Bickle's signal, those players pulled open the doors, allowing Bickle his grand entrance on the Harley-Davidson Electra Glide he'd purchased after getting the raise that came with the Master's in Education he'd gotten at Beaudelaire College.

After gingerly navigating the hump that lay between inside and out, Coach Bickle dipped his bald, bullet-shaped head so the sunglasses he'd balanced on top of it would slide onto his nose. He gunned the engine once, twice, a third time. Then the shiny black motorcycle took off, shooting onto the blue rugs those same football players had helped him lay in a path toward a spot in front of the microphone.

As Coach Bickle approached the center of the court, his football players burst from the gym's tunnel entrance, whooping and hollering. One of them (a back-up running back) even did a cartwheel.

The crowd took its lead from the football team and stood.

As Gray got up with them, he noticed something that stole his attention from the spectacle of the football coach and the motorcycle. At the far end of the second row was a girl with dirty blond hair. She was wearing a long dress of the sort that Gray had only seen on the people his friends had called "hipsters" back in Los Angeles. He couldn't tell if she was cute because he couldn't see her face. But Gray wasn't all that worried about her cuteness (or lack thereof). He was more interested in the fact that she wasn't watching the events that were going on at half court. She wasn't standing. She wasn't clapping. She had her head down, eyes buried in a book.

But before Gray could do any more reconnaissance, his attention was recaptured by what was happening at center court.

Harris Bickle wanted to be a motorcycle person more than he actually was a motorcycle person. This inexperience, combined with his natural overconfidence, meant he'd declined when Mr. Patterson had offered the gym that very morning so Coach Bickle could make a practice run. That refusal contributed to what was happening in front of the entire school, which was that Harris Bickle's Harley-Davidson was crashing into the microphone.

The crash caused two things to happen. First, a silence fell like a blanket over the student body of Beaudelaire High School, which couldn't know whether this was part of the stunt. And second, it made Bickle lose control of his motorcycle, such that it tipped and began to slide. Luckily for his own health, Harris Bickle knew enough about motorcycles to cut the throttle and let go. He tumbled clear of the bike, landing squarely on the padding in the thighs of his motorcycle pants—motorcycle pants he'd worn exactly once before this (on the way home from the Dick's Sporting Goods where he'd bought them).

There were gasps and oohs and ahs and winces and yet, no one knew: was this part of the show? In fact, they would never know. While not a very good motorcyclist, Coach Bickle was an excellent showman. He sprang to his feet and, tearing the bandanna from his bullet-shaped head, he screamed, "Who's ready for some football?!"

At this the crowd lost its hive mind, led by the football players, who were now jumping around on the court, bumping chests and fists.

Coach Bickle pulled the microphone off the ground and tapped its end. When the resultant pops were done, he said, "Hey, this thing is tougher than Bobby Murphy!"

He pointed at Bobby Murphy, who was standing near the front of the mass of football players. He was still wearing his green John Deere Hat.

On cue, Murphy flexed his right arm.

Bartholomew Karp thumped the bicep and mocked an overblown recoil.

The crowd roared in good-natured laughter.

"Now," said Coach Bickle, rubbing his waxed head. "Like I was telling Kurt down at the *Bee* this morning, I think coaching can only take you so far. You've got to have players if you want to win. And boy, I tell you, we've got players. Let's give this group a round of applause."

Bickle stepped away from the microphone to lead the crowd in applauding his players. But he didn't step far enough and his claps echoed across the gym like gunshots.

When the applause settled, Coach Bickle leaned back into the microphone.

"One of those players is someone you know danged well. This season he's thrown a school-record 44 touchdowns. Give it up for our very own Tom Brady, our own Peyton Manning, our own Joe Montana: Bartholomew Karp!"

This time, Coach Bickle didn't have to lead the crowd in applause. It took its cue naturally. So did the football team, whose members all looked down the line at the one player who wasn't applauding: their spiky-haired quarterback, Bartholomew Karp, who leaned over to say something to Bobby Murphy—something he said as he stared directly at Gray, making Gray's heart go Little Drummer Boy against his sternum.

"Thanks, Coach," said Bartholomew, accepting the microphone from Bickle. Then, with a look at the motorcycle, he clapped his coach on the shoulder. "Maybe don't ride that thing out to Ridley County tonight, though. We might need you, good players or not."

With a toss of his smooth head, Coach Bickle leaned back into a roaring laugh.

"So listen," said Bartholomew, rubbing his spiky hair in a way he knew wouldn't disturb the gel holding it in place. "Last night I had an interesting dream. But this dream was a little different than my normal dreams, if you know what I mean."

Bartholomew Karp stopped for a meaningful look, first at his teammates and then at a group of girls who had their chins in their hands in the front row of the bleachers.

"So in this dream, we're playing Ridley County. And it's going OK. I mean, we're not playing like we did against Ottawa. I only had-"

Bartholomew Karp held the moment again.

"-three touchdown passes."

This got a laugh, just as Bartholomew Karp had known it would.

"Anyway, the second half starts and it's back and forth, back and forth. And then it all comes down to the end. Now don't worry: we won."

"Duh!" shouted an offensive lineman, cupping his hands together in front of his mouth. This got a laugh, too. And again Bartholomew was wise enough to let the laughter die down before he went on, pacing and whipping the microphone cord.

"But what got us there was you guys."

He pointed at the crowd, three spots in turn.

"People like you. And you. And you.

Then Bartholomew Karp made one last point.

"And even you, Patra Patterson."

He held the moment, smirking at the girl Gray had spied in the front row. She still had the book out, a finger holding her place as she contemplated what to do. Meanwhile, Gray was putting it together: the girl was the principal's daughter. Her name was Patra. And in spite of his still-hammering heart, he had time to think: *that's a cool name.*

"Come on, Patra. You can give me a smile."

Bartholomew Karp waited.

The crowd waited.

Gray waited, too. Bartholomew seemed perfectly at home with the microphone cocked to one side of his head so it wouldn't pick up the sounds of his breathing.

"Pretty please," said Bartholomew, quiet now. Then he pointed at Patra Patterson and said, "Sold!"

This was a wise move by Bartholomew. In reality, Patra Patterson had used the book as cover to flash Bartholomew Karp her middle finger. Of course, Gray didn't know that. Which was why, up in the stands, he was shaking his head.

Cool name or not, she'd given in. It was another dark cloud in the storm that was taking over his brain.

Out on the court, Bartholomew had resumed his pacing.

"The best part about all this was the feeling I had when the game was over, which was that it wasn't just that I'd won or that the team had won. It was that *we'd* won. Everyone that was on our side. And no one-"

Bartholomew stopped, flopping the microphone down so its butt end was pointed into the crowd. He held it up like it was a gun sight with Gray at its end.

"-that wasn't."

Still aiming the microphone at Gray, Bartholomew held it out as if to drop it. But he didn't "drop the mic." This was only a signal to one of the football team's managers, who'd been stationed upstairs in the A/V booth, and who now pushed Play on the phone that was attached to the gym's speaker system, initiating the opening bars of a song that was all guitar.

And chanting. Weird chanting.

"Wah-ah-ah-ah-ah-ah-ah," over and over.

And then, "Thunder. Thunder."

Bartholomew tapped his front foot with the beat, the microphone held out to his side, his eyes on Gray in a duel only they knew about. And because of the isolated nature of this duel, Gray had the upper hand. Eventually, Bartholomew Karp would grow tired of staring at him, or the song (AC/DC's "Thunderstruck") would end, or the cheerleaders would interrupt, and the moment would be over.

But reality and perception are two very different concepts. To Gray, it felt like the entire school was staring at him. Which is why Gray did the worst thing he could have done, forgetting the rubber band and his pledge to himself.

He stood to go.

As he did, he felt like he'd just finished a math test that hadn't gone very well. He'd done his best. But maybe new starts weren't possible, at least not here. Maybe he could talk his mom into finding a school for him in a nearby town. Or maybe he could be home-schooled, wake up at 9 or 10, and spend the day in his pajamas. Or maybe they could go back to LA *now*. It would probably take some negotiating, and he'd feel bad about being the reason, especially after everything his mom had gone through to get them here. He was proud of her for trying. But weren't people always saying you had to make sacrifices for your kids?

Elmer—all 6'4" and 210 pounds of him—grabbed his elbow.

"Let go!" said Gray, tearing himself from Elmer's grasp.

Elmer could have doubled down on his attempt to prevent Gray from leaving, but when he saw the fury in Gray's blue eyes—blue eyes which had gotten bluer as Gray had gotten mad—he put up his hands and leaned back in his bleacher.

Gray pushed past Elmer, then past a girl in a black Misfits T-shirt that was too big for her. And then everything—Elmer and his sideburns, Mitzy and her cat sweatshirt, Coach Bickle's bullet head, Patra Patterson's dress, the principal's blazer, Bartholomew Karp's jersey, Bobby Murphy's John Deere hat, the girl in the oversized Misfits T-shirt—was lost to Gray as his eyes zeroed in on his escape route.

On the court, Coach Bickle was stepping to the microphone Bartholomew Karp was handing him with a satisfied smile. He noticed the commotion Gray was causing in the stands and, over the second chorus of "Thunderstruck," he said, "Looks like someone prefers Bon Scott!"

This extremely insider-y remark (which referenced the fact that AC/DC was founded with one singer but realized much of its success with another) didn't have any immediate effect on Gray, coming as it did in the midst of the fugue state that saw him tromping down the concrete stairs.

It did, though, cause most of the student body to look to where Coach Bickle was pointing. What they saw was a rail-thin boy in houndstooth-patterned pants turning the sharp corner into the brick-lined chute where only a few minutes before he'd nearly caused a fight with their football team's quarterback.

What they didn't see was that same boy sprinting through the brick tunnel and into the deserted commons area, where the TV hanging above the door to the office was flashing from one screen to the next. First, a brown turkey on a blue background, next to "Thanksgiving Break: Wednesday, November 25 – Friday, November 27."

Then, a football action shot, next to a reminder about that night's game. At the bottom, the screen read "Go Bearccats!"

This typo served to distract the boy sufficiently that he didn't notice, as he picked up speed on his way out the front door, the chest of Coach Desmond Rutherford.

Until he slammed into it.

Coach Rutherford pulled a red Blow Pop out of his mouth. The air around Gray got sweet like strawberry.

"Would you go back to LA?"

Gray's head jerked and Coach Rutherford chuckled.

"Ramona told me. You know, the other peppercorn in this salt mine?"

Gray didn't laugh at this. But he did manage an almost-smile.

"There we go," said Rutherford. "Before you take off, let me show you something?"

Gray hesitated, still attached to the momentum that had carried him out of the gym. But as his breathing slowed and his heart rate returned to normal, the realization dawned on him: even though he'd chickened out in front of the entire school and made the scene of all scenes, he couldn't go home. Especially because home was hardly home.

So Gray said OK and followed Coach Rutherford through the commons. By now, the AC/DC had stopped; the pep rally had moved on to a skit the dance team was performing. The sounds that filtered into the commons were of girlish voices imitating football players.

"Blue 32, blue 32, hut h-"

The last "hut" was drowned out by the creak from a door that was just off the commons area, buried behind a Coke machine. A current of cool air rose from the darkness that yawned from behind the door.

Coach Rutherford flipped a switch, but the only lights that came on were covered by wire cages, like something out of a prison movie. Or a mental institution.

Gray leaned around the door jamb and peered into the stairwell Coach Rutherford had already started down. He'd stopped on the third step.

"Yeah," he said. "It's a little creepy."

"A little?"

Rutherford put up his hands and wiggled his fingers, smiling and making a ghostly "Oooooo." His pale palms flashed in the dim light, the lines and wrinkles looking like topographical maps.

Gray followed Rutherford down the stairs past walls the color of limestone, pitted by their construction a hundred years before. When they got to the bottom of the stairs, a vast locker room with a low ceiling stretched out before them. The décor matched that of the stairwell, all metal and concrete and harsh light bulbs. Every so often, a concrete pillar broke up the monotony. There was one distinctive feature to the place: it didn't seem to end.

"Whoa," said Gray.

"I know," said Rutherford. "Gorgeous, right?"

"That's not exactly what I was going to say."

"Go on," said Rutherford. "Look around."

Gray took a step into the locker room. Then he looked back at Coach Rutherford. The basketball coach was smiling like he knew something, looking even more like Morgan Freeman.

Gray walked past one set of lockers that was bisected by a wooden bench. Then past another set of lockers that was bisected by a wooden bench. Then another. And another. Soon, he'd gone fifty feet. The locker room's back wall was still another ten yards away.

"Why's it so big?" he shouted.

Rutherford cupped a hand to his mouth and shouted, "Meet me in my office when you're done."

Gray waited until the coach was out of sight. Then he allowed himself a deep breath and waited for silence to descend. When it did, he noticed that it was almost complete. If he concentrated, he could hear a faint version of the pep rally going on in the gym. But that sound was limited to a dull thump every now and then. (This was the bass drum, playing its part in the school band's rendition of the school's fight song.)

Gray ran his fingers across one of the lockers. The face was metal lattice, painted desert tan. Over the years, the paint had been chipped enough times that the silvery metal showed through almost as often as it didn't. He opened the locker, surprised to find that it was empty. And not only was it empty, it looked like it had never been used. The metal hook at the top shone like it had just come from whatever factory produced metal hooks for lockers.

Gray noticed one thing out of the ordinary. At the upper right corner, someone had carved a romantic cross. There were two sets of initials. On top: NT. On the bottom: HB. Gray traced the initials, imagining who NT and HB might have been and what had become of them. Maybe they'd broken up the next day. But maybe, Gray thought, they were still together, happily married in this very town, his high school glory days having led to a job he liked; her high school glory days having led to a job *she* liked. Two kids, a decent car in the driveway, pancakes on Sundays-

"California!"

Gray's head jerked toward the sound. He saw Coach Rutherford at the end of the bank of lockers. The Blow Pop's white stick moved back and forth in Coach Rutherford's mouth like a pendulum. He moved it to one side so he could say, "Pep rally won't last forever. And you'll have to go back to class."

Gray closed the locker gently, with one last look at the initials. It was a nice story, but it probably wasn't true. More likely his first thought; they'd broken up the next day.

Coach Rutherford's office was protected by a heavy wooden door that stood open, revealing a desk the color of gunmetal, behind which rested an oversized neon-green ball.

"Keeps the core tight," said the coach.

"I know," said Gray. "Nobody in LA sits in normal chairs nowadays. I'm just surprised."

"Amazon delivers everywhere. Even Beaudelaire. Now have a seat. "

Rutherford pointed at a small leather couch that sat perpendicular to the desk and moved around the desk to sit on the physioball. He used the desk to help ease him onto it. Once he was settled, he stretched his arms over his head, lacing his fingers together.

"When'd you leave?"

"Sunday night," said Gray.

"And on your first day," said Rutherford. "All that business upstairs." He shook his head and pulled the Blow Pop out of his mouth, examining its cracked surface. "I'd want to get going, too."

This degree of understanding felt, to Gray, like he was getting a hug. And that felt good, but also like too much, too soon. So he changed the subject, pointing to the three posters that lined the wall behind the basketball coach.

"Who are those guys?"

Rutherford nodded at the furthest poster, where a defiant-looking man in a blue and orange uniform was standing over someone in a white and red uniform.

"John Starks. Smaller than everyone on the court, meaner than a cornered rattlesnake."

Gray pointed at the second poster, which showed a taller man in goggles and a yellow uniform. At the top, in blocky purple letters, it read, "Worth." And at the bottom, in script: "Every penny."

"James Worthy. The glue that held Showtime together. You know, your hometown team?"

"I went to a game once," said Gray.

"Did they win?"

"I don't know. I just remember there were tacos because they scored a hundred points. Or maybe it was burritos."

"We've got a long way to go."

The coach spun on the physioball toward the poster directly behind him, where a tall blonde man was shooting over another tall blonde man. One of the tall blonde men had on a green uniform with white accents; the other, a white uniform with green accents

"And this fella is Larry Bird. Won three World Championships and was the MVP twice."

"MVP?"

"Most Valuable Player. Of the entire league."

"So he was good," said Gray.

"That's why he gets this spot right behind me."

"He's your favorite?"

"Yep."

"That's weird. You wouldn't expect-"

"A black fella to call a white boy his favorite player?" Coach Rutherford shook his head and looked down at the Blow Pop as if he were conspiring with it on some sad secret. "We've come so far, but I guess we ain't come far enough."

"Sorry, it's just-"

Rutherford laughed, more a roar than a laugh.

"I'm messing with you, California. You're exactly right. And I catch no end of hell from Devon—that's my kid—when I wear his jersey 'round the house."

"So why then?"

"When you were upstairs, with all those other kids, you see a bunch of black folks?"

Gray shook his head.

"And when you watch basketball-"

Coach Rutherford waved the remains of the Blow Pop at Gray. "Oh right, you don't watch basketball. Well, if you *did* watch basketball, you'd see that there aren't a lot of white boys. And Mr. Bird there—he was the whitest of all, from a town in Indiana called French Lick, if you can believe it."

"So you like him because he was different. Like you."

"You got it. And better yet: that particular white boy didn't take any shhhh- crap from anyone. They say he was the biggest trash-talker in the NBA."

"And you're going to convince me to play basketball and teach me to be like Larry Bird and learn how to take no shhhh- crap from anyone?"

Coach Rutherford put the Blow Pop back in his mouth and moved the stick to one side.

"You would think that, wouldn't you? But here's the thing: I'm not sure I'm qualified to teach you that lesson."

"Why not?"

"Well, a little-known fact about Mr. Bird here is that before his illustrious college career at Indiana State, he went off to the University of Indiana. He lasted a week and then turned tail for home."

"This is a confusing lesson," said Gray.

Rutherford flashed Gray a wry grin. Then the grin disappeared as he crunched down on the last of the Blow Pop's hard outer shell.

"That's not the half of it," he said, pulling the bare stick out of his mouth and gazing at it like it was a match that had just gone out. "Your new friends and the Karp kid weren't wrong. We haven't been very good these past couple years. But I was thinking. Maybe, instead of leaving school, come to basketball practice tomorrow. Maybe you'll find something you like, help you ease into this new school. One misfit to another."

He tossed the sucker's stick into the trash can at the end of his desk.

"Why tomorrow, and not today?"

"No practice today," said Coach Rutherford. "Football game, you know."

"Alright," said Gray.

"Alright, you'll come?"

"Alright, I'll think about it."

"A little attitude! Larry would be proud. Now, let's talk about what you're going to wear to school tomorrow."

CHAPTER 6

"That's as fine a name as I've heard this year! Welcome to Western Civilization, Sir Gray!"

Walter Hoffman clapped Gray on the back. He pulled open the door to his classroom, whose desks were full of fellow freshmen situating themselves for class—searching for the right notebooks, building tiny nests with their sweaters and scarves, and reviewing the pep rally (and the kid who'd escaped it).

Gray snapped the rubber band, his eyes on an empty desk next to Elmer. Instead of slinking along the wall toward that desk, he strode down the middle aisle of the classroom. He was aware of the eyes that found him. And of the conversations that stopped around him.

"So you're staying," said Elmer, as Gray slid into the wrong-sided desk. People rarely accounted for the fact that in a room of 20 people you could assume that two of them would be left-handed.

"I did a survey," said Gray. "No one else will let you slam them into a locker."

This got a grunt out of Elmer—equivalent to a standing ovation from most people.

A girl walked past the wooden podium at the front of the room. She looked like she had stepped out of the pages of *Teen Vogue*, her blond hair falling in an even line that landed just past the shoulders on the pink Banana Republic blouse her mother had given her the previous Valentine's Day.

"Careful," said Elmer, his voice almost a growl.

Gray forgave Elmer the assumption; he had no idea that back in Reseda, there was a running joke about girls like this one. They'd take a picture and put a caption over it.

IS SHE PRETTY

OR

IS IT GOOD SHAMPOO?

"Who is she?"

"The A in your ABCs," said Elmer.

"The what?"

"*Ar*iel Bickle. *Barbarella* Destino. *Chris*ty Tisdale. A. B. C."

"Bickle, that's the football coach's name, right?"

"Yup," said Elmer. "And just like him, she's the boss."

The bell rang and Mr. Hoffman closed the door to the room. At the wooden podium at the front of the room, he switched on the attached green lamp. Tiny glasses rested on his nose—tiny glasses that he peered over so he could see the class.

"Does everyone feel appropriately rallied?"

Mr. Hoffman stuck out his arms.

"I SAID, DOES EVERYONE FEEL-"

He stopped himself with the same smile he'd flashed Gray at the door.

"I jest. It is fascinating, though, the way we respond to someone shouting at us in the front of a room...or gymnasium. Can anyone think of how this might relate to the subject of our most recent discussion?"

Ariel Bickle's hand went up.

"Ms. Bickle, enlighten us."

Ariel spun in her desk so her eyes were on Gray. "I think we should let the new student answer."

This time, Gray's heart didn't drop into his guts. After the talk with Coach Rutherford, he felt different, more confident. Or maybe he didn't care. Whatever the case, instead of glancing at Elmer or checking with Mr. Hoffman, he stared back at the girl named Ariel Bickle, pretending he was trying to bore out her eyes like the superhero his dad had been partial to. An X-Man, he thought. Or maybe he was one of the Avengers. It was hard to keep track these days. Whatever it was, that guy wouldn't have been afraid of some white girl in a pink *blouse*.

Meanwhile, Mr. Hoffman was momentarily frozen by the dilemma; the new kid was getting picked on again. His recovery was quick.

"How I love what you've done! Instead of *referencing* what Mr. Karp did in the gym, you've decided to re-*illustrate* the behavior. And perfectly! Isolate the new member of the tribe by encouraging the tribe's xenophobic tendencies. Well done!"

"Yes," said Ariel, her eyes still on Gray's. "That's exactly what I was doing."

Gray stared right back.

"Hitler," he said. "You guys are talking about Hitler."

Mr. Hoffman's head jerked back and he said, "Actually, yes. Bravo, Sir Gray."

Then Mr. Hoffman, who was thrilled that the situation had not escalated, glanced down at his notes.

"As 1939 drew to a close, Adolf Hitler was consolidating his support amongst the bourgeois with speeches all over Germany. This support would eventually manifest in the creation of-"

He turned for the chalkboard. When he did, Ariel Bickle put her hands together in silent applause directed at Gray. But Gray gave her nothing, pretending to focus on the board where Mr. Hoffman was making hash marks to denote various fortifications erected by the Luftwaffe.

It was the beginning of a twenty-minute lecture that Gray found surprisingly compelling. Back in Reseda, his teachers had been so worried about keeping everyone off their phones that they'd forgotten about teaching.

When Mr. Hoffman was finished reminding the class how slow communication had been in 1939 ("one must remember that much of the United States was mired in a depression, and it's not like they had pocket computers to tell them what was happening on the other side of the world"), he told the class to open their books to the page where they'd "find an excellent discussion of Hitler's association with Goebbels who was, despite history's assurance to the contrary, something of a buffoon."

Mr. Hoffman clicked off the green light and sat down at his desk.

"Sir Gray," he said. "You'll need some literature. Mr. Niehaus, you seem to have taken a shine to Mr. Taylor here. Why don't you walk him to the library? I believe Cleopatra Patterson will be there to assist you."

The Beaudelaire High School Library had been the crown jewel of the building's construction a century before. Shelves soared to a vaulted ceiling held up by massive, polished wood beams that were the same color as the rose-colored wood floor. There were two metal ladders, both attached to a track that ran along the outer circumference of the room. The library's floor was dominated by a dozen tables. Their legs were made of iron like the handle on the school's front door. And their tops were made of oak, like the doors themselves. Only one of the dozen oak tables was occupied, by two people. One was wearing a bright blue football jersey and leaning over the other, who was reading at the table. The person in the football jersey was Bartholomew Karp. The person at the table was Cleopatra "Patra" Patterson.

"So you're still here," said Bartholomew, rising to his full height and crossing his arms.

"Patra," said Elmer, ignoring Bartholomew. "We need to get Gray a book. How do we go about doing that?"

Patra Patterson methodically put her bookmark in the book she was reading. She looked up at Bartholomew Karp. "Don't you have a bus to catch?"

Bartholomew glanced at the enormous cast-iron clock behind the main library desk. "They're not leaving without me. But I'll see you tonight?"

"Maybe," said Patra.

"Hell yeah," said Bartholomew. He rapped the tabletop. "Have fun with Lenny and his pet rabbit."

"Don't tell me you're into him now," said Elmer, after Bartholomew let the library door click shut.

"There was the literary reference. And there's something about athletes that's sexy." Then Patra Patterson stopped herself and focused on Gray. "You must be the new kid."

"Ummm," said Gray.

Gray had forgotten how words worked because he was too stunned by the shape of Patra's face and the way her green eyes danced into all the corners of his, like she was processing everything about him faster than anyone had ever done before.

Patra gave up on Gray.

"So, Elmer, you and the Dali Lama need a book?"

Elmer's big forehead got a wrinkle. "Dali Lama?"

"You know how the Buddhist monks are always going, 'Ommm.'"

"History. Mr. Hoffman."

"Christ. Are we getting more of that pre-World War II stuff today?"

Then Gray remembered how to make words.

"Yeah, it's so boring."

Patra thrust both arms in the air. "The Lama speaks! So, it's not the material that's the problem. It's the way that he looks at it, from such a patriarchal viewpoint, like the only thing that matters is the men that fought the fights and not the women who were at home, cleaning up the messes."

"As you can see," said Elmer. "Patra's our resident feminist."

"Meh," said Patra. "I'm not a real feminist. That would be my mother. Sort of, anyway. Because let's be honest, some of her positions are kind of nonsensical because you can't argue with the fact that women are wired to be nurturing and kind-hearted. And a lot of the post-wave feminists neglect this little tidbit. But you know, she's got one or two good ideas."

Patra noticed that the attention of the two boys in front of her was wandering. She pulled a keyring out of a pocket in her dress and waved it at Elmer like she was shooing a cat. "Leave us. Unless that's a problem for you, Lama."

What Gray wanted to do was shake his head and say, "IT'S NO PROBLEM!" But what he did, instead, was to shrug and say, "That's fine."

"I'll see you back at class," said Elmer.

"Cool," said Gray. Then he wondered, did people here say 'cool'?

"Cool," said Elmer, heading for the door.

"Come on," said Patra, aiming them for a door in the back corner of the library. As they walked across the wood floor, the heels on her tall black boots clacked like a train, echoing into the ceiling above, from whose beams hung spidery chandeliers.

Patra stopped when she noticed that Gray was still taking in the room. "It's pretty, right?"

"It's OK," said Gray. "If you're into gothic décor."

"Do you actually know what gothic décor is, or did you just take a stab at that?"

"I dabble," said Gray.

"In gothic décor?"

"In knowing things."

"An educated man. I like that."

In truth, what Gray knew about architecture and interior design came almost exclusively from his mother's various online presences, which were full of pictures of buildings—the ways they were built, the ways they were decorated.

"Textbooks are in here," said Patra, putting the key to the lock in the wooden door. Inside, she reached for a light switch. "Some of these are a hundred years old."

When the fluorescent lights blinked on, Gray saw metal shelves running from floor to ceiling, filled with books of all sorts. Reference books, atlases, yearbooks. And textbooks, of course.

Patra started down the middle aisle. As she walked, she reached out a hand and ran it along the spines of a set of 1975 *Encyclopaedia Britannica*.

"I still can't believe they want to tear this all down," she said.

"These shelves?"

"The whole school. That's what the meeting Thursday is about. The one my dad was talking about during the pep rally. The bond thing. To finance a new school."

Then Patra concentrated on peering into the shelves.

"Let's see. Hoffman. That would be World History. I think the book's called-"

She pulled a thick red and white textbook from the shelf in front of her. She read its title: "Western History – 1800 – present."

"At least they got the 'Western' in there, right?" said Gray.

"Don't patronize," said Patra. She tossed the book and Gray caught it in his breadbasket, surprised by its weight. He thumbed through the pages, pretending to be interested. Really, he was stalling. He'd become conscious of the emptiness of the storage room— of the entire library.

"So Lama, what's your deal going to be?"

Patra had slid closer to Gray—close enough that he could see the dozen tiny freckles spread across her nose.

"What do you mean?" he asked.

"Everybody has their thing, right? Bartholomew is a football player and he's got the whole persecuted Native American cross to bear. Elmer *used* to be a football player. Ariel, Barbarella, Christy—they have the popularity thing. Bobby Murphy, he's got the brooding white trash thing. Mitzy and the bubbly gay girl-"

"Aha! I thought so. But, you know-"

Gray held up the history book.

"-books and covers and stuff."

"You're a hero. The question still stands: what about you? What's your thing, Lama?"

"To get a better nickname."

Patra tapped him on the chest, bringing with her a smell that was unlike any other girl Gray had been this close to. Like a spice. Although he didn't know which one.

"We'll work on that," said Patra. "After we figure out your thing."

"Why do I have to have a thing?"

"That's just the way it is. A mythology. To fit in."

"What's *your* thing?"

"That's easy," said Patra. "I'm the manic pixie dream girl."

"The what?"

"The manic pixie dream girl. It's the girl who you think is everything you've ever wanted but who can't actually live up to the expectation you've built for her. I read about it in the *New York Times* once and I thought—that's me."

"So you're dangerous," said Gray.

"You might say that. Or maybe you'd say I teach people what they need to know when they need to learn it."

"How are you so sure of yourself?"

"Do you know who Chuck Klosterman is?"

Gray shook his head.

"He wrote once that, in any relationship, the person with the most power is the one who cares the least. And I *always* care the least. It's kind of my specialty."

Gray focused his eyes on Patra's, like he'd done in Mr. Hoffman's class with Ariel. *Cyclops.* That was the superhero's name. "Sounds like a lonely way to live."

"I guess I never thought about it that way."

"Well," said Gray. "Maybe you should."

"Easy, Lama. I'm the one giving the lessons here. That's how it works. You know, new kid, wise girl, dark room."

Then Gray said something that he would not be able to believe he'd said when he replayed the moment that night. "Yeah, maybe we should kiss."

And for a millisecond, Gray thought his gambit had worked. It hadn't even required a stupid sign!

But Patra only patted him on the shoulder. "It won't be that easy, Lama. Now you need to get back to class."

Nicole Taylor waved at her son from the U-Haul. She leaned into the passenger seat to push open the door. A receipt fluttered out, from a gas station in Grand Junction.

Gray moved to catch the thin strip.

"Don't worry about it, honey! Just get in here and tell me about your day!"

Gray gave up on the receipt. He got in and shut the door. As his mother pulled away from the curb next to the high school, he watched in the rearview mirror as the receipt flipped and tumbled in the breeze behind them.

From behind the U-Haul's big steering wheel, Nicole Taylor asked, "So?"

Gray wanted to tell her everything. In fact, he *needed* to tell her everything: about Bartholomew Karp pointing the microphone at him, about Patra Patterson's boots clacking across the library floor, about how he was considering what the basketball coach had said and that maybe playing basketball *was* a good idea.

But as soon as he'd gotten into the car, all the strength in his body (and mind) had leaked out. So, instead of explaining everything that had happened—the several nicknames he'd gotten, the fight he'd almost gotten into, the talk he'd had with Rutherford—he resorted to the principal's walking orders.

"I guess there's a meeting on Thursday night about a new high school? They said to tell our parents. So I'm telling you."

"Like, they want to build a new one?"

"I think so."

Nicole Taylor glanced into the U-Haul's rearview mirror. "I guess that makes sense. I sort of can't believe that one's still there." She shook her head. "Is that it?"

"It was a lot," said Gray.

"Oh honey, I know. I'm sorry." She reached over and slid her fingers into Gray's black hair. "You know, this is getting-"

Gray lifted an eyebrow. The length of his hair was a source of contention between them.

"What?" she said. "I was going to say it's getting so it looks good."

Nicole Taylor winked and steered the truck down their new home street, which was paved with little red bricks. "Tell you what," she said. "Pancakes for dinner? I'll tell you my news, then, too."

She eased the U-Haul into the spot they'd found when they'd pulled into Beaudelaire only 24 hours before this—a spot that didn't seem to be regulated by a parking meter like the rest of the spots on the street. It had the *remnants* of such regulation: the pole, only without the gray head on top. It looked like a dandelion someone had already puffed into the breeze.

The parking spot was two doors down from Taylor's Downtown, the general store Nicole's parents, Gayle and Darby, had bought during a recession that coincided with their retirement. The building was made from the same red bricks as downtown Beaudelaire's streets. In front, there were two floor-to-ceiling displays where mannequins had once worn the clothes on sale at the formalwear store that had preceded Taylor's Downtown.

In one of these front displays, Darby Taylor was hanging a sign, his bearlike frame looking preposterous in the confined space.

BLUE FRIDAY

Underneath, there was a display of sweatshirts and hats emblazoned with the blue Bearcats logo shared by Beaudelaire High School *and* Beaudelaire College. The Taylors had negotiated a licensing deal with both institutions, making Taylor's Downtown the exclusive outside seller of their apparel.

From the U-Haul, Nicole Taylor nodded at her father. He was teetering at the edge of a foot-high pedestal. "Looks like your grandpa could use a hand," she said. "I'll get the pancakes going."

And then she was off, up the stairs to Number 268 ½. Because not only was that dandelion-like parking meter two doors down from Taylor's Downtown. It was also two doors down from their new home. The upstairs apartment had come with the store and had been unoccupied for two years. Darby said this was because they hadn't been able to "find a tenant worth a darn." But in reality, he'd always held out hope that his only daughter would someday need it.

Gray pulled open the door to Taylor's. A tiny bell announced his arrival.

"Gray? Is that you?"

Darby Taylor paused in mid-letter-hang.

"Hold on, Grandpa," said Gray, dumping his backpack on one of the refurbished piano benches that sat next to the front door at Taylor's. Behind it, postcards featuring black and white drawings of windmills rested in a tall stand.

"Could you-"

Darby Taylor was stretched to his limit. Gray picked up the piano bench not occupied by his backpack.

"Tarnation, that's a better idea. Bring that tootcatcher over here."

Gray positioned the bench underneath his grandfather, who smelled like minty aftershave. The bench creaked as Darby put his weight on it. But it held and, within thirty seconds, the sign was hung.

"Now get me down before your grandma gets back," said Darby. "She'll have my everloving hide if she sees feet on this bench."

Gray took his grandfather's hand. It was dry and leathery like a grandfather's hand ought to be. Then came two crackles. First was the crackle in Darby Taylor's ankle. Then a crackle from the bench, which sounded like a ship coming apart at its rivets.

"Look out!"

Darby was falling. This was problem enough on its own. Gray's grandfather was big and Gray was not. But the situation was exacerbated by the logistics: Darby Taylor was teetering toward the plate-glass window between them and the street. Gray reacted the only way he could. He lunged *into* his grandfather, hoping to generate enough momentum to keep them from tumbling through the window like they were in an action movie. His shoulder hit his grandfather's meaty chest and there was an "Oomph" as Darby's arms wrapped around him, pushing him closer and closer to the window. With two inches to spare, their momentum came to a stop. They looked at one another in relief just as the bell at the front of the store rang. Gayle Taylor shook her gray hair out of a white stocking cap and hung her red pea coat on a hook by the door.

"Anybody hurt?"

Darby said, "We remain uninjured, my dear!"

"Happy to hear it. Now Gray, come over here and give me a hug."

Gray released his grandfather and followed his grandmother's orders, allowing his heartbeat to return to a reasonable rate while also allowing his grandmother to do grandmotherly things: ask him how the day had been, how lunch had gone, how the teachers had treated him.

"Stop interrogating the boy," said Darby, easing himself down from the display window.

Gayle pulled Gray's head into her thin chest.

"I will not! What a treat we've got!"

"That's true," said Darby. "I'm glad we got you out of there, Gray."

"Darby," said Gayle Taylor. "What'd we talk about?"

Darby put up his hands while Gayle let go of Gray, straightening the clothes she'd mussed.

"Your mom said to send you up. Something about breakfast?"

"Thanks for the help," said Darby. "You saved my bacon."

There was a beat.

"You know, breakfasty things?"

Gayle Taylor rolled her eyes. But she also leaned into her husband of 43 years and, as Gray walked out the door and the bell tinkled overhead, Darby was kissing Gayle on the top of the head.

———————

Nicole Taylor appeared from around the wall that separated their new kitchen from their new living room inside the upstairs apartment, which had wood floors the color of caramel. She held out a spatula and motioned to the card table that was serving as one-third of the furnishings in an apartment that might have been called "grand," if not for the lack of furniture. It was a loft, really: ten-foot ceilings and hardwood floors, sturdy casings on its doorways and old-timey radiators for heat.

Gray sat and his mother deposited four of her "famous" pancakes on his plate and then put some of them on her own. She kicked off her shoes—a pair of off-white Chuck Taylors—and sat down.

With many of his mother's meals, Gray had to gather his thoughts before digging in, because a harsh truth that would go untruthed for all of Gray's life was that Nicole Taylor was not a very good cook. There were three exceptions: baked macaroni and cheese, chicken quesadillas, and pancakes. What made her pancakes especially good was her refusal to use cheap syrup on them, at least in California.

She hadn't yet been able to find real maple syrup in Beaudelaire, so the syrup Gray reached for was Mrs. Butterworth's.

"Sorry," said Nicole, noticing his hesitation. "It'll take a while before everything's back to normal. To say the least." She took the syrup from him and doused her pancakes. "Want to hear my news?"

Through a mouthful of half-mashed pancakes, Gray said, "Mmmhmmm."

"I think I might have a job."

"Grough," said Gray, trying to say "Wow."

"I know, right? First day." Then she shook her head. "I really thought it would take longer."

Gray swallowed his pancakes and cleared his throat of the too-sticky syrup. That was the thing about the cheap stuff—it never *felt* right.

"Where?"

"There's a Wal-mart in Ottawa."

"Ottawa?"

"It's a town near here," said Nicole.

"What would you be doing at this Wal-mart?"

"The pharmacy there needs an assistant."

"Have you told-"

Gray pointed at the floor with his fork.

"Just now," said Nicole.

"How'd that go?"

"It's not like I *want* to work all the way out there. They just don't need anyone here. Mom pretty well takes care of all the pharmacy work. They'll understand eventually, right?"

"It'll be fine," said Gray.

This got a smile out of his mother. She popped a forkful of pancakes into her mouth. "Now tell me about your day! But, like for real."

"You should see the windows they have in the library. It's like something out of a magazine or a movie. They go all the way to the ceiling."

Gray stopped when he saw the knowing look on his mother's face.

"Wait," said Gray. "Are you in the yearbooks?"

"I'd have to think so!"

Gray filed a new directive: keep his classmates away from the yearbooks. Or really any knowledge that his mother had gone to high school there.

"So," his mother said. "Did you meet anyone cute?"

Gray pointed at his face, which he'd only just stuffed with pancakes. It served as a good stalling tactic. He didn't really want to answer that question with the truth, which was that in spite of all of the madness that had marked his first day, there'd been Patra Patterson's freckles. And the way she smelled. Although he couldn't imagine how anything would ever come of that.

"Come on," said Nicole, dropping her fork and putting her hands under her chin. "Tell me!"

Gray swallowed but continued to point at his face as if he still couldn't talk. Nicole laughed and came around to his side of the table. She wrapped her arms around his shoulders.

"Tell me!"

Gray shook his head. This was just like his mother, who had this ability to shrink the world to a moment like this one. Sure, they'd just moved across the country and were living in an apartment above her parents' general store. But somehow it felt OK.

"Come on, Mom!"

"Fine. But whoever it is, she'll be lucky if you decide to talk to her." Nicole Taylor kissed her son on the head before rising to her full 5'10." "Oh and one thing I forgot to tell you: I start work tomorrow. And you know how I hate the idea of you being home alone after school."

"What do you mean?"

"I *mean* I'm not going to be home until 6 or 6:30. So maybe you could ask Grandma and Grandpa if you could help in the store 'til then?"

"Mom!"

Nicole shrugged as she picked up their plates and started into the tiny kitchen. "Sorry! But it's not that big a deal. I'll bet you can find something to do there."

While she busied herself with the dishes, Gray tapped the table in front of him. He liked his grandparents just fine. But working with them after school didn't sound ideal, especially when he considered what Patra had said:

There's something about athletes that's sexy…

And while the basketball coach—Rutherford—wasn't Barack Obama or Gandalf the Grey when it came to inspirational speeches, he wasn't wrong, either. Maybe basketball would help, when it came to his new start.

Gray picked up the Mrs. Butterworth's. He carried it to the threshold between the tiny dining area and the kitchen. His mother was staring at the bottle of bright green dish soap, considering how much to use. They'd had a dishwasher in Reseda.

"Hey, Mom?"

A few strands of Nicole's blond hair were hanging across her eyes. She blew them away. "Yeah, hon?"

"What if I were doing something else tomorrow after school?"

CHAPTER 8

As Gray got to the bottom of the locker room stairs at the end of his second day at Beaudelaire High School, he was thinking of the first time he'd been in a locker room. It had been one of his father's last fights and he could tell—even at five—that they didn't usually allow kids inside the locker room at the Long Beach Civic Center. He'd hidden behind his mother, refusing to come out from behind her legs even when his dad had grinned, tired and slick with sweat, patting the bench next to him.

"Let's go, California!"

Coach Rutherford was on the other side of the locker room, a few paces out of his office, tapping his silver watch.

Gray snapped the rubber band on his wrist. There was no

going back now. He hustled over to Coach Rutherford, who put his hand on his chin, rubbing the gray stubble there.

"Those pants are a step in the right direction," he said.

Gray glanced down at the jeans he'd put on that morning. They were the pair he wore when his dad had needed him to help work on his car. It had required repairs so frequently that Gray had begun to wonder if his dad kept it in that state on purpose.

"Speaking of wardrobes," said Coach Rutherford. "We need to get you some practice gear."

Gray followed Rutherford, grateful for the opportunity to avoid—for a few more minutes—the middle of the locker room, which was separated from them by a tall bank of lockers. He could hear the bustle of his new teammates as they prepared for practice. That was the thing he was worried about more than anything else: how to deal with a bunch of jocks. If he was learning anything about Beaudelaire it was that sports were celebrated above nearly everything else—a fact that had worked in his favor all day. The football team had won its state semifinal game the night before, and the accompanying jubilation meant that new kids were old news. In fact, after the madness of Gray's first day, Day 2 had felt almost *familiar.* Elmer had even invited him to come with his family to the state championship game that weekend.

Inside the tiny coach's office, Rutherford opened the metal locker next to the Larry Bird poster. He rummaged through a cardboard box that sagged like it had been inside the locker since the school was built. He came up with a practice uniform, shiny and limp. He tossed Gray the mesh jersey and shorts.

"Wash those at least once a week. I don't want them standing up on their own. Now let's talk about those Moon boots."

Gray looked down at his black Vans. "These won't work?"

"What the hell *are* they?"

"They're for skating," said Gray.

"Like, on ice?"

"No, on a board."

"Alright. Give 'em a shot until you can get some real kicks. Now get dressed. We start in ten."

Clutching his practice clothes to his chest, Gray spun for the interior of the locker room. His new teammates were scattered among three sections and Gray chose the section populated by only two new teammates: Dusty Rhoads and William "Bug" Biancalana.

Dusty was sitting on the wooden bench, his shirtless back against a locker and his eyes closed while his calloused feet aired out on the concrete floor.

Just beyond him, Bug Biancalana was working at a belt buckle that looked like it weighed ten pounds. A dark mustache matched the belt buckle in being regionally appropriate.

"Howdy," said Bug. "Take ya' a seat now, ya hear?"

"Don't listen to him," said Dusty, opening his eyes and shaking his floppy hair out of them. "It's a bit."

"I resent that, Dustin. You could have allowed me my fun." Then Bug looked at Gray. "You're the new addition to our institution, correct?"

Gray nodded.

"From California?"

Gray nodded again. A smile crawled onto Bug's face as he gathered his mesh jersey, preparing to pull it over his head.

"I've always wanted to know-"

Belt buckles.

White people.

Locker room.

Gray took a sharp breath.

"-how are the womenfolk in California?"

Gray exhaled, even though he wasn't completely in the clear. The story of holding Stefanie Espinosa's hand in seventh grade wasn't going to impress these two.

"Not…bad," he said.

"Hell yeah," said Dusty, holding out his fist for a bump.

Gray tapped the knuckles that were offered.

Bug wrenched his practice shorts out of his locker.

"Here's the unfortunate news, young friend: whatever behaviors you were participating in in California, you will soon look back upon those times fondly. Because the young women here-"

Dusty leaned back into his locker and finished the sentence.

"Not as cool, bro. Not as cool."

"Have you guys been to LA?" asked Gray.

"Alas," said Bug. "We have not. But we do own televisions."

"You've got cute girls here," said Gray.

Dusty thumped Bug's pale knee.

"Let's see how he feels after six weeks."

"What happens after six weeks?"

"You'll be real tired of looking at the same girls, that's what," said Dusty.

"Yes," said Bug, glancing behind Gray. "But you needn't worry about that now. What you need to worry about now-"

Gray inhaled abruptly. Was *this* when it happened—when Bug said something about borders or walls-

"-is getting your asses upstairs," said Coach Rutherford, pulling shut the door to his office. "Y'all ready?"

Gray looked down. He'd gotten his shoes off, but he hadn't put on a shred of his practice uniform.

"Almost?"

"Great start, California."

"That's our fault, Coach," said Dusty.

"Get that gear up over your head," said Coach Rutherford. Then he waved at Dusty and Bug. "You two, no time like now."

Dusty and Bug ambled out of the locker room with Coach Rutherford, leaving Gray alone in the cavernous space. He took off his pants. Then his shirt, leaving him in the underwear his mother had bought him at the Target on Kester—the one that stayed open until 11, where the security guards always huddled in the parking lot making it look like they were up to no good. He reached over on the bench for his practice shorts and slid them on, considering the encounter and how fascinated Dusty and Bug had been with California, which seemed almost mythical to them. Little did they know that where he'd lived—in a two-bedroom apartment with a window unit and only one parking space—hadn't been mythical at all.

Gray reached for his jersey. But it wasn't there. He checked under the bench. It wasn't there, either. Then it hit him: Dusty must have swiped it while they were talking.

Shirtless, Gray slipped on the shorts and his shoes. When he was dressed, a pile of street clothes was left on the floor. He picked them up and an idea occurred to him. He walked around the bank of lockers in front of him to the back of the locker room, opening and closing the metal doors of each of the lockers that seemed like candidates.

On his fifth try, he found it: the carving of NT + HB.

Gray smiled and dropped his jeans and shirt, wallet and keys. And then slammed the locker door and, still shirtless, jogged up the stairs, out through the heavy wooden door, past the Coke machine, and into the brick tunnel that led from the commons area to the gym.

Dusty was waiting at the tunnel's end.

With a smile, he tossed Gray's jersey to him.

"Welcome to the team, little homey," he said.

"California! Let's see what you've got."

Coach Rutherford's voice froze Gray. He pointed at his own chest. He'd only had five minutes to watch what they were doing on the court—a bewildering maze of weaves and traps and defensive drills.

"No," said Rutherford. "The other guy on the sideline. Come guard Bug."

Gray jogged onto the court, to a spot in front of Bug and his mustache.

Coach Rutherford threw the ball to Bug.

"Alright," he said. "Your education begins."

To this point, the totality of Gray Taylor's experience with basketball had come in two places: on the playground at his middle school and that one Los Angeles Lakers game he'd seen with his father, where there'd been tacos or burritos. It was into this vast reservoir of knowledge that Gray tapped when Bug caught the ball—a ball Gray thought was a good thing to keep his eye on. So that's what he did: he watched the ball.

William "Bug" Biancalana was no star basketball player. As the mustache and belt buckle indicated, he was better on horseflesh than hardwood. In the season prior to this one, he'd played only 12 minutes each game, averaging six points and shooting 23% from behind the three-point line. However, Bug knew a sucker when he saw one. When he noticed that Gray was watching the ball so intently, he faked a pass to the player in the middle of the court. When the fake happened, Gray followed the ball with his eyes. And because the fake was so exaggerated, his feet went with his eyes. This left Bug with just the space he needed to dribble past Gray and toward the basket, where he laid the ball off the backboard. It dropped through the hoop and into the net.

"First lesson," said Coach Rutherford. "You don't watch the ball. You don't watch the man *with* the ball. You watch the man with the ball's belly button. And crouch down, like a boxer."

When Rutherford said "boxer," something clicked in Gray's brain. His dad had said something about belly buttons when they'd watched a fight one time. (They'd watched a lot more fights than basketball games.) That something was, "You see how this man cannot move without his belly button? This is important when you are fighting."

"Now," said Coach Rutherford. "Let's try it again."

And just like that, Gray learned how to play man-to-man defense. For about four seconds. Because once Bug passed the ball, everything changed again.

On the other side of the court, Dusty Rhoads caught the ball, drove past his man, and dropped the ball into the basket.

Rutherford pulled a whistle from around his neck and blew it.

Gray pointed at himself again.

Coach Rutherford nodded and Gray stopped moving, expecting another lesson. He got it, but not from Rutherford. Instead, it was Dustin "Dusty" Rhoads who spoke up.

"Bro. You gotta help."

When he saw the blank look in Gray's eyes, Dusty sighed and grabbed the ball, which had settled under the basket. He tossed it out to the player who'd been guarding him and crouched in the middle of the court. He pointed at the kid with the ball, then at Bug, and then at himself.

"Imagine you're at a party and, like, your bud is off on the other side of the room. But he's talking to some lame-ass girl and you know he might need you to come grab him to get him out of this situation. But there's a girl you kinda like on the side of the room."

He pointed at Bug. "He's the girl you like."

He pointed at the ball. "And this ball is your friend. So you gotta stay in between 'em."

"That's not a bad analogy, Dustin," said Coach Rutherford.

"Anytime you need, coach," said Dusty, his face cracking into a smile as he rose from his defensive stance.

Rutherford looked at Gray. "You got it now?"

Gray nodded even though there was one thing that was bothering him: if all this happened with one pass, what would happen after three passes or six passes or when everyone was moving? How was he going to manage all this chaos? There were so many options—so many ways things could go wrong!

Coach Rutherford clapped his hands.

Gray snapped his rubber band.

And this time, as the ball moved around the perimeter, Gray moved with it. When Bug got the ball he dropped into a boxer's stance, one foot ahead of the other, and watched Bug's belly button. And sure enough, when Bug faked with the ball, he didn't lunge in the wrong direction.

Coach Rutherford blew his whistle.

"Good," he said. "Now switch it up."

Bug handed the ball to Gray with a smile.

"Your turn, my young friend."

While the rest of the team settled into their respective positions, Gray ran his hands across the basketball. The surface was smoother and softer than he'd expected, like a pair of shoes that's been broken in.

"OK," Rutherford said with a nod. "Have at it."

Gray glanced at Bug's feet. And then he took off for the basket. When he got there, he laid the ball off the backboard and into that basket, and the ball fell through the net with a rustle that matched the flutter in Gray's belly.

It had been so smooth! So natural! First, he'd conquered defense. And now: offense. And all of it in about eight minutes' time. Basketball was his best idea yet! OK, it hadn't been *his* idea; it was more Coach Rutherford's idea. But he'd been the one who'd put it into practice, taking advantage of his natural athleticism, granted to him by his father, and his natural sense of determination, granted to him….probably also by his father.

Gray's inner celebration bubbled into an exterior celebration marked by a screeching "Wheee!" that lasted exactly as long as it takes a basketball to drop from ten feet to the ground, which was also exactly the amount of time it took for the team's collective confusion to turn into collective amusement.

Coach Rutherford blew his whistle six times in an effort to stop the laughter.

Gray's head spun as he searched for an explanation—first to Bug, then to Dusty, then to Coach Rutherford.

What he got in return:

A wide-eyed look on Bug's face.

A bemused smile from Coach Rutherford.

And Dusty Rhoads saying the thing he'd say again that night at the makeshift dinner table he shared with his father and brother. "I mean, Coach is always saying you can get further than you think on one dribble."

This was the problem with Gray's maneuver: he'd only dribbled once in the forty feet between his starting point and the basket. He'd been guilty of at least three traveling violations on the way.

When Gray saw the reactions from his new teammates, his suspicions were confirmed. They'd all been lying in wait, hoping for just such a moment to humiliate the new kid—the new *Latino* kid.

He glanced at the brick tunnel. Within minutes, he could be dressed and free. His practice clothes weren't even sweaty; he wouldn't have to feel bad about giving them back to Coach Ruther-ford. Or he could just leave them in the locker, hanging from that shiny metal hook.

Gray took one step toward the tunnel. And another. What had he been thinking, anyway? He wasn't a basketball player. He was nobody.

Again.

It was this thought that stopped Gray. He didn't want to be a nobody like he'd been in Reseda—where everyone walked past him, where his own teachers didn't know his name. It was going to feel that way, if he jogged down those stairs and took off his practice gear and put on his street clothes. Sure, the people up here were laughing at him. But at least they were acknowledging he was here.

Plus, that locker room was scary.

So Gray snapped the rubber band, took a hard right, and jogged back to the spot where he'd been.

"OK, what'd I do wrong?"

CHAPTER 9

Gray heaved his backpack into the hallway that separated kitchen from living room. It landed with a thunk that gave away the weight of its contents—three thick textbooks, including the big one from Western Civilization. When it came to homework, the New Student Honeymoon was over.

He leaned into the doorway at the edge of the kitchen. "You know what I can't figure out?"

Nicole Taylor was finding spots for the bags and boxes she'd brought home from Wal-mart. She closed the door to the cupboard over the sink. "How we ended up in Kansas in a matter of five days?"

"That too," said Gray.

"Sorry. Long day." Then Nicole shook her head and it was like the color returned to the room. "Anyway, what can't you figure out?"

Gray picked up a can of black beans from the nearest counter. "Why everyone is so nice. Like, these two kids before practice today. I was expecting them to mess with me, but they were actually pretty decent. And this guy, Elmer, invited me to the football game Saturday."

"Right? I was, like, totally dreading my first day at work—and don't get me wrong, I'm tired—but the people were *amazing*. I'd kind of forgotten. You should go. To the game. Embrace it while it feels good. Because they do get a little boring, these folks."

"Yeah," said Gray, not sure what else to say. In truth, "these folks" didn't seem any more boring than the folks they'd left behind. And "these folks" seemed a lot less likely to try to sell you Adderall next to a dumpster behind a Subway on a scorching Thursday in August. Or pull a boxcutter when you said no. But what did he know? He'd been here for two days. His mother had grown up here.

Speaking of that.

"Was the old gym around when you went to school here?"

"What are you saying?"

"I'm saying you're old as the hills, Mom."

Nicole opened the cabinet. Then she slammed the door shut and threw a bag of rotini at her son. Pretending he needed to protect the can of beans in his hand, Gray let the pasta glance off him and fall onto the floor, where it did not burst like it would have in the movie scene and instead slid harmlessly up against the cabinets.

Gray picked up the bag of pasta.

"You dropped something."

"Just trying to teach you a lesson, mister. I may be old, but I'm still speedy!"

Gray tossed her the bag. She slipped the pasta into the cupboard in front of her and shut the door.

"To answer your question: yes, that gym was there when I was in school. And not only that, I played in that gym."

"Played basketball?"

"Second-team all-class."

"What? Why didn't you keep playing?"

"It seemed silly. You know, I don't really feel like cooking. And I kind of want to show you someplace—from the good *old* days. Want to go?"

"No," said Gray, holding up the can of beans. "I want to stay here and cook these."

"Really? I didn't think you liked beans."

"Mom. I'm joking. Let me get a coat."

Gray pulled open the glass door to Tundin's Family Diner, letting his mother lead the way into the tiled foyer. When he followed her inside, he almost bowled her into a set of ancient gumball machines. She'd stopped when she'd seen the battered hostess stand.

"Whoa, Mom," said Gray.

"Sorry," she said, shaking her head. "It's just, I never thought I'd be here again."

"Let's get a seat," said Gray.

"I can help with that," said a voice, after which Gray put the name of the place together.

Mitzy Tundin was behind the cash register at the end of a long, spotless counter lined with stools the same teal color as the outer walls.

Gray scanned the room for an adult.

"Yep," said Mitzy. "Inherited the place when my parents died and now I run it all by my lonesome. It's a hard-luck story about a girl overcoming all the obstacles the world might throw at her."

"I'm so sorry," said Nicole.

"I'm kidding," said Mitzy. "This *is* my parents' place. But they're alive. I just work here at nights."

"Mom," said Gray. "Mitzy Tundin."

Flaring her teal apron, Mitzy executed a quick curtsy before pointing to a teal booth in the back, two down from an older couple splitting a piece of pie.

The Taylors followed her and sat, Gray across from his mother. Mitzy set their menus on the tabletop.

"Thank you," said Nicole. But she wasn't looking at Mitzy when she said this. She was examining the miniature jukebox that sat in front of the window at the end of their booth. "This doesn't still work, does it?"

"Damn right it does," said Mitzy. "I'll get waters for the two of you.

After Mitzy left them, Nicole ran a finger along the tiny jukebox's teal metal trim. "When we started coming here, all the songs were from the fifties and sixties and we felt like we just *had* to get them changed."

She pointed at the song list and Gray read it aloud.

> Nirvana – *Smells Like Teen Spirit*
> Pearl Jam – *Black*
> Toad the Wet Sprocket – *Walk On The Ocean*
> Candlebox – *Far Behind*
> Metallica – *One*
> Cracker – *Low*

"That was my pick," she said, pointing at the last song.
"Cracker?"

"You've probably never heard that song, have you?"

"I think I'd remember a band called Cracker."

"Especially," said Nicole. "With, well, you know."

"Huh?"

"Cracker," she said. "Like me."

Gray snorted.

"What's so funny?"

Mitzy had returned. She eased two water glasses off her tray and pulled a pen from behind her ear.

"Oh," said Gray. "We haven't even looked."

"You don't need to. I'll tell you what to get."

Which is how the Taylor family came to have breakfast for supper two nights in a row. For Gray, this second breakfast-for supper was an introduction to biscuits and gravy, which are not really a thing in Los Angeles County. Most of the breakfasts in Los Angeles County fit into one of two categories: smoothies or Mexican food.

The novelty of the biscuits and gravy consumed Gray's focus for the next eight minutes—eight minutes that ended when Nicole Taylor dropped her fork and said, "Oh my gosh."

Gray's head whirled from the remnants of the biscuits and gravy. The football coach, Harris Bickle, was standing at the hostess stand in his bright blue Beaudelaire windbreaker.

"POWDER MY NOSE! NIKKI TAYLOR?"

Coach Bickle waved Mitzy aside so he could barge through the diner to get to the Taylor table. Nicole composed herself in time to get out of the booth for a hug.

"Harris Bickle," she said. "What a lovely surprise."

Bickle pulled back and said, "This is...what a... you look so good!"

Then Mitzy came into the frame and asked if she should make theirs a table for three.

Gray didn't want to see his mother uncomfortable, but he did want to know this story. He patted the tabletop. "I think you should."

Mitzy plopped a menu onto the spot next to Nicole. "Enjoy!"

Harris Bickle took off his blue BEARCATS windbreaker and hung it on the peg at the end of the booth, revealing a blue polo shirt with 'BHS' embroidered on the breast. He jerked it down so it would cover his ample midsection and followed Nicole Taylor into the booth, sliding jerkily across the vinyl seat.

"Gray, you didn't tell me your mother was *the* Nikki Taylor."

Gray glanced at his mother: the former Nikki Taylor—a name she'd given up at the suggestion of the scout who'd discovered her during her first semester at the University of Kansas, in order to avoid confusion with The Nikki Taylor, who was just finishing her domination of the market for tall, honey-blonde models.

"She never talks about high school," said Gray.

"You never tell Gray here about your glory days?"

"I like to think that those were the days *before* my glory days," said Nicole.

"That's us," said Bickle. "Launchpad to the stars." He winked at Gray. "Speaking of which, I saw you in that one video, by the guy who dates all the women. John something."

"Mayer," said Nicole.

Harris Bickle picked up his menu. "I've always wondered. Were those kisses real?"

"They were pretty real," said Nicole, with a glance at Gray. She didn't know how much Gray knew about those three months with John Mayer. Which, thanks to the internet, was a lot.

"Never know with Hollywood," said Harris Bickle, returning his attention to the menu, which he then dropped to the table.

"Don't know why I'm even looking at that. I practically have the thing memorized. It's going to be a shame when it's gone."

Nicole looked over at the man who'd once been the boy she'd gone to Homecoming with.

"They're closing?"

"All I know is that everybody's been going to the new Applebee's they built out on 56."

Then, his attention wandering like a puppy's, Harris Bickle glanced at the jukebox. "Remember when we picked out those songs?"

"Like it was yesterday," said Nicole.

"Wasn't yours the Cracker song?"

Nicole—or maybe it was Nikki—turned to Harris Bickle. This time her eyes were softer. "How'd you remember?"

Harris Bickle tapped the side of his head. "It's just in here."

Mitzy appeared at the table's end.

Bickle handed his menu to her. "Might as well make it five in a row," he said.

Mitzy put a hand on the football coach's shoulder. "At least there's bacon," she said.

Then Mitzy walked away and the unlikely threesome was left to pick up the conversational pieces. Gray glanced at his mother. She was looking quizzically at Mr. Bickle, who was rubbing his hands. Then his eyes popped up, focusing on Gray's. "Heard you might be playing basketball."

"I'm only one day in," said Gray.

"Don't let it distract you. We might need you next fall when football season comes back around. May have to chop that lettuce, though." He nodded at the top of Gray's head. "In the meantime, you'll get some good things from Rutherford. Good man, that one. Shame he's struggled like he has. Just goes to show. Can't be giving people things."

Then, as Gray was trying to figure out if what Coach Bickle had just said was race-related, Mitzy Tundin returned with Bickle's breakfast/dinner, sliding it in front of him as she reviewed what was on the plate.

"Two strips of bacon, two sausage patties, four eggs over *medium*. Sourdough toast."

"Thanks, darlin'," said Bickle, rubbing his hands together. "Nice to be able to eat this way again."

Mitzy leaned across the football coach so she could catch Nicole's eye. "Want your check?"

Gray knew this was going to be one of those times when he had to take charge. His mom was too polite to get them out of here.

"I do have some things I need to get done for school," said Gray.

Nicole glanced up at Mitzy. "Then yes, the check, please."

"Meet me at the front," said Mitzy.

Bickle set down the fork he'd just picked up. "Leaving so soon?"

"We should get home," said Nicole. "Just getting started, you know."

"Where are y'all living, anyhow?"

"Above my parents, for now."

"In the old apartments?"

"One of them."

"It's nice!"

The two adults looked at Gray in surprise.

"I'm sure it is," said Coach Bickle. He raised his eyebrows at Nicole as if it say, "Kids, right?" Then he dabbed at his mouth with his napkin so he could stand and allow Nicole Taylor to get out of the booth.

"Maybe I'll see you tomorrow night?"

"What's tomorrow night?"

Harris Bickle frowned at Gray. "You didn't tell her?"

"The meeting, Mom. About the bond thing."

"Oh right," she said. "Yes, I believe I'll be there."

"Good," said Bickle. "I think you'll be impressed by what we're proposing. It's disappointing that some people are holding up progress like they are."

Gray watched his mother's eyes light up when Bickle said the magic word. Progress. Where Gray had come from—where he'd lived until six days before this—the sorts of people who talked about "progress" were also the sorts of people who named their kids Meadow and Dash and thought vaccines were what caused their kids to be antisocial. But just because Gray had gotten suspicious of people who talked about "progress" didn't mean everyone had. And chief among "everyone" was his mother, who'd become increasingly fond of expressions about sharks (who will, supposedly, die if they don't keep moving forward) and mountain climbers (who will, assuredly, never finish if they don't keep moving up).

Nicole Taylor held up a finger. There was a light in her eyes that Gray hadn't seen since they'd arrived in Beaudelaire.

"You're exactly right about that," she said.

Gray kept his eyes closed for another second, allowing the satisfaction of a job well done to wash over him. He'd gotten position on Dusty Rhoads, taking what he'd learned was a "charge" by putting himself between Dusty and the basket. He'd absorbed Dusty's knee with his chest. And then absorbed the gym floor with his tailbone.

Gray opened his eyes to find Bug Biancalana standing over him.

"My land, Dustin. You nearly killed the freshman."

Gray allowed Bug to heave him off the floor. Coach Rutherford was clapping his hands and saying, "Alright, that's good for today."

Gray jogged over to the circle that was forming around the coach. Most of his teammates had their hands on their hips, a few had their hands over their heads. All of them were the same in one way: they'd spent the past two hours working hard. Now they were done. And Gray wasn't sure why, but he loved this feeling.

Coach Rutherford said, "Got anything, Dusty?"

Dusty Rhoads glanced up at the coach, surprise in his eyes. He was expecting Rutherford to say something—summarize the day or applaud Gray's play.

"Alright then," said Rutherford. "If anyone wants to do some extra work, the gym'll be open for another fifteen minutes. Then that meeting, the bond issue thing."

Rutherford put his hand in the circle and counted to three.

"Beau-beau, da-da, ee-ee-ee," the team chanted, the syllables poorly aligned, a far cry from Gray's first day when the syllables were lined up like rifle sights.

Rutherford was already walking slowly toward the tunnel, his head down. Meanwhile, the rest of the team scattered—a few to retrieve warm-up shirts they'd dropped at the start of practice, others to the water cooler, no one to do any extra work.

Gray watched Coach Rutherford go. Something was going on. He picked up a ball.

"Coach! Could you, like, rebound for me?"

A vision had come to Gray. The two of them, working on Gray's game while the lights got dim. Shot, rebound. Shot, rebound. The ball rolling off into the shadows. Coach Rutherford tousling his hair and telling him he'd done good work that day. He might even be able to warn the coach about Harris Bickle and what he'd said inside Tundin's, about how you couldn't "be giving people things." He still wasn't sure it was *racist*. But it hadn't felt *good*.

Rutherford sighed, looking like he was weighing a choice between death by hanging and death by firing squad. Just then, Trina Patterson peeked out from the dark tunnel.

"You two lovelies about done?"

"Yes, ma'am," said Coach Rutherford, the relief evident.

"Great!" said Trina.

She bent to pick up the two grocery bags she'd set at the tunnel's edge.

"Here," said Rutherford. "Let me take those."

If it had been anyone else, Trina Patterson would have gladly accepted. But what kind of picture would that paint if she, a white woman, allowed Mr. Rutherford, a black man, to help carry her bags? Trina Patterson believed herself to be very sensitive to issues of race.

"Oh, I've got it," she said. "And Patra will be along any minute."

At the mention of Patra's name, Gray forgot about the charge he'd taken, about the celebration that hadn't come, about his vision of shooting baskets with Coach Rutherford, and about racism, generally. He didn't want Patra to see him in his practice clothes. His shoulders looked like a pair of rakes.

"Alright," said Rutherford, tipping an imaginary cap. "Good luck with the meeting."

"I'm sure it will turn out just like it should!"

"See you later, Mrs. Patterson," said Gray, just as Patra appeared at the other end of the tunnel. She was carrying a pair of grocery bags of her own.

"Cool body," she said.

Gray blushed, assuming Patra was making fun of his thin frame. Little did he know: Patra didn't expect a 14-year-old's body to look like an Olympic weightlifter.

Gray recovered in time to say the first thing he could think of: "Cool shirt."

Still holding the bags at her sides, Patra looked down at her shirt, which was a black and yellow Nirvana T-shirt with a smiley face with Xs for eyes.

"Thanks," she said. "Wait, were you looking at my tits?"

Gray's eyes got wide. No he hadn't been looking at her "tits"! Or he didn't think he had been. Maybe he had? Then again, how could you look at a girl's shirt without also looking at her breasts?

"I'm just messing with you, Lama. I don't have any tits." Patra moved past Gray and set her bags on the gym floor. She blew a strand of her light brown hair out of her eyes. "I'll be in the library during the meeting," she said. "I mean, if you're staying."

And here Gray accidentally did something smart. He said, "I might."

Gray said this because there was a chance his mother was coming to the meeting; he'd reminded her about it at least three times. If she did come to the meeting, she was his ride home. That covered the "Yes" portion of "I might." But there was also a chance his mother wasn't coming to the meeting because Nicole Taylor couldn't always be counted on. And that covered the "No" portion of "I might." The reason this was smart was because when Gray said it, he was just tired enough from practice that it seemed flirtatious. That flirtatiousness was made all the more convincing by the way Gray raced out of the tunnel, leaving Patra with the impression that he had more important things to do. In reality, Gray was still thinking about how skinny he was and how he probably smelled awful.

But Patra didn't know any of that. Which was why, as Gray walked out of the tunnel, she was watching him go.

––––––––––––

When Gray got to Coach Rutherford's office the coach was at the whiteboard behind his desk, using a marker to scatter Xs and Os across a rectangle that represented an overhead shot of a basketball court.

Gray tapped on the door and nodded at the dry-erase board. "What's that?"

Coach Rutherford capped the marker. "Just something rattling around in my head. What can I do for you, California?"

Gray knew where he wanted to go in the conversation. However, he didn't know how to get there.

"An 'oop,' what's that?"

"Say what?"

"An 'oop.' Dusty said it today to Bug. Like, 'throw me that oop!'"

Coach Rutherford's grin bloomed and he motioned for Gray to sit down on the low couch. Then he sat, too, the physioball squeaking under the additional weight. In the background, the usual hoots and hollers came from the shower as the team unwound from the day of practice.

"*Alley*-oop. That's when one player tosses it to another player and he dunks it, but without coming down."

"I don't think Dusty can jump high enough to do that."

"You got that right, son."

Then Coach Rutherford's face drooped. Gray scanned the cluttered office. Dry-erase boards sat atop the file cabinet behind Rutherford's desk. A deflated basketball rested in the corner, looking tired and forlorn, the signatures on it faded by time. Then there were the posters.

Starks.

Worthy.

Bird.

What had Rutherford said about Larry Bird? That he didn't take shhhhhh- crap from anyone?

Gray snapped the rubber band. "OK coach, what's going on?"

Rutherford glanced at the door behind Gray. "Close that."

When Gray sat back down, Coach Rutherford picked up the deflated basketball and came around the desk. He perched on the corner nearest Gray and began tossing the ball into the air, an easy rhythm of up and down, up and down. After three of these, he finally spoke.

"You know what the problem is with, well, everything?"

Gray had some ideas. But he didn't think now was the time to lay them out. He shook his head.

"The problem," Coach Rutherford said, watching the ball move up and down out of his hands. "Is that everything changes. All the time. It never quits."

"No idea what you're talking about," said Gray.

Rutherford caught the ball. "See, you know what I mean. You probably weren't expecting to be here, say, a year ago."

"Or a month ago."

"Exactly my point." Rutherford looked at Gray like he was gauging whether he could trust him. "You know the principal, Mr. Patterson, right?"

Gray nodded.

"Pete and I played in together in school. Then I went off to play. Or try to. And that didn't exactly work out. Long story, different day. What's important is that a few years after my basketball adventures, Pete found out that we—Ramona and me and Devon—weren't doing so great. So he offered me this job. And I had all these ideas based on what I'd seen in Poland and-"

"You played in Poland?"

"Told you, long story. Anyway, things haven't gone…like we were hoping. We won four games last year, Gray. And five the year before."

"How many did you play?"

"Twenty-two."

"Each season?"

Rutherford nodded.

"Yeah, that's not very good."

"I know," said Coach Rutherford. "So I'm not surprised, but still-"

"Not surprised by what?"

"What Pete—Mr. Patterson—told me today. I guess, now that football's almost done, he's got his attention on the next thing. If I can't pilot this boat full of misfits to at least a .500 record, I'm done. Fresh starts, new horizons, just like with the school. Maybe Woody was right."

"Woody?"

"Jack Woodman, head coach of the St. Anthony Saints. Our arch rival, if you will."

"What'd he say?"

"That I should leave it to the big boys."

"So what can I do?"

Coach Rutherford looked up at the ball, suspended in mid-air.

"Kid, that's real kind of you. But you've played, what, two days of basketball?"

"Maybe-"

The ball landed in Rutherford's palm. He flashed a look toward Gray.

"Yeah?"

The answer seemed pretty obvious to Gray. The man across the desk from him needed to "suck it up," which was another thing his dad sometimes said. But he, Gray, couldn't say that. Coach Rutherford was right. He *had* only played two days of basketball. Not to mention that, in Gray's experience, grown-ups didn't usually like to be told what to do.

"Maybe we'll start by getting Dusty to quit calling for alley-oops."

Coach Rutherford held Gray's bright blue gaze for a second. And another. And another and in *this* second, Gray was reasonably confident that the message had been transferred—what he was saying without saying it, which was that the answer certainly wasn't to do *nothing*.

Rutherford chuckled, coming out of the trance. "Yeah, maybe so," he said. He nodded at the door to his office. "Now you need to hit the showers. Might as well give yourself the best chance with young Miss Patterson."

"How'd you-"

"Gray. Come on. You ain't that slick."

"Exactly! When you think about it, it's durn near certifiable it's taken us this long! I mean, look at what's going on at Edgerton. And they don't have a football team like ours!"

Laughter from inside the gym drew Gray to a spot just far enough into the brick tunnel that he could see what had people laughing.

On the court sat a long table, behind which were the five members of the USD 268 school board. To the side of the table stood the same microphone Harris Bickle had knocked down with his motorcycle on Gray's first day.

Bickle was using this microphone to simultaneously address the board of education and the audience, most of which was seated close to the front of the bleachers.

One exception was Nicole Taylor, who was near the top of the bleachers underneath one of the few championship banners that hung in the gym: *State Runner-up*, from Harris Bickle's senior year (and Nicole Taylor's sophomore year).

"But what about the money?"

This voice came from the audience and belonged to Griswold Karp, proud father of Bartholomew Karp and even prouder member of the Ottawa Nation.

Harris Bickle held out his arms behind the microphone. "Come on now, Grizz. You've seen the studies just like I have. New school means new residents. New residents means new property taxes. New property taxes mean a new stadium for that next quarterback of yours."

Bickle paused as he lasered his eyes on the father of Bartholomew (and Sebastian) Karp.

"That's right. I was at his eighth-grade game. Kid has a cannon. Chance to be just as good as his brother. Or his dad."

"Let's not get ahead of ourselves, Coach," said Griswold Karp.

This delighted anyone in the audience who knew their Beaudelaire football history, which was approximately 90% of that audience. This portion laughed along with Harris Bickle who, while an experienced leader of men, was still not an experienced user of microphones, which explained the amplified "HA HA HA" that dominated the gymnasium before the whine of feedback cut him off.

"Whoa, there," said Bickle. He tapped the microphone. "Ladies and gentlemen of the board, I think I've made my point. This bond issue would be good for the town, good for the school, good for all of us. It's progress. And progress is always a good thing."

Gray glanced up at his mother. She was nodding at that magical word.

"Now if you'll excuse me, I've got to get home so I can get ready. You know, little football game coming up. Go, Bearcats!"

Mr. Bickle hustled off to a round of applause that wasn't deafening but was impressive for an assembly about high school finance.

"Thank you, Mister—or rather, Coach—Bickle," came the voice of the middle board member. He pushed a pair of glasses up his nose so he could see the paper in front of him. "Next, we'll hear from our financial advisor on this-"

Gray stopped listening because Harris Bickle was going to have to come through the tunnel he was standing in. He took off, down the tunnel, through the commons, past the office and up the stairs, vaulting them two at a time. The hallway he landed in wasn't pitch-black, but it was close. The only light came from two sources: an EXIT sign above the stairway he'd just come up and from under the tall library door. But this light was far dimmer than he expected. That dimness was explained when Gray pulled open the door. There was only one light on in the library—a lamp with a shade made of burlap. This lamp sat at the end of a long oak table, illuminating a book that sat in front of Patra Patterson and her Nirvana T-shirt.

Patra looked up when Gray walked in, but she neither smiled nor said anything. And this didn't give Gray much to work with. Was she happy he'd come to the library? Disappointed he'd come to the library? But he'd come this far, so he let the door behind him close, careful not to let it slam. Starting across the library's polished wood floor, he snapped the rubber band as surreptitiously as he could.

"What's that about?"

Patra was pointing at his wrist.

"It's…nothing," he said.

Patra peered over the top of the burlap lamp shade. "This isn't going to work if you keep secrets," she said, leaning into the light. It made her hair shine in a way that almost stopped Gray's heart.

"It's a reminder to stop thinking so much—to just, like, stay here."

"It 'snaps' you out of it, then."

Patra hit an air cymbal as she backed out of the halo of light and slid the sliver of paper she was using as a bookmark into its place. "You going to sit down?"

"Yeah," said Gray. "Right after I do this."

He reached down and yanked the paper from the book.

Patra snapped her fingers. "Give it."

Gray plopped into the chair across from Patra. He held the piece of paper in front of his face as his heart whacked the middle of his chest. "Only if you'll tell me what's going on downstairs."

Patra snatched her bookmark and leaned onto the table. "Mr. Lama, we've got a little problem here. People are moving out of small towns and into big ones as the small farmer is run out of business by agricultural monoliths like Cargill. And as people leave the small towns, it's harder to get *other* people to come to the small towns. It's a death spiral."

"So what you're saying is, the towns start to die and the only ones that make it are the ones that do something big. Like, say, build a new school."

"More or less," said Patra.

"But if people are leaving, isn't there a chance the new school could be a problem if there's not enough kids to use it?"

Patra pointed a finger gun at Gray. "Bingo."

"So which side do you want to win?"

"I have my own side," said Patra. "Neither. I don't plan to be here either way."

Gray leaned back in his chair. He took a second to take in the library, with its tall windows and stacks and stacks of books. Coach Rutherford was right: everything was always changing. Some people, like Harris Bickle, wanted to speed it up. And some people, like Coach Rutherford, wanted to slow it down. Other people, like Patra Patterson, wanted to run away from it.

"What's so bad about this place?" asked Gray.

"Do you know how boring it is here? I mean, it must seem especially boring to you, coming from LA. Speaking of. What's it like? LA, I mean."

"It's hard to tell that time is passing there. And so people look young forever. But they also seem sad, somehow."

"Sad?"

"You have to understand that Los Angeles is there mostly to create entertainment. So it's like Oz, kind of."

"Oh boy," said Patra.

"What?"

"You're in Kansas," said Patra. "We don't like talking about Oz here."

"I didn't even think about that, Dorothy."

Patra glared at him. But there was a smile in there, too. "So how is it like Oz?"

Gray leaned forward, putting his arms onto the table. His eyes got big and blue.

"Everyone from outside LA sees it as this dream place. But everyone *there* is trying to find what you have here. Like, a community where people seem to know each other and care about each other. A school that doesn't have gang fights every day. Even a library like this one. I mean, if you think about it, everyone in LA is making movies and TV shows where they fantasize about places like this."

"It is a pretty great library, isn't it?"

"Exactly! So why do you want to leave it so badly?"

"There just has to be more, you know?"

"Maybe," said Gray, following Patra's gaze. "But I don't know. It feels like you ought to enjoy what you have while you have it."

Gray liked that line.

He thought Patra might, too.

But before either of them could consider Gray's words any further, the library door creaked open.

"So this place probably looks about the same," Peter Patterson was saying. Then he noticed the light coming from where Gray and Patra were sitting. He shielded his eyes and squinted.

"Patra? And…Gray?"

Patra flashed one last glance at Gray. "Yeah, Dad, over here."

Peter Patterson and Nicole Taylor exchanged a glance and walked toward their unexpected find: their children, huddled up in the school library, of all places.

"What are you two up to?" asked Mr. Patterson.

"I was explaining what's going on downstairs," said Patra.

"Funny," said Mr. Patterson. "I was doing the same."

"So," said Patra. "Are you, like, all in?"

Nicole put a hand to her chest. "Me? Well, sure. But I don't know that it'll matter. I don't know how long we'll be here anyway."

"Oh?" said Mr. Patterson. "Leaving us so soon?"

Nicole Taylor pushed a strand of her hair behind an ear. "Honestly, I don't know. The plan was that this was just temporary."

Gray glared at his mother, although she didn't notice it. She was busy absorbing the attention she was getting from Mr. Patterson, including a hand that found its way onto her arm. "Well, I for one think that would be a shame."

Patra said, "I don't blame you. I can't wait to get out of here."

Mr. Patterson sighed. "We know, Patra."

"Sorry, Dad," said Patra. "You shouldn't have brought us to this boring-ass town."

Mr. Patterson took a deep breath. "I know, darling. It'll all be over soon, I promise, and you can graduate early and go off to Berkeley or wherever it is you want to go."

"I was thinking Menlo Park, but whatever."

Gray wanted to say something, anything, to get back to the moment he'd had with Patra, back when the lamplight had made anything seem possible.

Nicole tapped Gray on the shoulder.

"Hey, squirt, you ready? We should get home."

"We should go, too," said Mr. Patterson.

Patra opened her book. "Can I stay for five more minutes? I've still got a few pages to go. Someone-"

She looked at Gray and Gray took some solace in the fact that there remained a small spark in her eyes.

"-interrupted me."

"Sure, Smurf. Just come downstairs when you're done."

Peter Patterson tapped Nicole Taylor's shoulder. "Come on. I'll show you the onion skins. That's what the architects—they're from Kansas City—call the blueprints."

Gray pushed his chair under the table, hoping the movement would catch Patra's attention. But it didn't. Patra's eyes were back on her book.

Then it hit him.

"The game!"

Patra looked up, blinking. "What game?"

"The football game. In Lawrence. You're going, right?"

"I am."

"Well, so am I. With Elmer."

"Alright then, Lama. I'll see you there."

"Sounds good, Smurf."

That got a middle finger out of Patra, but the right kind of middle finger.

Gray followed his mother and the principal out the library door. As he walked behind them—first through the dim library, then down the dim hallway, and finally through the not-so-dim commons—Gray was considering everything he'd just learned. His mother was serious about making this stop a temporary one. Patra was serious about going someplace else. The principal had a thing for his mother. And if he didn't miss his guess, his mother had a little bit of a thing for him. But most of all, no one here knew how good they had it. They needed someone to show them. And he figured that someone might as well be him.

CHAPTER 12

Bright green.

Bright red.

Bright blue.

The bright green belonged to the grass inside Memorial Stadium, usually home to the long-suffering football team of the University of Kansas. The bright red was the opposition: Pittsburg-Trident, which was swarming Bartholomew Karp and his bright blue uniform.

In the stands, forty-two rows above the colors, Elmer shook his head.

"Should've pitched it," he said, easing onto the aluminum bleacher behind him. He waved toward the field. "See how the line-

backer was already committed to Bartholomew? He should have
made that read and pitched it out. Probably would've gotten six or
seven more yards."

Gray caught Mitzy's eye. She made a cutting motion.
But Gray couldn't resist.

"If they're so bad, how'd they make it this far? You know,
state championship game and all."

"Probably because the Option's been out of style for so long
that it comes as a surprise to everyone who sees it. Back in the
Eighties and Nineties when Nebraska was running the Option, everyone else did, too. But that meant people were used to stopping it.
Like, their linebackers were used to reading the quarterback's hips,
which are really the key to stopping the Option—you've got to pay
attention to where his hips are."

Gray leaned forward so he could see Mitzy again.

"I can see why he got so mad at me for thinking he was a
football player."

"Zip it," said Elmer. "Or you're finding your own
ride home."

On the field, the two teams lined up for another play. The
Beaudelaire center snapped it to Bartholomew Karp, who faked
like he was going to run the Option again. But this time he stopped
short, took a step backward, and tossed a pass over the middle to
Bobby Murphy, whose copper-colored hair draped out of his blue
helmet just like it did when it was covered by hats with tractors
on them.

Murphy caught the ball in stride, and for a moment it
looked like he was going to sprint through the afternoon sun for a
touchdown. But a Trident linebacker got his arm around his ankle
and tripped him up, eliciting a groan from the Beaudelaire faithful.

"Need to hurry," said Elmer, his eyes dancing between the
field and the scoreboard in the end zone.

There were twenty-two seconds left before half-time. It was 21–6, Pittsburg-Trident.

A referee put the ball on the Trident 48-yard line and backed away, circling his arm to instruct the timekeeper in the grandstand to start the game clock.

Under center, Bartholomew Karp looked down his line at Bobby Murphy and jerked his head. The center snapped the ball and Murphy took off down the field. After a fake to his right, Bartholomew lofted the ball down the sideline where Murphy was running flat-out, keeping his defender on his hip just like he'd been doing since flag football in sixth grade when he and Bartholomew had started playing football together.

The ball arced downward toward the ten-yard line, just where Bartholomew had intended. Murphy reached up and the ball hit his left hand just like *he'd* intended. But as his right hand moved to cradle the ball to his chest, his defender got a hand on his elbow and Bobby Murphy tipped the ball, once, twice, and it tumbled out of bounds.

Back at the line of scrimmage, Bartholomew had his arms over his head while he screamed something unintelligible.

"Shit!"

This wasn't what Bartholomew said. This was what Mitzy said, right before her eyes got wide.

"Sorry," she mouthed to Elmer's father two rows down. The rest of the Niehaus brood had finally worked its way into the stadium. A last-minute diaper-change combined with everything else that was involved in getting nine people into a van (misplaced phones, lost headphones, final trips to the bathroom) had put their departure from Beaudelaire 45 minutes behind schedule.

There was time left for one play, but it ended harmlessly and the horn marking half-time sounded. Both teams trotted off the field while the announcer's voice boomed through the first half's details—first downs, rushing yards, time of posses-sion. Then, clearly turning a page in a guidebook in front of him, he said, "Now, stay tuned for our half-time show, featuring the Beaudelaire Belles!"

Beaudelaire's dance team, which included all three of the ABCs, stood at attention at the 50-yard line.

"Time to go," said Elmer.

He pushed himself off the bleacher behind him and into the stairs next to them, striding up toward the concourse that was 20 rows above.

Gray's head spun to Mitzy.

"What was that?"

With her eyes on the field, Mitzy's voice went explanatory. "In eighth grade, Elmer and Ariel were an item. He was the star run-ning back. She was the head cheerleader. Then he got hurt. She's still the head cheerleader."

"So he has to leave the stadium?"

"That's what he thinks. It's a shame. He was so much better back then."

Then three things happened simultaneously.

The first was that the stadium's sound system boomed with the first note of the bass line from the intro to Snoop Dogg's "What's My Name?"

The second was that Patra Patterson got up from a spot about thirty rows in front of Gray and Mitzy.

And the third was the germination of an idea in Gray's brain. If he was going to save Coach Rutherford's job, show the town it was being silly, and convince his mother not to cart him back to Los Angeles, he was going to need some help.

He snapped the rubber band. "I'm going to go, uh, stretch my legs."

Mitzy waved Gray away, riveted by the Belles.

Gray bounced up the concrete steps as the familiar lyrics washed over the stadium. He smiled at the reference to "creeping through the smog." It had been a long time since smog was an actual issue in Los Angeles.

When Gray emerged onto the concourse, the concrete apron in front of him wasn't teeming with fans. Memorial Stadium was built to hold 50,000 people, and the Class 3A championship game did not warrant the attendance of anywhere close to 50,000 people. It was thus easy enough for Gray to spot Elmer at the concession stand, his back to Gray and his eyes on the menu on the wall. And if it was easy for Gray to pick Elmer out of the crowd, it was also easy for him to find other people. Like, for example, Patra Patterson, who popped out of her own staircase wearing a pair of medium-tight jeans, a medium-tight T-shirt, and a blue scarf.

Gray didn't groan when he saw Patra but he might as well have. He allowed himself to imagine that she was trying to find him. When she saw him, she'd smile and they'd sneak behind a pillar and kiss.

Part of this fantasy came true. When Patra saw Gray she waved. And that was a start. Gray forgot about his Elmer-related mission and started toward her, just missing a portly Pittsburg-Trident fan who was carrying a tray with two hot dogs, two sets of nachos, and two enormous Cokes.

"Watch it, kid!"

Gray spun his head to apologize. This motion took his eyes off his route and he almost ran over a child who was backing away from the ketchup-and-mustard stand, a tiny paper cup of each in either hand.

"Whoa!" said Gray, juking to his left.

And then he was in front of Patra. She held out her arms for a hug. "You came! How was the trip?"

"Full," said Gray.

"There's a lot of Niehauses."

"And somehow it was the quietest ride of all time."

"I love Elmer's dad," said Patra. "He's so precise."

Gray switched to his best German accent. "Ees very exact, thiss mann."

Gray checked for Patra's reaction. He was disappointed to see that she was looking past him, into the mass of people. It hadn't been his best material but he hadn't thought it was *that* bad. It was time to go for broke.

"I think I need to get Elmer to play basketball. How do I do that?"

Patra's eyes swiveled to Gray's, her pupils regaining focus. "Elmer? Basketball? Why?"

"Because I think he loved it."

"You figured that out after three days?"

"Am I wrong?"

"No. Plus, you're going to need him to protect you from Bartholomew and Bobby."

"They play basketball?"

"Of course," said Patra, her eyes going past Gray again.

"So how do I do it?"

"With most people, if you can figure out what they want, you can figure out how they work." Patra put her hand on Gray's forearm. "Here's the thing: Elmer wants to play again, but he's taken a stand. So give him an excuse."

Patra squeezed Gray's arm before brushing past him into the crowd.

Gray's fingers went involuntarily to the spot on his arm. He held the position for a little longer than he wanted to—long enough that Elmer had time to sneak up behind him and chuck him in the shoulder.

"How'd that go?"

Gray's hand was still on his arm. His mind was spinning, to wins and celebrations and post-game kisses.

"It went-"

Gray was about to say "pretty great," but then he saw what he saw next, which was Patra rushing toward a guy wearing a green military jacket, his hair tied into a bun on top of his head. The guy was leaning against one of the stadium's pillars. In addition to the jacket, he was wearing a sly grin as Patra pulled him behind the pillar, and Gray didn't need to see what happened next to know that the wish he'd made had come true. For someone else.

"Just fantastic," said Gray.

Elmer followed Gray's line of sight. "Ah. Sorry."

Gray took a deep breath. So after all that: Patra had a guy, an older guy. Maybe he was in college. Maybe he went to high school in Lawrence. Whatever the case, things had just gotten very different, very fast.

Gray brushed his hair out of his eyes, which were doing that burning bright blue thing.

"I'll make you a bet," he said.

"A bet? About Patra?"

"About the game."

"Okaaaaay," said Elmer.

"If they somehow come back and win this game, they're going to be state champions, right?"

"That would be the implication, yeah."

"If they're state champions, they're going to be insufferable."

"Also true," said Elmer.

"And I can tell that your man Bartholomew Karp—he doesn't like me much, and he's going to make my life difficult. And you don't want that, do you? Especially after-"

Gray pointed to the spot where Patra and Man Bun were locked in their embrace.

"I guess not," said Elmer.

"So here's the bet: if they—I mean 'we'—somehow come back and win this game, you play basketball and you protect me from Bartholomew Karp. If they—I mean 'we' lose, which is probably what's going to happen, what with them being down by 15—no problem, you go back to your lonely mountaintop."

"What if, instead of all that, you just didn't play basketball?"

This stopped Gray. It was a good point. He could just *not* play basketball. Then he recalled the feeling he'd gotten on his second day, which had come again on his third: united with his teammates in a common purpose and like everything else—everything he was prone to worrying about—had melted away.

"Nope. I'm playing basketball. I have to. You'll see why, eventually."

Elmer peered into Gray's electric blue eyes, calculating his options as he took a pull on the lemonade he'd gotten at the concession stand. Gray had been right when he'd guessed that Elmer needed an excuse to come back to sports. And he'd been right to play upon Elmer's natural inclination toward being a protector. He'd felt guilty about slamming Gray into the locker ever since he'd done it, and now he felt guilty about what Patra Patterson had done to Gray's heart. But Elmer Niehaus was not a sucker.

"I'm not saying yes. But let's say I did. I'd need something in return."

"Let's hear it," said Gray.

Then Elmer did something Gray wouldn't have predicted in a billion years. Elmer blushed from his chin to the tops of his ears. "If they win and I play basketball, you have to, well, keep me under control."

"I don't totally understand."

"You'll see why, eventually."

Gray pulled his hand from his side like he was yanking it out of a holster. "You've got a deal."

When Elmer and Gray got back to their seats, Mitzy Tundin was sprawled across the bleachers. She waved across the vista containing the bright green field.

"That was almost too much," she said.

"The half-time show?" said Elmer.

"The Belles, man. Things were jingling and jangling and…whew!"

"The Belles had bells? Like, real bells?"

Mitzy sat upright.

"Elmer," she said, as if she were about to clarify things for him vis-à-vis her sexual orientation. But then she sighed. "Nevermind. Let's concentrate on this comeback."

"Let's," said Gray, nudging Elmer's thigh.

Mitzy's chin rotated from Gray to Elmer and back again. She tilted her head as if she was going to say something.

But just then came the kickoff from Pittsburg-Trident. The ball spun through a sky so blue it seemed like a cartoon, sailing harmlessly through the far uprights, thanks to the wind that had picked up at half-time.

Mitzy's arms shot into the air.

"It's goooooood," she shouted.

And even though this was the obvious joke, Gray laughed an enthusiastic, devil-take-the-details kind of laugh. He'd done everything he could, making his deal with Elmer and learning the bad news about Patra's boyfriend. Now it was a matter of sitting back and observing what unfolded.

Bartholomew Karp started the second half with the Option that Elmer had explained in the first half. Only this time something different happened. Not only did Bartholomew pitch it to his running back, but that running back tore around the end, smashed the

Trident free safety, and ran the ball all the way down the field into the Trident end zone.

"What in the world?" asked Gray.

"That," said Elmer. "Is Devon Rutherford."

"Like, Coach Rutherford's son?"

"One and the same," said Elmer.

"Refuses to play for his dad," said Mitzy.

Gray shook his head. "What is it with you people?"

On the field, Beaudelaire was going for two. The center snapped the ball to Bartholomew Karp, who headed left with Devon Rutherford on his outside. But this time, Karp handed the ball to Bobby Murphy, who was wheeling around from his spot at wide receiver. Murphy trotted into the end zone untouched.

The bottom half of the scoreboard blinked:

> *Trident 21*
> *Beaudelaire 14*

Gray pointed at the scoreboard.

"Zip it," said Elmer.

Mitzy whirled from one seatmate to the other, her eyes in a squint. "OK, what's going on here?"

"I want to tell her," said Gray. "Can I tell her?"

"Fine," said Elmer.

So Gray explained the deal they'd made at half-time, leaving out the part about his heartbreak at the hands of the guy in the cool military jacket. By the time he was done, Mitzy was beaming.

"I had a feeling about you, Gray Taylor," she said. Then a different voice dropped in like a paratrooper.

"What feeling?"

The oldest of Elmer's younger sisters had settled into the bleacher behind Gray. This sister's name was Katya and she looked like the rest of the Niehauses: pale and blond. Although, to Gray's way of thinking, the pale and blond worked quite well on Katya.

Mitzy leaned toward her from her bleacher.

"Gray bet Elmer on the game," she said. "If we win, Elmer's going to play basketball."

"Oh, thank God," said a voice that didn't belong to Katya Niehaus, but did belong to the mother of Katya Niehaus (and to the mother of Elmer Niehaus). When Katherine Niehaus had asked her son to give up sports, she hadn't known he'd take it so seriously; it had been one of those things that had come out before she'd known what she was saying. And frankly—as she told her colleagues in the social sciences department at Beaudelaire College—she wanted him to get out of the house.

And so, the Beaudelaire cheering section got a little more exuberant, bolstered by an uptick in support from five of the six Niehauses. (Elmer couldn't let on that he cared, one way or another.) Unfortunately, that cheering section didn't have much to inspire it through the rest of the third quarter. The football see-sawed back and forth in the middle of the field, with each team gaining only a few first downs. Their progress was stymied by the erratic wind, causing footballs to whistle out of bounds when they should have landed in friendly arms. As the fourth quarter began, the score remained the same, which did not bode well for Gray's plan. And when he thought about it, it didn't seem likely that Bartholomew Karp was going to be all that easy to be around if he was a state runner-up.

Gray asked Elmer, "If we lose, can we go double or nothing?"

"How would we do that?"

"Arm wrestle for it?"

"I'd advise against that," said Mitzy, slapping one of Elmer's superhero shoulders.

The fourth quarter brought more of the same, the middle of the field tearing and clumping in a way that was going to leave the head of the grounds crew with the monumental task of getting that field back into shape in time for the University of Kansas's next game.

10 minutes.

8 minutes.

6 minutes.

4 minutes.

And then, with 3:42 on the clock, the Pittsburg-Trident running back blasted through Beaudelaire's line and into its defensive backfield where only an arm—this time belonging to one of Beaudelaire's linebackers—kept him from scoring.

Gray felt a pinch on his shoulders. He flip-topped his head to find an upside-down version of Katya's face a few inches from his own.

"That was close," she said. Then she noticed that she still had Gray's shoulder in a vice-grip. "Oops! Sorry!"

Resisting the temptation to gaze at Katya Niehaus for any longer than might be allowed by her brother, Gray snapped his head back to the game. Trident had lined up for a first down play at the Beaudelaire eighteen yard-line: as close as either team had gotten since Beaudelaire's early score in the half.

The quarterback dropped back and nearly everyone in the stands could see what he was about to do. The team's tight end was fading toward the corner of the end zone and that's where the quarterback was going to throw the ball.

But the fans weren't the only one who'd seen what the quarterback was doing. Bartholomew Karp, playing cornerback, saw it too. And the sense he had as a *quarter*back combined with the mean streak that made him a good football player allowed him to read the play correctly. So correctly, in fact, that he ran in front of the tight end, caught the ball, and raced out of the end zone.

"Beaudelaire's got it!" came the announcer's voice, his voice rising with the Bearcat cheering section, all of which was rising to its tiptoes. "He's at the 30. The 40. Midfield! He's got a couple of Trident players to beat. But here comes help!"

"Help" was Bobby Murphy, who'd come screaming over from the other cornerback position when he'd seen the interception take place. Bobby sprinted past midfield. The Trident running back leapt to tackle Bartholomew Karp. And Bobby Murphy leveled that running back with his shoulder, giving Bartholomew Karp an avenue toward the end zone.

"He's at the 20, the 10, and that's a touchdown for Beaudelaire's cornerback, Bart Karp!"

In the end zone, the team was bouncing around Bartholomew Karp, slapping his helmet and bumping his blue chest. But Bartholomew Karp had his eyes on the press box.

Mitzy threw her head back in a laugh, clapping her hands together. "He's worried about the announcer!"

"Why?" said Gray.

"He hates being called 'Bart,'" said Elmer.

On the field, Bartholomew "Bart" Karp had settled down enough to get under center.

"They're going for two," said Elmer. "I wouldn't expect this out of Bickle."

Mitzy pointed to the sideline, where Harris Bickle was screaming at his quarterback.

"It isn't Bickle," she said. "It's Bartholomew. He's gone rogue!"

Emboldened by his anger at the announcer and in spite of his coach's protestations to the contrary, Bartholomew Karp took the ball from his center, ran to his left, faked a pitch to Devon Rutherford, and then ran the ball toward the end zone, straight through Trident's biggest linebacker. He dove and the stadium gathered its breath as it awaited word from the closest referee.

The referee put up his arms.

Seeing this, Bartholomew Karp rose from the scrum with the ball and held it in front of him like it was the idol in *Raiders of the Lost Ark,* screaming something unintelligible while his teammates piled onto his back.

On the sidelines, Harris Bickle began nodding furiously as he screamed at his team, "That's what I'm talking about! Heart! Balls! Guts!"

Mitzy looked at Elmer, her hands covering a grin.

"It's not over yet," said Elmer.

Elmer was correct in a technical sense. There were 97 seconds left in the game. But he was wrong in a practical sense. The fight had gone out of Pittsburg-Trident when it had seen its linebacker mauled in the end zone by Bartholomew "Bart" Karp. After one first down and a series of plays of increasing desperation, the horn inside Memorial Stadium sounded and Beaudelaire High School was the Class 3A football state champions.

On the bright green field, the Beaudelaire players ran to the fifty-yard line and piled onto Bartholomew Karp.

On the sideline, Harris Bickle went to his knees and thrust his fists out of his bright blue windbreaker and into the sky. In the end zone, the dance team tossed their silver pom-poms into the air.

And in the stands, Gray Taylor grinned at Elmer Niehaus.

CHAPTER 13

"You watching, California?"

Coach Rutherford was standing with the ball on his hip at the top of the "key"—the half-circle above the free-throw line.

"Yes, sir," said Gray, his voice amplified by the enthusiasm borne of a fresh start.

Since the state championship football game, everything had seemed right with the world. Thanks to three hours of Sunday cleaning and a couple of Amazon deliveries, his bedroom no longer looked like a flophouse. And Elmer had made good on his promise: he was suited up in his practice clothes and had already made several stunning plays that had left Coach Rutherford trying to cover a smile.

On the court, Rutherford returned to his explanation of where he wanted Dusty Rhoads to be in the 1-3-1 zone they were installing.

"Wait, Coach," said Dusty, scratching the top of his head. "You're saying I have to cover here-"

He pointed first to the court's right wing—the spot where the free throw line would intersect the three-point line if it extended that far—and then to the other wing.

"-*and* over there?"

"Nah," said Coach Rutherford. "You just cover one side of the court. We'll let 'em shoot on the other side."

It took Dusty a second to figure out that Rutherford was being sarcastic. Gray, though, picked up on it right away. Since their meeting about Dusty and the alley-oops, Rutherford had gotten, well, not *funny*, exactly. He just seemed quicker, more hooked up to the proceedings in front of him. This wasn't entirely because of what Gray had said (or not said).

As Gray had suspected, Coach Rutherford had needed to come to his own conclusions, which had happened that same night when the old ball coach, as he liked to call himself, had gone to the only real bar in Beaudelaire for a night of rumination. At Sandy's Social he'd resolved that if he was going to go out, it was going to be on his terms. Hence the add-ons—a full-court press that had confused almost everyone, a set of plays that were based entirely on "reads" by the players involved, and the 1-3-1 trapping defense that had the sockets in Dusty's brain working overtime.

Coach Rutherford backed away from the play, toward the half court line. He tossed the ball that had been on his hip to Bobby Murphy, who was among the four football players who'd joined the team.

Bobby faked a pass to the corner nearest him and then lofted the ball cross-court, to the far corner, to another late-comer from the football team: Dusty Rhoads's younger brother. This Rhoads's real name was Richard but everyone called him Rocky—a name that was far tougher than the boy it belonged to. Rocky Rhoads was even wispier than Gray. He had glasses, too. They were held onto his face by a yellow band that drove Dusty crazy.

Rocky caught the ball, took one awkward dribble, and shot the ball. It missed and ricocheted harmlessly into the middle of the free-throw lane.

"You know what to do," said Coach Rutherford, pointing at the baseline.

Rutherford had prohibited dribbling in the drill. As he'd explained before the start, the goal was to get the 1-3-1 zone used to moving to particular spots. Not to "show me how good you are against a zone that don't even work right yet." The punishment for such transgressions was a torturous Burpee, which consisted of a long sprint interrupted by push-ups at both free-throw lines, half court, and the other end of the court.

Gray jogged to the baseline, joining the ten players on the court in a long line strung across the end of the gym. The policy was that everyone in the gym had to come along for the punishment. Unless you were still in street clothes like a particular star quarterback. Unlike Bobby Murphy, Bartholomew Karp hadn't yet suited up.

"Git."

This was Coach Rutherford's version of a starting gun.

Gray dashed to the free-throw line and dropped into the push-up position, his elbows straining. He bounced up, hoping he'd be somewhere near the front of the pack. He was disappointed to learn that he was already close to the back. Bobby Murphy and his brother (another newcomer from the football team) were ahead of him. As were the Rhoads brothers. And Bug Biancalana. And Elmer, of course.

Gray dug his left shoe into the court, putting his head down as he tried to gain some kind of edge. By half court, he was only two strides behind Dusty. By the far free-throw line it was one stride. Gray allowed gravity to pull him to the floor for the push-up, firing his triceps and rocketing back to his feet for the last burst to the baseline.

When he glanced down that line he saw that he'd finished just ahead of Dusty Rhoads. He caught Elmer's eye and saw a small smile there, right before Elmer jerked his head back to the court.

Another newbie, Oskar Haart, was lowering himself into the last required push-up. It wasn't a *bad* push-up. It was just slower than most of his teammates' efforts. Oskar spun out of the push-up position like a breakdancer, finishing in a cross-legged position before lifting his lineman-sized body up with his hands.

"Not bad, Haart," said Coach Rutherford. "Now let's see you do that every time this year."

Oskar snapped his heels together and whipped a salute for Coach Rutherford.

"Yes sir! Every time, sir!"

"OK," Rutherford said with a half-smile. "Let's try it again. Only this time-"

He looked straight at Gray.

"-you get Bug."

Gray's heart sped up. Since the return of the football players, he'd spent most of his time in his spot on the sideline. His moments of on-court Zen had gotten very rare, which meant he needed to make the most of this chance. Should he do a quick stretch? Warm up somehow?

"Jesus. Tapdancing. Christ."

This came from Bartholomew Karp. Who, until now, had ignored Gray on the sideline.

Gray snapped the rubber band and trotted onto the court to take Bug's position.

From what Gray had picked up, his job in the 1-3-1 zone defense was to stay between the ball and the basket, except for one specific instance: if the two players trapped someone with the ball in the corner, he was supposed to lie in wait for the obvious pass to the guard on the wing. And then steal that pass.

"Letsgoherewego," said Rutherford, again tossing the ball to Bobby Murphy. This time, Bobby threw the ball across the top of the court to his brother, Darren, who wasn't quite as athletic as Bobby—his muscles weren't as defined, his movements not as smooth. His hair was just as red, though.

Gray moved with the pass, keeping himself close to Dusty Rhoads in case a pass came into his area.

Darren Murphy threw the ball to the corner opposite him, and Gray's brain sounded the alarm. The corner was the magic spot.

Oskar Haart lumbered out from his position under the basket, joining the guard from the far end of the 3 in the 1-3-1 formation to set the trap in the corner.

As Bobby Murphy edged toward the three-point line, calling for the ball from the corner, Gray raced across the free-throw line to get into position. He thought back to what Rutherford had said. The goal wasn't to keep the ball from coming out of the corner. The goal was to bait the offensive player into thinking he had a safe pass so he, the rotating middleman, could steal it.

He waited, waited, waited, and then he saw it: the ball coming out of the corner toward Bobby Murphy, just like Coach Rutherford had said it would.

Gray lunged for the ball, already planning for what would happen next. He'd transfer his momentum, now angled at the sideline, toward the other end of the court, starting a fast break with whomever from his team came with him, maybe—hopefully!—Elmer. He could see the high-five after they completed the fast

break—an easy, casual one because this was how things were supposed to go.

Gray stuck out a hand to deflect the ball, preparing to slap it
out toward half court and fast-break glory. But as he reached he felt
a rush of air. It was Bobby Murphy, snatching the ball and jetting
toward the basket.

"Too late," Murphy said as he slipped past Gray and laid
the ball in.

Gray assumed this would be a "teaching moment." And
it was a teaching moment. Just not in the way Gray wanted it to
be. Coach Rutherford was waving at Bug with two fingers on his
left hand.

Gray was planted on the court as he felt his guts spin. He
wasn't entirely surprised. But still—this fast?

He put his head down and jogged to the sideline, where he
anchored his thumbs in his jersey. His thoughts scrambled over one
another like snakes in a pit.

Stupid add-ons.

Stupid football players.

Stupid him, for thinking he could do this at all. He wasn't
built for basketball. Who was he kidding?

"Don't worry, freshman," said Bartholomew Karp behind
him. "You'll get it."

Gray almost dared a hopeful look at Bartholomew Karp.
Maybe when Bartholomew saw someone struggling he knew to let
up. Or could it be that now that he was a state champion he'd mel-
lowed out—learned how to take it easy on the little guy?

"In about a hundred thousand years."

Bartholomew Karp moved down the sideline, a smirk on
his lips.

Gray knew he shouldn't let this get to him, especially because Bartholomew's line had hardly been cutting. Or creative.

But it was. Getting to him, that is. Because it seemed like maybe Bartholomew Karp was right. Since the return of the football players (and the addition of Elmer), he—Gray—had gone from mostly overmatched to completely overmatched on the court.

Gray kept his eyes on that court, trying to keep from thinking about the enormity of the job he'd taken on: a new town, a new school, and now a new sport.

There was one problem with Gray's resolution. His vision was starting to blur because his blue eyes were filling up with tears. If he'd had to explain why this was happening, he would have said that it wasn't that he was *sad*, exactly. More like overwhelmed. He would also say that he only needed a second—like, seriously, one second—to catch his breath.

Gray snapped the rubber band. Then, as surreptitiously as he could, brought his jersey to his face, pretending he was wiping sweat from his brow. It was this movement that betrayed him, causing an about-face from Bartholomew Karp.

"What the? Is that, are you, is he-"

Bartholomew hot-stepped to a spot in front of Gray and leaned forward, craning his neck around so he could inspect Gray like he was a museum exhibit.

"-crying?"

"It's just sweat!"

"Yo, B Murph," said Bartholomew. "The freshman look sweaty to you?"

Bobby Murphy took a step toward the sideline.

"Nah, he don't look like he's sweatin' too much," said Bobby. "But he does look he's about to start bawling like a cut calf."

This got a laugh out of Bobby's brother Darren, who, like Bobby, had seen more than a few calves castrated.

Gray blinked several times and returned to the staring-straight-ahead thing, waiting for Coach Rutherford to give the ball to someone, anyone, to get the drill going again. But time was not cooperating. Everyone on the court was waiting to see what would happen. Would Bartholomew Karp keep at it? Would Bobby Murphy do the same? Was Gray Taylor really sobbing on the sideline at basketball practice? Even Coach Rutherford seemed intrigued.

Bartholomew Karp edged closer to Gray, contemplating the next thing he might say to the freshman whose existence he was trying to erase for no other reason than to see if he could. And then, just as he was about to ask one of his rhetorical questions—something along the lines of "So what are we going to do with the wittle baby freshman?"—Gray reached deep into his memory banks, back to when his father had taken him to learn jiu-jitsu at the strip-mall studio on Ventura Boulevard. His dad had been reluctant, at first, not wanting to give Gray the impression that he cared whether Gray followed in his fighting footsteps. But when Gray had shown some aptitude for the subject Fausto had signed him up and their trips to jiu-jitsu class had become a Saturday morning ritual, complete with donuts after.

Gray thought he'd forgotten most of the jiu-jitsu, but muscle memory has a funny way of being sticky. And it was this muscle memory that Gray accessed when he shifted his weight to his left leg and, with his right, swept a kick at Bartholomew Karp.

When Gray pivoted into the whip-kick he'd learned from his sensei, a man from Hawaii who pretended to be from Japan for the sake of the parents of his clients, he was planning to kick Bartholomew in the thigh or maybe the stomach. And if this had happened, the kick might not have had the repercussions it did have.

But Gray did not kick Bartholomew in the thigh or maybe the stomach. He kicked Bartholomew in the testicles.

The reactions to Gray's kick were as predictable as a bad action movie. First, Bartholomew went down like he'd been shot by a sniper, howling in pain. Then Bobby Murphy's eyes went wide as he began processing what had just happened. Then there was Darren Murphy who, while not possessing his older brother's athleticism or social ease, wanted to.

It was this envy that led to Darren Murphy's overreaction: he sprinted over and vaulted himself toward Gray, throwing a punch that landed squarely beneath Gray's left eye, officially ending Gray's practice for the day and giving him something much more defensible to cry about.

CHAPTER 14

"Honey! Your face!"

"Mom. Just drive."

Nicole Taylor started to reach across the front seat of the U-Haul. But then experiential training overcame her maternal instincts. After dating—and then being married to—a professional mixed-martial artist, she'd seen more than her share of black eyes (and bruised knuckles and broken tibias and shattered elbows).

She also knew that the more acute damage was that which was done to pride. And that the longer she hesitated, the more that pride suffered. So Nicole Taylor faced forward, concentrating on piloting the truck from one pool of streetlight to the next so she didn't direct too much brainpower toward the desire to murder whoever had done this to her only son.

Her resolve lasted until the first turn. And then, still facing forward, she said, "OK, let's have it."

Gray—also facing forward—explained what had happened. He left out only a few minor details, like that the kick in the story had been delivered to Bartholomew Karp's nether regions. He figured he'd pay for that plenty in the upcoming days.

When Gray was finished with the explanation, Nicole Taylor paused long enough that Gray felt compelled to say, "Mom?"

He was afraid that she might be crying herself. But here Nicole Taylor surprised her son. Oh, she would cry later, in her bedroom, a mess of not only self-pity but also son-pity. For now, though, Nicole Taylor was tapping into some deep-seated instinct that what her son needed now was for her to play both mother and father.

She asked Gray what he was going to do.

Gray said, "I was thinking we could get some more ice on it. Coach Rutherford said that there was no reason to ease off on the ice, like probably every hour or so."

This wasn't the only thing Coach Rutherford had said to Gray. Once he'd gotten practice back under control (there'd been Burpees, again) and once he'd conducted the rest of that practice and once he'd gotten Gray into his office with a curt, "Taylor, in here," Rutherford had sighed and asked Gray what he was going to do with him. He'd explained that, yes, Bartholomew Karp could be cruel but that that didn't excuse "kicking him in the jewels." Gray had sat quietly while Coach Rutherford worked himself around to the conclusion he couldn't help but reach, which was that while he couldn't condone the behavior, he also didn't hate it. Then he'd shooed Gray out of his office with a request that the next time Gray tried something similar, he should just "aim a little higher, or lower."

As she wheeled the U-Haul onto Main Street's cobble-stones, Nicole Taylor frowned.

"No, Gray. I'm asking you what you're going to do about basketball. Is this it?"

Gray growled his answer: a No that made Nicole Taylor think of a young Fausto Torres, when she'd met him at that magazine party three months after the breakup with John Mayer and 22 fights (and zero losses) into Fausto's then-promising career.

She parked the truck in their spot in front of Taylor's. She reached over and squeezed Gray's leg.

"Well, you're going to have to do something."

"Yeah, Mom. I know."

Gray pushed open the U-Haul's door and put a foot onto the curb just as another door slammed. A truck door.

"What's going on, Taylors?"

Harris Bickle was getting out of an enormous black Ford F-250 that had two tires on each side in the back. He was carrying something encased in aluminum foil.

Gray flopped back into the front seat of the U-Haul. This was not what he needed.

"Um, hi, Harris," said Nicole Taylor. "What's that?"

Harris Bickle held up the aluminum mummy. "It's a casserole. The only one I know how to make. Sort of a welcome-back present. Now the season's over, I've got time."

Nicole Taylor cocked her head, an action Gray watched from the front seat as he prayed that his mother would conjure a way out of this situation.

"That's really nice of you," said Nicole Taylor. "I guess you should, um, come up and have some."

"Great!"

And so the Taylor family ushered Harris Bickle up-stairs to their upstairs apartment, where they sat down to eat a lukewarm tuna-and-noodle casserole with the coach of the state football champions.

Gray scooped into the casserole with the lowest of expectations, both of the casserole itself and of Harris Bickle. But he was in for a surprise. Or two surprises. The casserole, though reliant on cheddar cheese as its chief source of flavor, was delicious. And second: Coach Harris Bickle managed to behave himself on the conversational front. The topics were not what anyone would call "intellectual" but they stayed within reasonable bounds. There was talk of the bond issue. And the inevitable question regarding how they were "liking it here."

But by the time Gray had plowed through not one, not two, but three helpings of tuna-and-noodle casserole, Harris Bickle hadn't brought up his black eye. Until:

"They say basketball isn't a contact sport," said Bickle, waving at Gray's eye. "But that ain't true. I mean, you don't quite have the collisions we get in football but still."

"Plus," said Nicole Taylor. "No pads."

"Good point," Bickle said, pointing his fork at her. "And sometimes the pads make people move even faster. Makes for even bigger crunches."

He slammed a fist into his hand.

Nicole recoiled at the impact.

"Sorry," said Harris Bickle. "I get a little worked up about football."

"I've noticed," said Nicole Taylor.

"I'm going to grab something for this," said Gray, pointing at his eye.

As he slipped into the kitchen, he heard Harris Bickle say, "Ice is like magic. One time-"

The rest of the story was drowned out by the hum of the freezer when Gray opened the tiny compartment. Inside: a package of mixed berries (fodder for smoothies), a packet of fish (fodder for emergency dinners), and a bowl of grapes (fodder for nostalgia; frozen grapes were a Fausto Torres original).

Then, above the hum came a knock on the front door, rat-a-tat-TAT.

Gray snatched the fish packet.

"I'll get it!" he said.

A zany thought had popped into his head: what if the knock at the door was Patra, coming to check on him after hearing about his black eye? Maybe it was just that kind of night.

Then his mother's voice called out from the tiny dining room.

"Gray, I totally forgot. Mom and Dad said earlier today that they wanted to come by and take us for dessert."

"I'll *still* get it," said Gray. It wasn't Patra, but it was a welcome reprieve.

When Gray opened the apartment's front door, his grandfather leaned into the room, lifting his glasses and squinting. "Pickle me and put me in a petunia patch. Whatcha got there?"

Gray moved the packet of fish so his grandfather could see the eye in all its glory.

"Fist or elbow?"

"Fist," Gray said, a touch of pride in his voice.

"The girls'll love it."

Then Darby Taylor noticed that this wasn't just a family gathering. "Is that Harris Bickle?"

"He brought us a casserole," said Gray.

"How was it?"

"Better than it should have been."

Darby Taylor nodded and winked at Gray. Then he engaged his big voice.

"Harris Bickle, if you're not in here treating my daughter like the princess she is, there's going to be hell to pay."

Gayle Taylor slipped into the space left by her husband and did her own inspection of Gray's eye.

"Do I need to hurt someone?" she asked.

"Not yet," said Gray.

Gayle pulled Gray into a hug while, in the kitchen, Harris Bickle was standing to shake the hand of Darby Taylor.

"Congratulations on that championship," said Darby. "You're making us proud."

Meanwhile, Gayle Taylor was releasing Gray from her hug.

"Yes," she said, loud enough for the kitchen to hear. "That was quite a run!"

Like most Midwestern women, Gayle Taylor knew how to toss in a subtle dig. "Run" implied "streak," which bordered on implying "fluke."

"We had a nice group of kids," said Harris Bickle.

"I'll say," said Darby Taylor. "I wish we'd had a couple more of those in my time."

Darby Taylor had spent 12 years as the athletic director of Beaudelaire High School. He'd spent two of those years doubling as Beaudelaire High's football coach. His career record of two football wins and 22 football losses haunted the outer reaches of his brain.

By now, Gayle Taylor had made it to the kitchen, prompting her daughter to stand for her hug.

"I didn't realize you had company," said Gayle.

"It was unplanned," said Nicole. "And I think we're about done."

"We can always do dessert another time," said Gayle.

"Don't be silly," said Nicole. "Just give me a few minutes. I'll clean up and then we'll go."

Then an idea occurred to Harris Bickle in the way that ideas always occurred to Harris Bickle: visibly. His eyes got big and his chest swelled.

"Why don't y'all go ahead with Gray and I'll help Nikki, er, Nicole clean up. I can drop her at Tundin's on my way home."

"Seems reasonable to me," said Darby. "This'll give us a chance to hear about the fisticuffs."

"Indeed," said Gayle Taylor. "And plan our revenge."

"I'm not going to ask," said Mitzy, when she saw Gray's black eye.

Behind Gray, Darby Taylor barreled through the front door, his big body making Tundin's ancient gumball machines look extra small.

"You should see the other guy!"

"Mr. Taylor," said Mitzy, beaming as she pulled menus from their home next to the hostess stand. "How are you?"

"I'm A-OK, Mitzy. How's that painting coming along?"

Mitzy blushed.

"It's OK, sir."

"Well, you keep at it, eh?"

"Hon," said Gayle Taylor, putting a hand on Mitzy's arm. "Do you have a table for us?"

Mitzy squinted into the empty restaurant like she was searching the horizon for a smoke signal.

"I don't knowwww...."

"It'll pick up," said Gayle Taylor.

"It better," said Mitzy. "Or I'm going to have to start selling my body."

Mitzy directed the group of Taylors to a back booth, where Darby Taylor stepped aside to let his wife slide in before sitting down across from Gray.

Darby reached across Gayle to touch the top of the jukebox menu, shaking his head. "Remember the big deal they made out of these, babe?"

Gayle Taylor nodded, a faraway look in her eyes. Like many mothers, she couldn't help but think back with some sense of regret on those days, which had seemed so hectic then but which she'd give almost anything to do over.

Darby released the song list. "Let's have it," he said. "Before Ms. Tundin gets back."

Gray took a deep breath and told his grandparents everything that had happened at practice. This required him to explain what had happened on his first day—Bartholomew's call-out during the assembly. He left out the part about his cowardly escape. When he was finished with the story—the exclamation point naturally provided by Darren Murphy's punch—his grandmother was shaking her head.

"I knew those Murphys were trouble the first time I laid eyes on them," she said.

"They are hellions," said Darby. "But Gray, this is about you. What are you going to do about it?"

Gray shook his head and said he didn't know, and it seemed like they were all going to sit in silence for a few moments. But then came movement from Gayle Taylor's direction. She reached into her purse and pulled out a tiny, wire-bound notebook, opening it to a blank page as she took a pen out of the wire binding.

"OK," she said. "Let's talk about assets."

Darby Taylor leaned over and kissed his wife on the head.

"I've got Elmer," said Gray.

"The Niehaus kid is playing basketball?" asked Darby. Gray nodded.

"You have something to do with that?"

Gray nodded again.

Darby reached out to tap his wife's notebook.

"Put 'negotiating skills' on that thing."

Gayle did just that.

Then Darby Taylor's eyes narrowed. "Your dad teach you any *more* of that jiu-jitsu shit?"

Gayle whacked her husband with her pen hand.

"What?" Darby Taylor said. "That would definitely go under 'assets.'"

Gayle sighed. Then she looked at Gray. "Well?"

"Three years," said Gray.

"I knew something good would have come out of that relationship," said Darby.

In saying this, Darby Taylor was behaving according to a protective fatherly instinct. The past four years had only served to confirm what he'd always suspected: that the tattooed professional fighter his daughter had inexplicably fallen for would let that daughter down, sooner or later.

From Gray's perspective, though, he himself was the "something good" that had come out of the relationship. But he couldn't exactly defend his father's behavior. So Gray didn't react to his grandfather's words, other than to reach down to the zipper on his sweatshirt and absently move that zipper up and down.

Gray was saved from further reflection by the appearance of Mitzy Tundin, who was trailed by the mother and daughter of the inhabitants of the booth.

"Look who I found," said Mitzy.

Nicole Taylor waved in the way she had, always a little awkward even with the people she knew best. She slid in next to Gray and asked the table what everyone was getting.

"Haven't even ordered," said Darby, his voice a little louder than normal. As Darby had played back what he'd said to Gray, he'd realized the implication.

"I think you're going to like what we've done with the pecan," said Mitzy.

"Pecan it is!" said Darby.

Gayle handed her menu to Mitzy.

"Cherry for me, dear."

"I think just a coffee," said Nicole.

This provoked a growl from Darby. "Nikkiiii."

"Fine. Coffee and pecan."

Mitzy pointed her pen at Gray. "Pecan for you, too?"

Under normal circumstances, Gray would have gone along. But he hadn't forgotten what his grandfather had said.

"Do you have milkshakes?"

"Now what kind of diner would this be, if we didn't have milkshakes?"

"Strawberry," said Gray.

"Coming right up," said Mitzy. "Two pecan pies, one cherry pie, one strawberry milkshake, for Doubting Thomas here."

Mitzy left for the kitchen and the table's attention focused on Nicole Taylor.

Darby was the first to speak. "So?"

Nicole Taylor ran her fingers through her hair. "So what?"

"So what's up with Harris Bickle?"

"Nothing's up with Harris Bickle," said Nicole. "He dropped me off and then he went home."

"Are you going to see him again?"

"I think it was nice that he brought the casserole, and that's it."

"Sorry," said Darby Taylor, putting up his hands.

"How was work today, dear?" asked Gayle.

Nicole Taylor slumped into the teal vinyl.

"It's long," she said. "Back in LA, I always thought I'd give anything to be less busy. But now that I am, goodness gracious, the days go by slow. Then again, I shouldn't complain. I'm glad I found it so fast."

"Yeah, that was lucky," said Darby Taylor.

"What's that supposed to mean, Dad?"

"I just mean it was good fortune that they had the opening!"

Mitzy arrived with a tray holding their orders. She set the tray on the next booth over and whisked each plate (or glass) in front of its respective recipient. Then she put both her hands on her hips, staring down at Darby Taylor.

"Did you spit in this?" he asked, his fork poised above his piece of pecan pie.

"I'm waiting for your report," said Mitzy.

Darby mashed his fork into the end of his piece of pie. When he'd gotten the pie into his mouth, he closed his gray eyes and chewed as if he were contemplating a Zagat review.

Then those eyes snapped open.

"Why, Ms. Tundin, this is even better than usual!"

"I thought you might like it. We couldn't get it from our supplier anymore, so I learned to make it myself."

"What's your secret?"

Mitzy held up her hands.

"These. I made about a hundred pies, until I figured out how to do it. Sometimes there is no secret. Sometimes it's just a matter of, like, doing more."

Mitzy Tundin didn't say this to Gray. She didn't even look at Gray. She definitely didn't know that Gray was hoping for guidance regarding what to do, vis-à-vis basketball, the Murphy Brothers, and Bartholomew Karp. Or that he was going to use what she said to find his answer.

"Whatever it is," said Darby. "It's working."

"I know," said Mitzy.

"Whoa, Taylor! Let me get a look at that thing."

Like most days, Principal Peter Patterson was standing outside Beaudelaire High School, shaking hands, giving high fives, and cracking "jokes" such as the one he delivered after taking hold of Gray's shoulder and peering at his eye.

"Let's see. Black. Blue. Green. Orange. Yellow. Only color I don't see in there is GRAY."

Gray faked a smile before hitching his backpack further onto his shoulder and stepping through the tall door that had seemed so intimidating a week before. As he wove through the morning crowd he felt like a fugitive in an airport, dodging looks from kids he didn't yet know.

This was something Gray had planned for in the time between the trip to Tundin's and leaving the apartment that morning. Gray knew you couldn't walk into high school with a black eye and expect no one to notice. What he hadn't planned on was the rumor machine that revved up as soon as he arrived.

The first story to make the rounds was that Gray had *punched* Bartholomew Karp in the testicles. Gray caught wind of this rumor thanks to Mitzy, inspiring a hallway debate with Elmer regarding why it mattered whether Gray had used his fist or his foot. They came to no real conclusion, other than it had something to do with premeditation. You could imagine a person reacting in the heat of the moment with a kick. But a punch?

"You have to aim a punch," Elmer had said in conclusion.

By midday, Gray's choice of physiological weapon wasn't the only bit of misinformation floating around the school. There was also a sub-rumor that Gray had injured both Bartholomew Karp *and* Darren Murphy and that this was why the Murphy brothers weren't in school. The truth, which was that the Murphys had had to stay home to take care of their father, who'd spent the night in the Dewey County jail after a bender gone awry, wasn't discovered until the next day.

It didn't matter all that much to Gray, what a person thought about his eye. What mattered was that people were leaving him alone. He had a job to do and the fewer people he had to talk to, the better.

Gray's job commenced when the day's last bell rang and he scurried as quickly as he could through the hallway, into the commons, and down the dark stairway to the basement locker room. He yanked his practice clothes out of his locker and onto his body.

As he was pulling on his jersey, Coach Rutherford leaned out of his office. "Larry would be proud," he said. He nodded behind him, at the poster of Larry Bird.

"Let's not get ahead of ourselves," said Gray.

Then, hearing his teammates coming down the stairs, Gray got up and tiptoed across the room. He waited until the group that had just entered got past him. Then he darted to the next bank of lockers. Then another bank and another group, and he was clear to jog up the stairs into the commons area and into the gym. Which was cold enough to make him shiver.

Gray shook off the goosebumps and jogged to the storage closet where the basketballs were. He took one off the top rack and bounced it once, gauging its inflation. He'd noticed that it was far easier to deal with a ball that wasn't inflated to capacity.

He smacked the ball between his hands.

It was time.

Gray's plan was a simple one: he wasn't going to talk and he wasn't going to kick anybody else in the balls.

He was going to work. And eventually he'd get better, just like with Mitzy and her pies.

This work started before practice, with twenty minutes of stoically shooting and chasing down his own rebounds. It continued during practice, even when Bartholomew Karp blocked his shot during a three-on-three rebounding drill and said, "Not today. Or ever."

In response, Gray smiled. It wasn't a big smile. In fact, it was, at most, a thin smile. Nevertheless, the smile took Bartholomew Karp by surprise and contributed further to Bartholomew's general confusion regarding what to do about Gray Taylor.

Bartholomew hadn't appreciated getting kicked in the testicles. But according to the principles of frontier justice, Gray had paid his dues by way of the black eye delivered by Darren Murphy—the younger Murphy's last act as a basketball player. He'd quit the team the next day, a move that had baffled even Coach Rutherford.

When practice ended, Rutherford went through the upcoming itinerary, reminding his players that their first game was only a week away. He explained what they'd be doing the next day—specifically, that they'd be working on a series of plays to combat the zone defense their first opponent, Linwood, ran every year.

Gray watched Coach Rutherford from only eight feet away. But it might as well have been 800.

Gray knew he wasn't going to play in the game against Linwood. And he wasn't the only one who knew this. Hierarchies were being formed within the team and he, Gray, was at the bottom. Even Elmer, a reluctant participant in the proceedings, was slipping out of Gray's orbit and into the one populated by the team's best players: Dusty, Oskar, Bartholomew.

"And that's it!" said Coach Rutherford. "One, two, three."

"Beau-dee!" they said as a group, the syllables crisp and clear.

As they dispersed, Gray took another deep breath. He walked to the ball rack, again, and got out a ball. Then he dribbled that ball to a side goal and set up a few feet away from it. He started shooting: one miss, two misses, three misses.

As he took his fourth shot, he heard a voice come past his shoulder—the one he'd been hoping to hear.

"Try again," said Coach Rutherford, pointing up at the net.

Gray did as he was instructed, trying to loft the ball up and through the net like he'd seen his teammates do so easily. And for about the millionth time that day (or so it felt), the ball bounced off the rim.

"You're shooting with your arms," said Coach Rutherford. "You shoot with your legs."

Gray resisted the temptation to say what came to mind, which was that what Coach Rutherford was saying didn't make any sense.

He held out the ball.

Rutherford took the ball.

Then, resting the ball on the flat part of his hand, he bent his knees and pushed the ball up toward the basket. The ball rose (rather slowly, Gray felt) and slid through the net.

"See how my legs generate the power?"

Gray didn't see this at all. But he said OK in the way people do when they're trying to be agreeable.

Then, with Coach Rutherford at his side, he missed four of his next five shots, trying to think about using his legs. Then he *made* three of the next five, as he tried *not* to think about using his legs.

"Not bad," said Coach Rutherford. "Now, close your eyes."

Gray raised an eyebrow.

Rutherford said, "Trust me."

So Gray closed both eyes. (And not just the one that was nearly swollen shut.)

"Now," he heard Rutherford say. "You know where the basket is. So just shoot it in there."

"Like *Star Wars*?"

Gray was thinking of the scene on the Millenium Falcon, when Obi-Wan is training Luke Skywalker, telling him to "trust the Force." His dad had shown him the movie when he was seven. Beforehand, he'd barely been able to contain his excitement. But while Gray had liked Han Solo a fair amount, the rest of it had seemed kind of amateurish. He hadn't told his dad that, though.

"Yeah, like that," said Rutherford, even though he'd never seen the original *Star Wars*.

Gray imagined where the basket was. Then he bent at the knees and shot. He opened his eyes to see the ball whipping swiftly through the air on the right side of the basket. He'd missed completely.

But Coach Rutherford was unfazed.

"Don't worry about it going in," he said. "I just want you to think about how you felt when you shot."

Gray thought back. It was true – when his eyes had been closed, he'd been much more attuned to the sensations in his body. He clapped his hands for the ball.

"That's what I like to see," said Rutherford.

Gray bent at the knees with the ball in his right hand. Then, instead of concentrating on where the basket was, he focused on his body's muscles as he pushed off the floor. First, his lower legs, then his hamstrings. Butt, stomach, shoulder, elbow, hand, release.

He opened his eyes to see the ball arc up and over the rim, before nestling itself in the net.

"Nice like Mark Price," said Coach Rutherford.

"I thought you said it didn't matter if it went in."

"It doesn't. But it feels good when it does, right?"

Gray nodded as he caught the ball Coach Rutherford bounced back to him. They stayed like this for ten minutes—Gray shooting with his eyes closed, Coach Rutherford rebounding. Then it was time, Rutherford said, for him to turn off the lights and for both of them to go home.

The coach started for the tunnel. But as he got to the entrance, Gray held up a finger.

With his eyes open, Gray took a shot that felt far different than any of those he'd fired up at the beginning of the day. It was smoother, calmer, easier. And sure enough, the ball plopped into the bottom of the net, just like more and more of his shots had begun to do.

"That's it," Coach Rutherford said. "Soft like a peach at the bottom of the pile."

Gray gathered the ball and dribbled it over to the entrance to the tunnel, where Coach Rutherford was waiting.

"I left the light on in the locker room," said Rutherford. "And I put something in your locker."

"What?"

"I'm not going to ruin the surprise. When you're done just turn the lock on the inside of the door so it locks behind you. Got it?"

Gray nodded slowly, awed that his coach was giving him this much responsibility.

Coach Rutherford pulled on a weathered Kansas City Royals ballcap.

"More tomorrow."

When Coach Rutherford was gone, Gray went back into the gym and put the ball in its rack. Then he walked through the pitch-black tunnel, into the commons area that was lit only by the green blink of an Exit sign. When he got to the door to the locker room, he checked the back of the doorknob. Sure enough, there was a tab that could be turned to vertical to lock the door. He left it in its horizontal position for now; it seemed strange to lock himself in.

Gray shook his head as he started down the stairs. There was no way that a teacher (or coach) would have let him have the run of the school like this back in Reseda.

Downstairs, Gray opened his locker, where he found a weathered DVD case. He opened it. Inside was a blank disc with a yellow Post-It note stuck to it.

He read it aloud.

"The beginning of your education."

The echo of his voice bounced around the walls and made Gray realize just how alone he was.

This realization, though, was inaccurate.

While Coach Rutherford had been telling Gray how to get into and out of the locker room, Patra Patterson had been hiding in the stairwell to the second floor. Prior to that, she'd been upstairs, reading in the library. She'd been surprised to hear the voices of Gray and Coach Rutherford; she'd thought she'd had the school to herself.

Curious, Patra had stolen down the wooden stairs in her socks to listen to the exchange between coach and player. Then, when Coach Rutherford left, she'd slipped all the way down the stairs and into the commons in time to see the basement door slam shut.

Like everyone at Beaudelaire High School, Patra had heard the rumors about Gray's altercation with Bartholomew Karp. She didn't really care who'd thrown the first kick (or punch). She just liked that someone had stood up to Bartholomew and the rest of the football team. So, with intrigue as her guiding principle, she opened the door to the basement and eased down the stairs. She tiptoed past one bank of lockers, and then another, and then she positioned herself on the far side of the bank of lockers next to the one Gray's was in.

She could see him through the lattice, haloed by one of the yellow lights above him. She watched him close the DVD case and plop it into his locker. Then, without any warning, he stripped out of his practice clothes, dumping them in a pile at his feet.

Patra covered her eyes on instinct. But then, when she recalled that there was no one watching her, she peeked through her fingers. By then, Gray was on his way back into the shower. So Patra didn't *see* anything, at least not anything pertaining to Gray's private parts. She did, though, see his naked rear end. It was a cute rear end, she thought.

Patra heard the shower turn on. Then Gray's voice. She couldn't make out the words, so she took one more chance and slipped over to the edge of the bank of lockers so she could hear.

"No barking from the dog, no smog, and Mama cooked a breakfast with no hog."

Gray was rapping Ice Cube's "Today Was a Good Day," which had been one of his dad's favorites.

Patra knew the song. That wasn't what made her giggle. What did make her giggle was the thought of Gray Taylor (and his black eye) rapping, alone in the shower.

In that shower, Gray heard the giggle. Or he heard something. Which is why he stopped rapping, right around, "but didn't pig out."

Patra noticed that Gray had stopped and slipped back behind the lockers, just in time for Gray's head to peek out behind the white concrete wall that separated the shower from the rest of the room. His hair was matted to his head on one side. On the other, it was sticking up, making him look like an owl.

When he didn't see anything (or anyone) he shook his head and went back to the shower.

As for Patra: she'd had just about enough of this adventure. She slid across the concrete floor on the opposite side of the locker room. Then up the stairs and, carefully, through the oak door at the top.

Just before she let it close—softly, of course—she heard Gray Taylor start up again.

"Get me on the court and I'm trouble. Last week, messed around and got a triple-double."

Patra Patterson didn't know what a triple-double was. But that didn't keep her from smiling as she let the door close.

Among the school's marginalized populations, Gray's assault on Bartholomew Karp's nether parts became known as Wounded Peen. The event became a way to keep track of time, much like the massacre after which it was named. Kids would ask if something (a test, a makeout, a fight) was BWP or AWP.

For Gray, Wounded Peen marked the start of a new routine. Every day AWP, he rushed into the locker room in order to put on his practice gear so he could race up the stairs to start shooting. Then, when practice was finished, he stayed as long as Coach Rutherford would allow—sometimes twenty minutes, sometimes thirty, sometimes an entire hour—working on his shot, his ballhandling, his passing.

After each of these long days, Nicole Taylor would ask how practice had gone. And each of these times, Gray would ask her if she was going to ask him that every day. Then he would smile and tell her something about how practice had gone better than the day before.

Gray wasn't being deliberately vague when he described his progress. It's always difficult to tell if we are making progress when we're the ones making that progress. In Gray's case, that progress was especially difficult to quantify because it wasn't just happening on the basketball court. A lot of it happened after his mother asked her question, after they ate a quiet dinner together (sometimes at home, sometimes at Tundin's), and after Gray retired to his room where, on a tiny DVD player Nicole had dug out of a shoebox, he watched basketball game after basketball game.

Coach Rutherford knew Gray hadn't seen enough basketball to know how the game really worked. That was why he'd put the first disc in the locker. And then, when Gray had dropped that disc on the coach's desk the next day, a second disc. And so on, until the trade became something that both people—master and student—counted on.

All this repetition had a predictable effect: Gray *was* getting better at basketball. And not just in his personal shooting sessions. He was better in practice, too. And yet, he knew he wouldn't play in any games first semester because Coach Rutherford had said outright that he wouldn't play in any games first semester. When Coach Rutherford had said this, Gray had first assumed that the coach was being harsh—giving him a lesson in patience. But the truth was that Gray *couldn't* play in any of first semester's games, having transferred into the school only that same semester—a fact the ever-efficient Ramona Rutherford had brought to her husband's attention.

"But what about Winter Carnival?" Gray had asked when Coach Rutherford was finished explaining Gray's situation.

"That's still first semester," Coach Rutherford had said.

"Not according to the calendar," said Gray. "School will be done for the semester, right?"

The Winter Carnival game took place at the end of the last day of the first semester and was followed by the Winter Carnival dance: winter's answer to homecoming. This year's would be the school's 99th edition...sort of. The "sort of" because technically it was only the 18th edition of *Winter* Carnival. Before that, it had been called *Christmas* Carnival; the name had run afoul of the same committee who'd changed the school's mascot.

"I'll have to check on that," said Coach Rutherford. "And anyway, we've got a few games between now and then, bub."

Four games, in fact.

The first was in a town called Lecompton—a name that had, when Coach Rutherford said it at the end of practice one week before that game, caused Gray to snort a laugh.

Everyone looked at him.

"Oh, you're serious?"

Coach Rutherford said, "Why wouldn't we be?"

"Is our next game in LeWatts?"

This got a chuckle out of Coach Rutherford.

"Yo, I don't get it," said Dusty Rhoads.

"I'll explain it to you later," said Coach Rutherford, who never did get around to explaining what had tickled Gray: the two neighboring sections (Watts and Compton) of Los Angeles known to anyone familiar with West Coast hip-hop from the 1990s.

Coach Rutherford could be forgiven the oversight. He was more worried about that game against Lecompton, a game Beaudelaire High won thanks mostly to Elmer Niehaus, who danced through Lion defenders like they were nailed to the gym floor, scoring 21 points, pulling down 8 rebounds, and mixing in 5 assists.

The second game of the season went like the first, the only real difference being that it was at home. Once again, Elmer was the best player on the court. Once again, Beaudelaire won, this time against a team from Marais de Cygne.

But then things went awry. Beaudelaire lost its next two games—both on the road, both against teams whose mascots were birds. In each, Elmer's scoring was limited to single digits, but not because he was missing shots or because he'd stopped caring. No, the cause of the abrupt failure was a predictable one: Bartholomew Karp, who'd decided he didn't like sharing the spotlight.

The solution to this problem seemed obvious enough to Gray from the real estate he'd made his own at the end of the bench. Coach Rutherford needed to be quicker with the hook whenever Bartholomew began keeping the ball from Elmer by way of poorly timed shots and errant passes.

Unfortunately, Coach Rutherford wasn't ready to take this step. This wasn't because Coach Rutherford was being myopic. There were some politics involved. Bartholomew's father, Griswold, was at every game, and Griswold Karp had the ear of the man who had the most power at Beaudelaire High School: Harris Bickle. And if Coach Rutherford was too hard on Bartholomew Karp, he risked angering Griswold Karp, who would likely transfer his anger to Peter Patterson by way of Harris Bickle.

And so, going into the 99th/18th edition of Winter Carnival, Beaudelaire High had a disappointing 2-2 record.

Two wins wasn't the number of wins Deacon Rutherford wanted Peter Patterson to spend Christmas Break with, especially when Peter Patterson was already considering relieving him of his job. This anxiety about his job contributed mightily to Coach Rutherford's terse answer, when Gray asked him, again, one hour and forty-five minutes before the 99th/18th Winter Carnival game, if he'd found out anything about Gray's eligibility for the game.

"Just stay ready," said Rutherford.

But that was *all* he said, leaving Gray in a confused state—did "just stay ready" mean he was eligible to play? Or was Rutherford just distracted?

Gray put up his hands, backed away, and retreated to the interior of the locker room, where he took off the clothing ensemble he'd prepared for the Winter Carnival dance (Mitzy had talked him into going with her).

When he was finished dressing he went upstairs to shoot. When he was finished shooting he came back downstairs to listen to Rutherford's pre-game talk. When he was finished listening to Rutherford's pre-game talk he went back upstairs for pre-game warm-ups.

Then, as the Winter Carnival game tipped off, he found the seat he was getting used to occupying: at the end of the bench next to the round-headed Rocky Rhoads, younger (and less skilled) brother to Dusty.

"Dude," said Rocky, nodding toward the bleachers across from them. "Your mom is hot."

Gray sighed.

"Sorry, man," said Rocky. "It's just—it's the truth."

Gray glanced up at his mother. For the Winter Carnival game, Nicole Taylor had taken a seat three-quarters of the way up the bleachers across from the bench. And the thing about it was: Rocky was right. His mom *was* pretty. She almost shone in a red sweater and white scarf—both of them more cosmopolitan in fit and cut than anything else in the gym.

Rocky leaned back on the wooden bench, which was really just the first row of bleachers. He pulled his glasses out of the yellow elastic band. He rubbed them on his shorts and squinted through them.

"It'll make it hard for you to find a wife someday. Everyone compares their girlfriends to their mothers. And your mom is tough to compare to."

Rocky put his glasses back on. His brother had just snatched a rebound. Bug Biancalana was calling for the ball so he could take it upcourt.

Gray stared at Rocky for an extra second, wondering if this explained why he hadn't really cared about girls until now—a thought that reminded him to look for Patra. He found her at the end of the bleachers nearest the baseline, book open in defiance of her father's request to "just come to the game, for my sake."

Gray wondered if Patra would be at the dance that was set to start, according to the posters that had been up in the hallways for two weeks, thirty minutes after the final buzzer. Maybe if she *was* at the dance she'd say hello and that she was bored and then they could have a talk about life and Beaudelaire and what she saw in that guy in Lawrence—the one who'd ruined his day at the state football game.

"California!"

Gray swiveled his head to find that Coach Rutherford was staring at him, his hands on ample hips that had gotten slightly less ample in the past month. In addition to retaking ownership of his basketball philosophy, Rutherford had retaken ownership of his workout routine.

"What was wrong with that play?"

Gray thought back, holding the image in his head: after Bug had brought the ball upcourt he'd passed it to Bartholomew, who'd dribbled three times before taking an off-balance 17-footer.

"The defense was set when he shot it."

Coach Rutherford stood still for a second, surprised by the accuracy of Gray's answer. Then he said, "Exactly. Shot like that, gives us no chance at a rebound because nobody's moving."

Rocky nudged Gray's knee. "Nice catch."

"Damn right," said Gray, allowing himself a small smile. He hadn't been paying all that much attention to what had been going on in the game. But he'd noticed that this didn't always matter. He could usually hold in his head not only the surroundings of the game, but also the events of the game itself.

Nonetheless, he resolved to pay more attention.

Gray's self-assigned directive was a challenging one because the game in front of him—against Tonganoxie High and their bright red jerseys—was a dull one, especially when compared to the games Gray was now used to watching on the ancient DVD player in his room. His favorite so far was a game in the 1986 NBA Finals when Coach Rutherford's spirit animal, Larry Bird, had struggled, forcing his replacement—a shooter named Scott Wedman—to see more time than he might have otherwise. Wedman had gone 8 for 10, leading the Boston Celtics to a come-from-behind win. Games like that one were capital-E exciting. This was one lower-case-b boring.

But, boring or not, time will pass during a basketball game just as it will pass during every other activity, and soon enough, there were only 30 seconds left in the first half and Elmer was trapped on one side of the court. Bartholomew was on the other side, calling for the ball by clapping repeatedly. But Elmer wasn't able to see Bartholomew. He bent over the ball and motioned to the referee for a timeout.

As the team jogged off the court, Bartholomew Karp was chirping at Elmer, questioning his eyesight, his athletic prowess, even the way he'd called timeout. Then Bartholomew was at the bench, dropping onto the wood and kicking it with his heel. His arrival was like a small thunderstorm: heat and wet and fury.

Coach Rutherford eyed Bartholomew Karp as the huddle formed around his team, calculations rattling around in his head.

He flashed a glance at Griswold Karp.

Then Bartholomew forced his coach's hand. He found a towel behind the bench. After making a show of wiping his face with it, he draped it over his head.

Coach Rutherford started quiet. "Bartholomew," he said.

He didn't get a response. Bartholomew's attention was on the empty court, where the cheerleaders were doing their best to draw a response out of the sparse crowd.

"Bartholomew Karp."

"What?"

"Take the towel off your head."

Glaring at Rutherford, Bartholomew Karp shook his head until the towel fell from the top of his head.

Rutherford jerked his chin over his shoulder. "Meet us in the locker room."

The buzzer sounded and the nearest referee leaned into the huddle. "Time to go, Coach."

The four players who'd been in the game wandered onto the court in a daze. Meanwhile, Bartholomew continued to glare at Rutherford.

The referee spoke up again, apology in his voice. "Need one more, Coach."

Rutherford released Bartholomew from his gaze so he could survey the available players. His eyes landed on Gray and Gray gulped a breath. Was this it?

"Rocky," said Coach Rutherford. "Get Bartholomew."

Rocky Rhoads put his hand to his chest as his eyes went round like his head.

"Yeah, you. Go!"

Rocky Rhoads tore off his warm-up and scurried to the scorer's table, leaving Gray to find his way back to the end of the bench, where he settled his butt bones just as the Tonganoxie center inbounded the ball to their point guard. Who, when he noticed the confusion on the round face of Rocky Rhoads, launched the ball upcourt to the player Rocky was supposed to be guarding. This player caught the ball on the block nearest the goal, where he spun toward that goal at the very moment Bartholomew Karp began his defiant walk of shame to the locker room.

The Tonganoxie forward's tiny hook shot fell into the net as Bartholomew passed the scorer's table, where the bow-tied Social Studies teacher, Mr. Hoffman, put two points on the board for the road team, which gave Tonganoxie 32 and a five-point lead.

As Bug Biancalana brought the ball up the court, Bartholomew Karp was ambling around the edge of the court, toward the brick-lined tunnel that would take him through the commons and down to the locker room. He was moving slowly enough to draw half the sparse crowd's attention away from the game. Because that crowd was so thin (and because the game was so slow), anyone watching Bartholomew knew he wasn't reporting to the locker room because he was injured.

Bartholomew knew this about that crowd, which was why he clapped three times and shouted, "Let's go, Beau-dee!"

If Beaudelaire hadn't been a small town, and if the people in the stands hadn't known everything about their football team's star quarterback, they might have taken Bartholomew Karp's exhortation as a legitimate bit of cheerleading. But that, of course, wasn't the case. The crowd could tell Bartholomew Karp was being viciously sarcastic—sarcastic enough to have some kind of atmospheric influence on the shot taken by his replacement, Rocky Rhoads.

Rocky's shot missed, badly, and as Bartholomew got to the tunnel (whose wood edge he slapped while passing through), a Tonganoxie player gathered the rebound with eight seconds to go. He dribbled through a crowd of Beaudelaire players to half-court, where he heaved a shot that arced straight into the basket just as the buzzer sounded.

The players on the court jogged into the tunnel. So did the players on the bench.

Most of them, anyway.

Gray was still on the bench, watching Coach Rutherford, who was staring at the basket the ball had just splashed through. His stillness told the story more effectively than if he'd written his thoughts on cards.

Then came a pitter-patter of feet in the brick tunnel and the Beaudelaire Belles were rushing through the tunnel and onto the court, their timing both perfect and awful.

The Belles lined up across the court, each member of the dance team bending over, legs straight, one pom-pon on a hip, one pom-pon on the ground, all of them perfectly still until:

Ba-duh-duh-da-da.

Ba-duh-duh-da-da.

These were opening beats of "Kiss Kell" by Kelli Uzi, a song Gray knew almost by heart because he was a human being alive at the same time as Kelli Uzi.

He watched arms move along hips, legs bend along knee lines, midriffs slide like charmed snakes. Their skirts were so short and whose hair was so long and….and…this was good news! He was impressed by these girls! Gray filed this away to tell Rocky Rhoads in the second half.

"California."

Coach Rutherford was watching him watch the Belles.

"Let's go figure this out," he said.

"Listen up! We're too good to be this bad. And I want to know: what are y'all going to do about it?"

One arm draped against the bank of lockers, Coach Rutherford was talking to the whole team. But he was aimed at his upper-classmen: Dusty Rhoads and Bug Biancalana.

Dusty said, "We need to play harder, coach."

Rutherford inhaled—long, low, and slow. "That's true, Dustin. But it's a little more than that."

Upstairs, the music gave way to applause that was only barely audible in the locker room. It sounded like rain, which only added to the claustrophobic feel of the situation.

"Whatever it is, we ain't leaving 'til we figure it out," said Rutherford. "I don't care if we have to stay down here through the whole second half."

Above them, the band started on the school's fight song—the same fight song that had been playing overhead when Gray had gotten his first tour of the basement locker room, on the day he'd nearly run out of the school before Coach Rutherford stopped him.

Gray snapped his rubber band.

"I know what the problem is," he said.

The locker room froze. And for Gray there was no turning back now. He went full Cyclops on Bartholomew, like he'd done with Ariel Bickle.

"You shoot too much."

"Oh yeah?"

"Yeah," said Gray. Then he forced himself to hold the eye contact. "Because no one has ever told you not to, and you think shooting a lot makes you good, when everyone knows that it's not about shooting, it's about *making*. I mean, all the research shows that a missed shot is the same as a turnover, unless you get the offensive rebound. But we can't get any offensive rebounds because you shoot the shots when there's no chance at a rebound."

Gray stopped and glanced at Coach Rutherford, not entirely sure what he had just done.

"Do you want me to keep going?"

"By all means."

Gray returned his guns to Bartholomew, whose eyelids had gotten narrow and scary.

"The real problem is that no one thinks you can do anything wrong because you won state in football, so you must know what you're doing. But you don't. Know what you're doing. And you can, like, beat me up or whatever, but it's the truth."

Bartholomew took a step toward Gray.

"You think you can do better?"

"I can't do much worse."

Bartholomew made a half-hearted lunge toward Gray, but Bobby Murphy held him back. Meanwhile, at the front of the semi-circle of players, Coach Rutherford was rubbing his chin.

"So, Cali-, I mean, Taylor, what do you think we should do about this?"

"You're the coach," said Gray. "I'm just outside counsel."

This got a grin out of Coach Rutherford—a grin that preceded another deep breath.

"Alright," he said. "Here's what we're going to do."

The rest of Coach Rutherford's half-time talk was surprisingly mild. When he was finished, he called the team into a huddle.

"On three, we're going to say, 'Team together.'"

This was a rallying cry Rutherford's own coach had used at Emporia State, back when Deacon Rutherford had been leading that team to so many wins that he'd left the school at the top of the all-time list. The only thing that had stopped *Coach* Rutherford from having his teams say "Team together" was another thing that coach had said, which was that if any of his players coached, they'd be surprised at how much they stole from him.

"1, 2, 3-"

"Team together!"

The rendition of the new battle cry wasn't perfectly in unison, but it was better than it should have been. Bartholomew even joined in, albeit with a supervillain's glare at Gray while he mouthed the words.

There was one silver lining: as the huddle dissolved and the players prepared to return to the court upstairs, Bobby Murphy *wasn't* glaring at Gray. Oh, he was *looking* at Gray, but he was doing so in the manner of an alien who's trying to figure out if the intrud-

ing humans should be given alien dinner and alien wine or shot with
an alien laser cannon.

Upstairs, the team was clustered outside the tunnel waiting
for the high school's rotund janitor, Mr. Edison, to finish sweeping the floor for the second half. The Beaudelaire Belles were in a
cluster of their own, their silver skirts swirling in the corner of the
commons opposite the doorway to the basement.

When Mr. Edison gave them the sign, the team rushed
through the tunnel and onto the court for halftime warm-ups.
Throughout those warm-ups, Gray was careful to avoid Bartholomew. Then half-time came to an end and Gray sat in his spot
next to Rocky Rhoads as the referee handed the ball to Oskar Haart
and blew his whistle, signaling the start of the second half.

"Nice speech," said Rocky.

"Thanks. I think," said Gray. "Oh and by the way, about my
love life-"

But Gray never got around to explaining how his distrac-
tion by the Beaudelaire Belles was a good sign for him because
Rocky Rhoads was pointing at the scorer's table and saying, "What
the hell?"

Coach Rutherford was sending Bobby Murphy in for Bartholomew Karp—all because Bartholomew had gone to the wrong
spot in the play Bug had called.

A minute later, when Bobby jumped into the air without
anyone to pass to, Rutherford sent in Bartholomew.

It was the beginning of a pattern.

At first, each was reluctant to take the other out, slouching
his respective way to the scorer's table. But soon enough, Bobby
and Bartholomew started to see it as a game within the game. On a
play during which Bartholomew screwed up a defensive coverage,
Bobby Murphy bounced out of his seat like it was electrified and
headed for the scorer's table. Two minutes later, Bobby threw the

ball into the stands and it was Bartholomew's turn to dash to the scorer's table.

There was another benefit to this game within a game: it freed Elmer to do what he did best, which was to dominate a basketball game. In the third quarter, Elmer scored eight of Beaudelaire's points during a fourteen-point run.

The fourth quarter started the same way. Bartholomew and Bobby were competing with each other. Elmer was singlehandedly destroying the Tonganoxie Tornadoes.

And the gap on the scoreboard kept growing.

A 10-point lead.

Now 15.

Now 20.

"This is awesome," said Rocky Rhoads.

"Totally awesome," said Gray.

"Well, I meant it in the literal sense. Like, it's filling me with awe."

"Isn't that what *awesome* means, all the time?"

Rocky's chin bounced back and forth.

"I guess so."

And then, with one minute and 24 seconds left in the 99th edition of the ~~Christmas~~ Winter Carnival game, it happened: Gray remembered what he was going to tell Rocky Rhoads about the Beaudelaire Belles vis-à-vis how he thought *several* of them were quite cute and so he had a chance no matter how "hot" his mother was

However, Gray *still* never got to say this. Because another thing happened with one minute and 24 seconds left in the 99th edition of the ~~Christmas~~ Winter Carnival game.

"Taylor!"

Coach Rutherford was facing the court.

"Dude," said Rocky, tapping Gray's knee with his own. "I think you're going in."

Gray leaned forward so he could see Rutherford. He pointed at his own chest.

"Yeah," said Rutherford. "Get your bony ass up off that bench and into the game."

Being summoned into the game was exciting. It was also frightening because, among other things, Gray didn't know what you were supposed to do when you checked into a basketball game.

Here, though, he had help.

Rocky Rhoads pointed down the bench.

"Go to Mr. Hoffman, with the bow tie. Tell him who you're going in for. And then go get that person."

Gray began to stand.

Rocky grabbed Gray's wrist.

"Make sure you take off your warm-ups."

"You alright, son?"

Coach Rutherford had him by the shoulder. They were walking to the scorer's table.

Gray nodded quickly.

"OK good. Now just breathe easy. You're going to get Bartholomew. Trial by fire."

The coach slapped Gray on the lower back and retreated to the bench.

Mr. Hoffman leaned over the scorer's table, his arms wide.

"Sir Gray! Are you prepared?"

Gray nodded as a whistle shrieked behind him. The ball had slipped out of a Tonganoxie player's hand, squirting out of bounds.

"And whom will you be replacing?"

Gray glanced onto the court, where the team (and the referee) was waiting. Everyone's hands were on their hips.

"Bartholomew."

"Number, please?"

"Really?"

"Protocol."

"Looks like...13."

"And yours?"

"22."

"Excellent."

Gray spun for the court, where a referee was waving him onto the court with the urgency of a man who wants to get home.

Mr. Hoffman's voice again.

"You'll want to remove your outerwear."

Gray held up a hand for the referee. Then he pushed his warm-up pants to the ground and pulled his warm-up top up over his head. He tossed both of them behind him and ran a hand through his hair, snapping the rubber band as he did so.

He found Bartholomew.

He pointed at him like he'd seen his teammates do.

And that was all well and good. It was the next part that was scary because now he had to *replace* Bartholomew Karp. And what *replacing* Bartholomew Karp meant was running past him and slapping his outstretched hand. In this encounter, all manner of awful potential outcomes awaited: a snide remark, a withdrawal of the hand, maybe even a quick punch in the stomach—retribution for what had happened at half-time.

But, curiously, none of these things happened. Instead, after Gray successfully tapped Bartholomew's palm with his own, Bartholomew smiled.

He smiled!

And said, "Looking good."

If Gray's brain hadn't been concerned with the debut he was about to make, he might have grown suspicious. If he'd learned anything it was that Bartholomew Karp was not known for his compliments. But Gray *was* concerned with the debut he was about to make, so he took Bartholomew's compliment at face value, thinking

that perhaps the game-within-a-game had made Bartholomew forget about half-time.

He turned to find the Tonganoxie player he was supposed
to guard.

It was this person who clued Gray in.

"Jersey's on backward, kid."

Gray looked immediately to his chest. And sure enough,
there was no *Beaudelaire* there. Just a number (22) that was bigger than it was supposed to be because it was supposed to be on
his back.

CHAPTER
18

"I just can't imagine how I put it on backward. Like, how did I not check that in the mirror? Or feel it during the game? I'm such an idiot."

"Let's get punch," said Mitzy, pointing to a table at the edge of the darkened dance floor.

"In an actual punch bowl?"

"Where else would they keep it?"

"Back home," said Gray, "the teachers would have been too scared about what the kids would put in it."

"Welcome to the heartland," said Mitzy, sweeping her hand across the gym, whose transformation had been swift and thorough. After the game's end, the Beaudelaire Belles had shooed everyone out the door so they could get to work. The theme was "Tangled Up in Blue" because Ariel Bickle had seen a "cool pic" of the Bob Dylan album of the same name. The décor was centered around a literal interpretation of the album's title. The chairs were "tangled" in blue by way of streamers wrapped around them. The DJ—DJ Earthquake—was tangled in more streamers that hung from his arms. And the dancers were tangled in Silly String that DJ Earthquake was spraying on them.

The punch was blue, too, with Gummy Worms "tangled" inside it. As Gray dipped the ladle into the slimy, sugary mess, the beat dropped on a remixed version of "California Love" by Dr. Dre and Tupac Shakur.

"California!" said Mitzy. "Do you miss it?"

Gray gulped his punch, drawing a gummy worm into his mouth for effect.

Mitzy cuffed his shoulder.

"I'm serious!"

"I don't know," said Gray. "My mom seems a lot happier here, even if she won't admit it."

"I'm asking about you. Are *you* happy here?"

Gray looked up from his punch just as Patra Patterson slipped into the gym wearing black tights and an oversized jacket with brass buttons that ran up the front, like a Civil War soldier's uniform.

"I think I could be," he said.

Mitzy followed Gray's eyes. "What about the fella in Lawrence?"

"Oh," said Gray, sputtering. "I didn't mean Patra. That was just a coincidence—that she walked in. What I meant is, I think I could be happy here if, for example-"

Gray nodded at the dance floor, where Bartholomew Karp and Bobby Murphy were rapping along with Tupac Shakur, much to the delight of Ariel Bickle and Barbarella Destino.

"-I stopped pissing them off."

"They don't seem so mad right now," said Mitzy.

"They'll get bored," said Gray.

"Won't Elmer protect you?"

Gray frowned.

"Oh," said Mitzy. "You don't want to *need* to be protected."

"Maybe. How'd you know?"

"Lots of time to observe people."

"Because you like girls?"

"Probably. People don't know what to make of me, so they don't pay much attention to me."

"This may not be helping."

Gray stepped back and waved a hand at Mitzy's outfit: mismatched Chuck Taylor's, blooming genie pants, and a scoop-necked blouse that made her top half shapeless.

"California Love" ended and DJ Earthquake moved to the other deck in his booth as the next song started up: INXS's "What You Need."

Mitzy grabbed Gray's hand. "We're dancing."

Gray's wanted to protest. After screwing up his debut on the court, he wasn't in the mood to dance. Plus, he didn't think the song could be danced. Then he noticed that Bartholomew and Bobby were headed their way, making the dance floor a comparatively safe space. He allowed Mitzy to drag him over. When they got to the edge of the dance floor, Gray cocked his head at the song.

"INXS. RIP," said Mitzy. "But here's the important question: can you feel it down here?"

Mitzy pointed at her hips, which were shaking in time with the downbeat of the song.

Gray checked the table where the punch bowl was. While it was true that he'd made a mess of his first attempt at playing basketball *and* that he'd annoyed Bartholomew Karp to a degree that would undoubtedly have future repercussions, it was also true that they'd won the game and that he'd survived the semester and that he hadn't gotten beaten up by Bartholomew Karp (yet).

So he let his hips slide from one side to the other. He looked down at his own waist as if surprised by what was going on there. Then, up at Mitzy. Thanks to the disco ball overhead, his eyes were even bluer than usual.

"I don't know," he said. "*Do* I?"

Mitzy stuck out her hand again and pulled Gray to the center of the dance floor and before Gray knew what was happening, he no longer knew what was happening. Instead, he was there, in the moment, sometimes catching Mitzy's hand, sometimes not catching Mitzy's hand; sometimes laughing, sometimes not; all the time being serenaded by Michael Hutchence and a song that was telling him a truth he needed to hear.

Then, in the midst of all this non-thought, Gray caught a different hand: the hand of a person who'd been drawn to his dance moves because of a universal truth—that having fun is the best way to attract people.

Without really processing whose hand it was, Gray swung the dancer past him, to Mitzy, who swung the dancer back just as the last strains of "What You Need" slithered out of the giant speakers at the side of the gym.

Then the song was over and Gray became aware of whose hand he'd been holding: Barbarella Destino's.

The song that started up next was a slow one: a remix of a backward-looking crooner from London by a forward-looking mash-up artist from Berlin.

Barbarella slung her arms around Gray's shoulders.

"Can I have this dance?"

"Yes you may," said Gray, as his arms found Barbarella's hipbones—a move that concealed his surprise.

Since Elmer's first-day warning about the ABCs, he'd had exactly one encounter with Barbarella Destino—a "You go, no you go" at the water-bottle refill station that had been installed by the go-getting Class of '18.

"You looked pretty cute out there," said Barbarella, sliding close enough to Gray that Gray could feel the heat from her stomach.

Gray said, "You look pretty cute out *here*."

Barbarella smiled and moved closer to Gray—close enough that her face was only a few inches from Gray's shoulder. This freed Gray's eyes for the peek he was desperate to sneak. Barbarella's body was mythical among the males of Beaudelaire High, mostly because of her CDs—the code name those males used for her breasts because no one knew for sure if they were Cs or Ds.

Emboldened by INXS and sugary punch and the night he'd had, Gray risked a glance, following a tiny rivulet of sweat that was sliding down Barbarella's collarbone. The bead of sweat hesitated and then dropped onto Barbarella's left breast, sliding past its rounded inner edge before disappearing into her black bra.

Barbarella moved her head back from Gray's shoulder in time to notice where his eyes were.

Gray's heart banged into his ribs. You weren't supposed to look down girls' shirts, that much he knew. And so, he was tempted to apologize. But Gray did not apologize, because of the game and the dancing and Mitzy and INXS and the song DJ Earthquake had picked, which was simultaneously heartbreaking and fun. Instead, he said the first thing that came to mind: "So, no tan line, huh?"

Barbarella leaned into Gray's ear. "I could say the same about you."

Gray's brain did a little jig. His gamble had paid off!

"All that beach time," he said. "California, you know."

"Really?"

"No, not really. My dad's Venezuelan."

"Oh, I love tamales!"

"That's not–"

Barbarella moved Gray's left hand further around her waist and Gray forgot about correcting her geography, allowing Barbarella to pull him closer.

Up to a point.

Because, while Gray was thrilled that Barbarella was pulling him close and while he was enjoying the moment for a change, he also needed to keep a certain amount of distance between his midsection and Barbarella's midsection because all the music and the dancing and that rivulet of sweat were causing Gray to get an erection.

As this was happening, it occurred to Gray that getting off the dance floor in his condition might be challenging. But Gray exiled that thought just as quickly as it arrived. Like many males in similar straits, his planning skills had abandoned him. And in reality, getting off the dance floor probably wouldn't have been a problem for Gray thanks to two factors: the darkness in the gym and the Silly String that would soon fly onto the dance floor participants.

Wouldn't have been a problem, that is, but for the arrival of Bartholomew Karp.

Bartholomew's first words weren't directed at Gray at all. Instead, holding out his cup of punch like it was a pistol, he spoke to Barbarella.

"What are you doing dancing with this *fresh*skin?" he asked.

Gray kept his eyes forward, on Barbarella's eyes, willing her to stay strong while he willed his penis to return to its natural state.

And at first, Barbarella *did* stay strong. She said, "Why don't you not worry about it, Bartholomew."

Bartholomew took a sip of his punch. Then he pointed downward. "Just thought you should know, he's got a boner for you."

Gray felt Barbarella's hands go slack as she pulled back so she could evaluate Gray's pants. There was one upshot to this movement: Gray got to see almost all the way down Barbarella's dress. And what he saw was glorious—something he'd tell Mitzy about later. If there was a later. Because, right then, Barbarella gave up. Conditioned by years of picking the right side based on popular opinion, Barbarella put her hand to her mouth and said the words that would sear themselves into Gray's brain: "You dirty wetback!"

The music stopped. Like, really stopped. This didn't happen because of the slur Barbarella had hurled at Gray. It was a coincidence; DJ Earthquake had decided his next dance was going to be a "Snowball"—one of those dances that involve participants picking a new dancer each time the DJ stops the song and says "Snowball!" He was planning to explain the rules before the song started.

However, the silence served as an exclamation point for what Barbarella Destino had just let slip from her mouth, which was something her father said whenever he was faced, on the news, with talk of Hispanic immigration to the United States.

"What's up?"

Bobby Murphy had just arrived on the scene, with a plastic punch glass of his own.

"What's up," Bartholomew said. "Is this Mexican's dick."

Even though the situation was quickly going from bad to more bad, Gray wanted to raise a few points with Bartholomew. There was the geography issue, same as with Barbarella. Then there was the math. He was *half* "Mexican." And there was the sociological perspective: it didn't seem like Bartholomew, a *Native American*, should be critiquing someone's semi-exotic heritage.

Bobby slapped Bartholomew in the chest. He was far less reserved than usual thanks to the contents of the flask in his back pocket, one-half of which were in his cup.

"He got wood?"

Bartholomew nodded at Barbarella.

"Thanks to that slut right there."

This might have worked in Gray's favor if Barbarella had had a more liberal mother. But Mrs. Destino believed in old ways and old customs (and would have been appalled if she'd seen Barbarella's dress, which Barbarella had had to smuggle out of her house in her Belles bag). Thus, Barbarella did not take the sex-positive position. Instead, her voice shrill, she said, "I'm not the one who got the hard-on!"

This was a good point, as far as Bartholomew was concerned.

"What do you have to say for yourself?" he asked.

What Gray wanted to say for himself was that he couldn't understand why the DJ hadn't started the next song. The answer was that DJ Earthquake—real name Sawyer Putthoff, age: 20—thought there'd been an injury on the dance floor and was debating whether or not he should radio in for an adult. He did not need an emergency harshing the mellow he'd been cultivating between song breaks.

What Gray *did* was to put his hands on top of his pants and sprint for the tunnel.

———————

As Gray rocketed through the school's tall front doors and onto the sidewalk, he was forgetting something: his bags, both gym and school. But Gray's mind was decidedly not on his bags—one of which was in his blue hall locker, the other of which was in his tan gym locker. Gray's mind had more urgent matters to attend to. He needed to get home, get to his room, speak to no one. And possibly talk his mother into moving back to California. Now that the semester was over, he could start fresh in January. He could go to school in Sherman Oaks or Van Nuys or any of the other suburbs that were close enough to where they'd been without being Reseda.

Gray slapped at a twig hanging from one of the oak trees that dominated the front walk. It was within slapping range thanks to a small coating of ice that had fallen during the dance. The twig snapped off, bringing with it a larger piece of the branch than Gray could have thought possible.

He ducked just in time as it landed behind him.

"Whoa," he said.

"*Whoa* is right."

Patra Patterson's hands were on her knees.

"They ought to put you in the game just to outrun the other team," she said.

"Did you come out here to finish me off?"

"Do I seem like the sort of person who would do that?"

"Right now, maybe."

Gray picked up the branch. He tossed it into the semi-frozen grass next to the sidewalk they were on. It skidded to a stop in front of a small sign that was jammed into the frozen ground.

VOTE!
Tuesday, January 23rd

Patra took a step toward the branch. She broke off a twig and twirled it between her fingers. "It's high school. That's how it works."

"Is that why you date someone out of high school?"

"He's in high school. Just a different one."

"And that's good?"

Patra nodded back at the school.

"It's better than that. But it has its own challenges. Let's just say: he's got other options. But I'm not here to talk about that. I came to make sure you're OK."

"Came to check on the wetback?"

"Sure," said Patra, plucking another twig from the branch. "Except I don't know what that means."

"It's a term for Mexicans that are new to the country. Like, their backs are still wet from crossing the Rio Grande."

"Oh," Patra said. Then her face cracked into a smile, which she quickly covered with a hand.

"You're not supposed to like it," said Gray. "It's offensive!"

"I know," said Patra. "But it's kind of funny."

"Yeah," said Gray. "It's kind of funny."

"So you're Mexican. That's cool."

"That's the thing. I'm one-half Venezuelan. Which is way further from Mexico than here. If I were a wetback, it'd be because I had to swim across half an ocean."

"I know," said Patra. "Hugo Chavez screwed that place up bad."

"Impressive," said Gray.

"We Midwesterners may not know all the latest slurs, but we know how to read," said Patra. "Or some of us do."

Then Patra kicked the branch further into the grass, just missing the sign.

Gray jerked at the sudden, violent movement.

"Sorry," said Patra. "It's cold out here and we need to get down to business."

While Gray considered what "business" might be, Patra took a step toward him and straightened his shirt. As she did, Gray wondered if she would notice that his heart was beating against his ribcage like one of those upside-down five-gallon drums the Dominicans played on the boardwalk next to Venice Beach.

When Patra was finished with Gray's shirt, she patted his chest. "What are you going to do?"

"Do I really have to *do* something? It seems like every time I *do* something, something goes wrong."

"Alright, let's start with this: what do you want?"

"A home. For me, and for my mom. And this place feels like a home. I mean, it did, before, you know-"

"Bonerdance?"

"It already has a name?"

"It does now."

"Bonerdance or not, this place feels more like a home than LA ever did. But now that I'm here, everyone's trying to turn it into something else."

He nodded at the VOTE sign.

"I get it," said Patra.

"You do? I was kind of talking out of my ass."

"I guess I like it when you talk out of your ass."

Patra patted Gray's chest once more. "I have to go," she said, retreating down the sidewalk and pulling her coat close. "But when we come back from break, we'll make a plan. Because if anyone ever needed a plan, it was you."

Then Patra pointed toward Gray's pants.

"Oh, and don't ever let anyone make fun of you for that. When you're sixty-five, you'll wish it worked as well as it does now."

When Gray Taylor got home from Bonerdance after a walk long enough to calm himself both emotionally and physically, Nicole Taylor was on the couch she'd dragged from the darkest, dampest reaches of her parents' basement. On the side table that had come with the couch, a half-empty bottle of white wine sat in a pool of light provided by a second-hand lamp.

"So," she said.

"Check my uniform before I go in, I know."

Nicole leaned over and poured wine into her glass. "Yes, also that. But that wasn't the reason for my *So*."

"OK, *so*?"

"*So*. Your dad called."

"*So?*"

"He's saying he screwed up."

"Mom. He always says that."

For several years, the pattern had been a familiar one. Fausto made a mistake. Nicole froze him out for a while. Fausto apologized. Nicole took him back. Until one Friday night after work. It was a woman on the line—a woman who was *also* worried about Fausto because she didn't know where he was, either. That time, they'd gone to stay at the world's most depressing motel for the rest of the weekend while Fausto packed up the few possessions he had.

From the lumpy couch, Nicole Taylor was pleading with her eyes. "What if what we had is the best it gets?"

"Oh come on, Mom."

"What?"

"You know what."

"I really don't."

"Mom."

And it was in this moment that Gray's brain decided to pop in and remind him that he'd forgotten two bags at school. "Son of a *bit-*"

"Gray!"

"Sorry! It's not you. I mean, it's not *not* you. But it's my bag. Or bags. I left them at school."

"Can't you get them on Monday?"

"It's Christmas break, remember?"

"Do you want me to take you?"

Gray leaned across the couch and grabbed the wine bottle. He swirled the remaining contents, of which there were not many.

His mother's eyes followed the miniature wine hurricane, her eyes glassy. "I'm sorry," she said.

"It's fine. It's like four blocks."

"No, I mean, for everything.

Gray sighed. How did she do this? One second, he was ready to kill her. The next, he wanted to fix her.

"It's OK," he said. "Just don't decide anything right now."

Then he returned the wine bottle to the coffee table with a thunk that was a little harder than he'd planned.

———————————

Back at the high school, the gym's back door was open and yellow light from the sodium-vapors was streaming onto the ice-coated grass. The dance had ended ten minutes after Gray's escape, and the participants had fled for assorted house parties to which Gray had not been invited.

Gray followed the light to the back door. He leaned around the metal edge and saw Coach Rutherford guiding a push broom across the gym floor, gathering used cups and dried Silly String. There was music, too—music that had replaced DJ Earthquake. It was coming from a small boom box sitting at half court. Coach Rutherford was humming along as he (and the broom) reached the court's baseline. When Rutherford turned, having dumped the broom's filthy contents into the collection at the end of the gym, he saw Gray peeking through the back door.

"You wouldn't make much of a spy," he said, leaning into the broom.

Gray stepped into the gym. He pointed at a line of Silly String the broom had left in its wake. "You wouldn't make much of a janitor."

"They don't pay me well enough to be much of a janitor."

"Yeah, why *are* you doing this?"

"Because I've got a wife and a kid, and I have to make up for lost time. And union rules keep Mr. Edison from staying this late. This falls under the category of 'chaperone.' Not 'janitorial.'"

The song that had been playing faded out. It was replaced by one that featured a choir singing.

Coach Rutherford ejected a quick bark of a laugh.

"What?" Gray asked.

"Clean out your ears and listen for a second."

The choir faded into the strumming of a guitar. And then a voice that made Gray think about Patra, even though he wasn't previously thinking about Patra.

I saw her today at the reception
A glass of wine in her hand
I knew she was gonna meet her connection
At her feet was her footloose man

Coach Rutherford held up his finger as the chorus came in.

You can't always get what you want
You can't always get what you want

Gray rolled his eyes; it was a little much.

You can't always get what you want
But if you try sometimes, you might find
You get what you need

And then, after resisting for thirty seconds, Gray gave up and started laughing. But this wasn't just any laugh. This was one of those laughs that comes when there's nothing to be done *but* laugh.

"The Stones are good," said Rutherford. "But I don't know if they're *that* good."

"Sorry," Gray said, wiping his eyes. "It's just-"

"While you're filling me in, why don't you catch hold of that other broom?"

Gray snapped a salute. "Yes, sir!"

"If I could get the whole team to do that, we'd be in business," Coach Rutherford said, as he started his broom moving again.

Gray found a broom in the supply closet and caught up around the free-throw line. He stayed behind, picking up anything Rutherford's broom pushed off to the side.

As they moved up and down the court, "You Can't Always Get What You Want" became "Gimme Shelter" became "Midnight Rambler."

Then, just after the first time through the chorus of "Let's Spend The Night Together," Coach Rutherford said, "Nah, I'd rather not."

He bent over the ancient CD player.

"Coach!"

Rutherford stopped, his finger suspended above the Stop button.

"Yeah?"

"Can I talk to you about something?"

"I reckon so," said Coach Rutherford, standing to his full height. "Especially after what you said at half-time. That took guts. Now we just have to work on you putting on your jersey properly."

"If only that were the worst thing that happened tonight."

"The dance?"

"You heard?"

"It's a small town. But I'm guessing that's not what's on your mind."

"It's my dad," said Gray.

"I'd been wondering about that."

"Why didn't you say something?"

"I figured it'd come out, one way or another. Plus, my dad didn't have much call for me, when I was growing up. That's probably why I'm so hard on Devon. Wish I could get him to see-"

Rutherford stopped himself.

"Sorry, this is about your dad, not Devon's dad. So, what about yours?"

Gray explained what had just happened, about the call that had been made—the call he'd been waiting for, really. Even though it had been three years, he'd known it was coming, like winter or a dentist appointment.

When he was finished, Coach Rutherford's chin was resting on his hands on top of the broom handle.

"Miss him?"

"That's the question, isn't it?"

"Yeah," said Rutherford. "That's why I asked it."

"Yes. And no. I miss the fun times we had. But he always kind of scared me. And my mom, I think. So it feels like this is what's best—the way we're so far apart now."

Coach Rutherford nodded. Then he leaned down to the CD player and pushed a button that made the songs scroll. When he'd found the one he wanted, he mashed the Play button.

> *Under my thumb*
> *The girl who once had me down*
> *Under my thumb*
> *The girl who once pushed me around*

Gray crinkled an eyebrow.

"That dude's got his girl under control, so what?"

"First of all, 'that dude' is Mick Jagger, the greatest rock singer of his—or any—time."

"You like a lot of white-people stuff."

"Son, the Rolling Stones ain't white."

"Wait, the Rolling Stones are black?"

"OK, *tech*nically they're white. But also English, so it's a different thing. Like Bowie. Or Led Zeppelin. Anyway, yeah, this song's about a girl, but it applies here, too."

"I don't know if you've been paying attention, but I've got zero girls under my thumb."

"You know that's not what I mean."

"You're talking about basketball and how I've got a chance to be good at it—get it under my thumb."

"I think you know it's not just basketball."

"Yeah," Gray said. "But do you think I can be any good?"

Rutherford looked away.

"Oh," said Gray.

Then Coach Rutherford's eyes came back to Gray's, and he looked at Gray. Like, *really* looked at him.

"Gray. You could be great. But lots of people *could* be great. You have to figure out if you want to."

"Alright. I want to."

"Then go get a ball."

Gray scampered to the supply closet. He picked out a ball, massaging the soft leather. It was neither too new nor too old. He even liked the way it smelled, which reminded him of his grandfather.

He dribbled back to Coach Rutherford.

"You like that one?"

"I do."

"Good. It's yours. And over break, you're going to learn how to handle it."

"How?"

"That's up to you."

Rutherford took his keys out of his pocket. He pulled a set of two off the ring and held them out.

"Make copies tomorrow and bring me these. By the end of break, I expect things will look a little different, on the basketball front. But more important, I'll bet they'll look a little different on the home front."

"When can I start?"

Coach Rutherford picked up the CD player, looked up at the lights, over at the basket, and then back at Gray.

"No time like the present."

"Is that a Rolling Stones song, too?"

"Nope. But maybe it should be."

CHAPTER 20

Gray lasted an hour that first night.

It was by far the shortest period of time he spent in the gym over Christmas break. When it came to his newfound resolve, he had one important thing working for him: the alternative wasn't all that attractive.

His mother's workdays left him in the care of Darby and Gayle, where "care" meant indentured servitude at Taylor's Downtown. Around Christmas, business was less slow than usual, and the last-minute shoppers kept Gray bouncing around the maze that was the stock-room.

Whenever he was finished filling shelves or folding carryout bags or directing old people to the various powders and supplements they needed, Gray yanked over his ears the wool cap his grandfather had given him at the end of his first Monday as an employee and walked through the frigid air to the gym, where awaited his ball and the set of drills he'd invented with the help of various objects he'd found inside the gym's supply closet. Blue plastic chairs became defenders. Orange cones were his cues to change direction when he was dribbling the length of the court. Jump ropes laid out parallel to one another were safe zones he could dribble inside. A yoga mat made for an uncertain surface.

Then there were the body-sized punching bags. Each had two handles because they were meant to be used with someone else. One person held the handles, the other person ran into the bag. But Gray didn't have another person, so he tied a jump rope through one handle and tossed the rope over the rim. Then he did the same with another cushion. And then another, and pretty soon, he had three bags hanging there. He jerked them to and fro and installed himself in the middle. He dribbled and the bags slammed into him and he figured if he could keep hold of the ball through all that, he could keep hold of it when there was a person slapping at his arm.

It was this drill that Coach Rutherford saw Gray in the middle of, the one time he checked in on Gray from the edge of the concrete tunnel. The coach didn't say anything, though. He only nodded, went home, and told Ramona he had a feeling he was going to have a new starting point guard come second semester.

Not that Gray knew this. What Gray knew was that the ball—which he carried everywhere—was beginning to feel like an extension of his hand. And that he was going to miss having the gym to himself when school started again.

But whether Gray liked it or not, school *was* going to start again.

It snowed the night before the first day of second semester, and the next morning Gray could see his breath as he walked through the plowed streets, catching up to the clouds that puffed out in front of him. His backpack bounced behind him, and the basketball he was carrying might have bounced beside him, except that Gray could tell the cobblestones would scar the leather.

As he walked, Gray was thinking about how practice would go, and about his mother and LA. He was also thinking about Patra Patterson and whether she would remember what she'd said, the night of Bonerdance—that thing about coming up with a plan. Together.

Gray didn't have to wait long to find out. Before school, the commons was a war zone, everyone catching up, sharing stories of Christmas presents and Christmas trips and what they'd done in the snow. Then the bell rang and Gray went to his locker to stow the backpack (and the basketball, which squeezed just past the locker's blue edges).

That's when Patra bumped into his locker, dropping a note on the floor before striding off down the hall.

Gray covered the note with a shoe—a new pair of Vans his mother had given him Christmas morning.

When Patra turned the corner, Gray picked up the note.

Library.
Third period.
It's time.

———————

Patra was in her usual spot at one of the long wooden tables. She had a different book in front of her.

Gray slid into the heavy oak chair across from her. "New semester," he said. "New book?"

"You got it," said Patra. "What'd you tell Hoffman?"

"That I had to, uh, *schieze*."

"You learned the German word for poop?"

"I did."

"*Sehr gut.*"

Then Patra opened her notebook, took out a piece of paper, and slid it across to Gray.

"Seriously?"

"I had some time over break," said Patra

Gray nodded, whispering, "Psy-cho."

Patra reached across and thumped Gray's finger.

But Gray kept his head down. This, he was learning, was how flirting worked. And flirting was a lot easier when you had something in your life that you felt good about.

At the top of Patra's page was this:

Gray Day
(Gray Taylor Saves The Daylor)

And underneath:

Copyright: Patra Patterson

"Like Dre Day," said Patra. "I thought you'd enjoy the California reference."

"Not bad," said Gray.

Then he held up the paper.

"But it's blank."

"Not completely."

Gray spun the piece of paper so he could see it. At the bottom, in red, was a date.

"What happens on January 23rd?"

"Are you paying attention to anything? The vote. On the bond issue. To pay for a new school."

"That's soon," said Gray. "So what are we going to do between now and then?"

Patra put her elbows on the table. "Do you agree with me that it's pretty silly that they want to tear down this place so they can replace it with something sterile?"

"I do," said Gray.

"We're going to make sure that bond issue doesn't pass— show these idiots the error of their ways."

"How?"

"That's what we're here to figure out."

So they got to work, huddling over Patra's paper under the library's iron chandeliers. They scribbled and erased and wrinkled their brows and pointed at things they thought would work and things they thought they wouldn't and laughed and argued and twenty minutes later they had the beginnings of a to-do list.

First came "Teamprovement."

(The team needed to start winning.)

Next was "Grayball."

(Gray needed to play more than 54 seconds. And with his jersey on the right way.)

Third was "The World According to Karp."

(Someone had to do something to get Bartholomew Karp off Gray's case.)

Fourth: "Turn That Frown Upside Downtown."

(Because this wasn't *just* about the school.)

Gray held up the paper.

"We're getting there," he said.

Patra snatched the sheet. She scribbled something and spun the page.

"Sundae Fundae?" asked Gray.

"If we get to 80," said Patra. "Everybody gets free ice cream at Tundin's."

"Reminds me of something I saw once. At a Lakers game."

"What's a Laker?"

"The basketball team in LA. They're called the Lakers."

"Lots of lakes in LA?"

"Like two? You're right: it doesn't make sense. So, with Sundae Fundae, who's setting that up?"

"You are," said Patra.

"Why me?"

"Mitzy's mom can be…challenging. And I've already failed that challenge."

"Fine," said Gray. "Give me that."

Patra slipped the list across the table and Gray scribbled out #6 on the list. When he was finished, he held up the paper for Patra.

"*Fancy dancing*?"

Gray dropped the page and tented his hands atop it.

"Indeed. There's something else going on around the time of that bond issue vote. Vote's on Tuesday the 23rd. On Friday, the 26th, there's a dance. I think you call it King of Courts."

"King *and* Queen of Courts."

"Right, that."

"And you want to set up a deal, like you did with Elmer," said Patra. "If we beat them, I go to the dance with you."

"Nope," said Gray. "I want the opposite. I want you to go to the dance with me if we fail."

"I don't get it."

"It's simple. I'm trying to set up a win-win situation here. If we lose, I still get something out of the deal. And if I *don't* get to take you to the dance, that means I got something out of it, too."

"Clever," said Patra, crossing her arms. "There's only one problem."

"Your boyfriend?"

"Let's just say that probably won't be an issue by then. I was talking more about another thing: what if I wanted to go to the dance with you, either way?"

"Well, it sounds like you're refusing my deal. And I think I'm fine with that."

"Agree to disagree," said Patra.

"Exactly," said Gray, standing from his chair. "Now if you'll excuse me, I have to get the *schieze* back to Social Studies."

Gray got an early break on the first item on the list (*Team-provement*). When, over ~~Christmas~~ Holiday Break, Devon Ruther-ford heard his father telling his mother about Gray Taylor's ded-ication to basketball, he'd asked his dad if maybe he could play basketball second semester. Desmond Rutherford had been wait-ing several years for his son to ask just this question. But he knew too much enthusiasm might scuttle the deal. Which is why, after a few seconds, he said, "Only if you're OK with me pretending you're not my son when we're on the court."

Devon Rutherford said, "That sounds perfect."

As for the second item on the list (*Grayball*), something had congealed inside Gray Taylor during his solo sessions in the gym. This progress felt to Gray like something magical had happened.

In fact, it wasn't magical at all. It was only that Gray's basketball experience had reached what the armchair philosopher Malcolm Gladwell might have called a tipping point. If someone had asked Gray, he would have said that it felt like things had slowed down. He was also more self-assured and less bothered by the looks he got from teammates when something went wrong, and at no time was this more evident than during a particular play in the team's first practice after Holiday Break.

The drill was called 3-on-2-on-1. It started with three players attacking two players at one end of the court, followed by those two players attacking whichever player had last passed the ball on the other end of the court.

Gray had been this last passer, tossing the ball to Elmer for a short jump shot that Elmer missed. According to the rules of the drill, Gray needed to get back on defense.

So that's what Gray did—or started to do—and this made his attackers relax. Dusty Rhoads tossed the ball to Bobby Murphy and then, just as Bobby was tossing it back, Gray dashed forward to intercept the ball, which he then laid into the basket he'd just come from. The reason this showed so much progress on Gray's part wasn't just the interception; it was the timing he'd shown in getting it. He'd waited just until there was no going back for Bobby Murphy. Then he'd sprung forward, snatching the ball out of the air at its highest point.

Coach Rutherford blew his whistle and began a jog toward half-court.

"Good!" he said. "Now let's huddle up."

Coach Rutherford spent most of his post-practice talk being hard on the team. But this, Gray could see, was a cover. Secretly, Coach Rutherford was overjoyed with the team huddled around him, thanks in no small part to the addition of his own son.

When the talk was finished (with a reminder that they had only four days until their next game), Gray put his hand in the middle, like everyone else, and said, after Dusty Rhoads's three-count, "Team together!"

Gray turned for his beloved ball rack, ready to start his post-practice routine while everyone else reported to the showers. But something was different about today. Gray wasn't the only one taking a ball from the rack. Elmer and Devon snatched balls and took up position near one of the side baskets. The same was true for Bug and Dusty, at one of the other side baskets.

"Looks like you're having some kind of influence," said Coach Rutherford. He'd followed Gray to the ball rack.

Gray didn't say anything in response. Instead, he got to work. He had three hundred shots to shoot, albeit a little faster than usual because he also needed to get home to work on numbers four and five on the list, plus a little sabotage he was cooking up after learning about a speech his mother had once made.

———————

Tundin's was busier than usual—a couple in a booth on the side, a family of four in the back corner, and a pair of old men huddled at the counter over decaf coffee and pecan pie.

This didn't mean, though, that it was difficult for the Taylor family to get their usual booth in the back. When they were settled in their spot, Mitzy held out menus.

Gray waved her off.

"I know that thing by heart," he said.

"Look at you," said Mitzy. "Like a real regular."

"I might still need one," said Nicole Taylor.

Mitzy passed Nicole a menu.

Before she could get away, Gray caught her wrist.

"Can I talk to you in thirty minutes?"

"Someone's feeling his oats. But sure."

After Mitzy had gone, Nicole Taylor stared at her son for a few seconds. Then she gave up trying to figure out what was going on and refocused on her menu.

"Have we had the chicken fried steak?"

"Two times ago. You tried mine and liked it."

Nicole Taylor nodded, put down her menu, and asked Gray how the day had gone. Gray explained to her the magic he'd felt on the court.

His mother's eyes went to the window, which mirrored the table thanks to the dark night outside.

"I remember that feeling," she said. "Like, the world slows down and makes sense for a while."

"Exactly," said Gray.

And had this been all Gray had wanted to say to his mother about practice, this is where the conversation would have ended or switched topics. But this wasn't all Gray wanted to say to his mother about practice.

"You know what helps?" said Gray.

Nicole Taylor shook her head, her face still studying the window.

"The old gym," said Gray, letting his voice get spacey. "I feel like that place has something special about it. Something kind of mystical."

"Mystical?"

"Yeah," said Gray, pretending this had just occurred to him. "It's like there's something there that connects everyone in the gym to everyone who came before them—everyone who's ever, I don't know, played a game in there, or done a play in there, or given, like, a speech in there."

"You know," said Nicole. "I gave a speech in there once. I was good."

"I'll bet," said Gray, pretending he didn't know (thanks to Harris Bickle) that the speech in question had come when his mother had been running for junior class vice-president. Her campaign speech had been, according to Bickle, "gol-darn magical."

Mitzy appeared at the end of their table. Nicole Taylor—buoyed by the remembrance of a past when she'd been the sort of person who gave speeches in front of a gym full of people—said, her voice clear, "I'll have the chicken fried steak."

Gray ordered what he'd known he would get since he'd proposed this trip: the chicken fingers. He knew they wouldn't take long to arrive (or long to eat), thus giving him time to get to #4 and #5 on the *Gray Day* list.

When Mitzy left, Gray picked up the thread of the conversation. "It's just such a shame, that they're thinking of getting rid of the gym."

"What?"

"Yeah," said Gray, picking up his glass to further display his nonchalance. "If the bond issue goes through."

"Wow," said Nicole. "I hadn't thought about that."

And that was enough for now. Gray changed the tack of the conversation, asking his mother about work. She told him about her boss and the To-Do lists he kept leaving her on Post-It notes, but by the way she did this telling, Gray could see that he'd planted a seed.

Then it was time for food—the chicken fingers that Gray chomped down while also checking the teal clock behind the counter every few bites.

At one of these checks, Nicole said, "You must really need to talk to Mitzy. If it's a girl, you know you can always talk to me about it."

"I know," said Gray, putting his hand on the table so his mom could take it. "But there are some things that you just have to talk to a friend about, you know?"

Even though Nicole Taylor was a little disappointed, this fit with what she expected her son to say in this situation. So she said, "I know what you mean, hon," and reached for Gray's hand.

Gray glanced at the teal clock once more.

8:01

"Oh, jeez," he said, bringing a napkin to his mouth and tossing it on his plate.

"What's the rush?"

"Nothing," said Gray. "I just don't want to keep her waiting."

"It doesn't look like her dance card is full."

Mitzy was wiping the counters like someone who's trying to make wiping the counters take all night.

"I know. But you know Mitzy."

Gray said this as if Mitzy Tundin had no patience for delays in her life. In truth, Gray had seen a certain black pickup truck arrive in Tundin's parking lot and wanted to be out of his booth in time.

"I'll be back in a little while," he said, balancing his dishware as he took off for the front counter.

Nicole held up her mug. "If you get a chance, ask her if I can get some coff-"

The bell tinkled over the door. Harris Bickle got his bearings. And Gray caught the look his mother flashed him from across the booth. It was a look of disappointment, mixed with complete understanding, mixed with appreciation.

Now standing in front of the counter with Mitzy, Gray put his hands to his cheeks, *Home Alone*-style, while the football coach's voice boomed across the restaurant.

"Nikki Taylor, fancy seeing you here! You hoping they'll put some kale on the menu?"

Bickle sauntered across the diner and slid into the booth across from Nicole Taylor.

"You can lead a cornball to water," said Mitzy, still wiping the counter. "Now what's up?"

"Nothing much," said Gray. "Just thinking about a way to save your restaurant."

Mitzy let her sponge skid to a stop in front of a table tent advertising Sunday's "Bunches of Brunches."

"Apparently," she said. "My parents already have that un-der control. Remodel. Top to bottom. Get rid of this thing-"

She patted the counter.

"-and put in more tables."

"That's not going to work."

"I know," said Mitzy. "But what can I do?"

"That's where I come in," said Gray. He nodded toward the kitchen. "Either of them back there?"

"Mom's cooking. But you don't want to talk to her. The re-model was her idea."

Gray looked over his shoulder, to the booth. Harris Bickle had an arm over the back of his side. He looked like he was going to be there awhile.

"I can't go back over there," he said.

"Just don't say I didn't warn you," said Mitzy.

Gray lifted the drawbridge contraption that kept customers on their side of the counter. He slipped through the narrow space between the counter and an industrial sink. Then he was in the back kitchen, which smelled like ammonia and fried food.

"Mitz?"

The question was punctuated by the crash of a pan.

"No, not Mitzy. I mean, no, *ma'am*, not Mitzy. It's Gray Tay-lor. I'm a friend of your daughter's."

Gray leaned around a set of wire shelves holding jars of pickles and peaches.

He waved at Mitzy's mom.

Theresa Tundin wasn't big, but she wasn't small. She was also neither old nor young, the type of person who looks the same from age 30 to 75. Her hair was tightly bunned and she was wearing an apron that didn't have the Tundin's logo on it because she'd decided that would be an unnecessary expense.

She held up a pan. "You handy with a scrub brush?"

"I don't know!"

"Only one way to find out."

Mrs. Tundin dropped the pan in the soapy water in front of her and moved out of the way like a matador.

Gray walked to the sink and plunged his hands into the vat of murky, lemony water.

"Yowch!"

Gray yanked his hands out.

Mrs. Tundin stopped stacking plates on a shelf that was behind the sink and bent to a tiny cabinet underneath. She came up with two bright yellow rubber gloves, which she tossed to Gray.

"Try those on for size," she said.

Gray pulled on the gloves, pretending for a moment that he was a surgeon. He dunked his hands, more slowly this time.

"Better?"

Gray felt around in the murky water for the sponge. When he found it near the back corner of the sink, he started working on the side of the pan that was under the water.

"Much," he said.

"Good," said Theresa Tundin. "Now focus on the bottom of that pan while you tell me what you want."

"Mitzy tells me you're thinking of a remodel."

"We are. Only way to beat the Applebee's."

"What if I told you there was another way?"

"I'd be willing to give you two minutes to explain what you mean before I threw you out of my kitchen."

Gray scrubbed the bottom of the pan as he outlined the theory behind *Turn that Frown Upside Downtown* and *Sundae Fundae*. When he was finished, Mrs. Tundin put her hands on her hips. "So that's it? Free milkshakes?"

"I mean, that's not-"

Mrs. Tundin's arm shot from her hip.

"Get the hell out of my kitchen!"

"You haven't heard the best part," said Gray.

Mrs. Tundin took her hand down, replacing it on her hip. "Out with it."

"The best part is that we're going to get the school to help."

"Really?"

Gray took the pan out of the soapy water and plopped it, upside-down, on the metal shelf that drained into the sink.

"Yeah, really."

Mrs. Tundin's arm flew toward the drainer.

"You have to rinse it!"

"Sorry," said Gray. "I don't really know what I'm doing."

"I can tell," said Mrs. Tundin. She grabbed the pan and rinsed it for Gray. "But I like your attitude. Now finish that next pan and tell me the rest."

The commons area at Beaudelaire High was a kaleidoscope of sights, sounds, and smells. Some kids had their heads on tables, still sleepy after being rousted in the dark of midwinter. Some kids were loud: a rumor about a quiz, a crack about someone's mother, the slurp of a coffee from the Casey's on the highway. Some kids were finishing breakfasts they'd brought from home, dumping the remnants of those breakfasts into bins meant for a compost pile that was half-heartedly maintained by Trina Patterson but mostly served as a feeding station for several coyotes that had learned her schedule.

In the eye of this kaleidoscopic storm sat Gray Taylor and Patra Patterson. They were across from one another at a table that would stay out all morning and through lunch, until the roly-poly janitor, Mr. Edison, stowed it and the rest of its brethren away at 1:20, like he did every day.

At this table, Gray had his eyes closed and his arms crossed, looking like a toddler caught in a lie.

Patra was leaning toward Gray like the parent who's caught the toddler.

"Look," she said. "I like the reverse psychology with your mom. And that sounds like progress with Mrs. Tundin. But may I remind you: we don't have much time left? And we haven't even talked about *Grayball* and *Teamprovement*. I mean, you all have a game tomorrow night, and then there are only, what, two weeks left before St. Ant's? And what are we doing about Bartholomew? What do you have to say for yourself?"

"I've got a couple more tricks up my sleeve," said Gray, opening his eyes.

"Oh really? Like?"

"Like-"

Gray jerked his chin to the corner of the commons area, where the janitor, Mr. Edison, was emerging from his closet/office with a copy of the *Beaudelaire Bee*.

"-Mr. Edison."

"Got it," said Patra. "You're going to kill the janitor, build a hideout inside his office, and use it as headquarters for your new role as a superhero. Should we call you The Gray Ghost? Or maybe The Graymaker?"

She put her fists in front of her and threw one into an exaggerated punch.

Gray caught her hand.

"Mr. Edison's going to help us," he said. "Number one and number five."

"You mean *Teamprovement* and *Sundae Fundae*?"

"Those are the ones."

"How?"

Gray lowered Patra's hand to the table as he fought the urge to tell her what he was thinking—a way to embrace the mistake he'd made with his first appearance in a game. That is, if Warren "Eddie" Edison had the supplies he thought he might.

"It's a surprise," said Gray.

"And what about you playing for more than 54 seconds? That's kind of integral to the plan."

"Well, I've been killing it in the Shell Drill, and it feels like things are making sense out on the court, at least on offense. If Coach *doesn't* put me in, I guess it might be because he's just not sure. And anyway, Bobby and Bartholomew have calmed-"

Gray trailed off because he'd noticed that Patra wasn't paying attention any longer. It made him think of the time at the state football game, when she'd been distracted by the guy in the military-style coat.

He spun in his seat, dreading what he would see. He was both relieved and not relieved to find that the answer was Barbarella Destino, advancing on them from across the commons. She was wearing low-slung jeans that were entirely wrong for the weather—low-slung jeans whose top edge caught her hand when she got to the lunch table, instinctively affecting the Instagram Hip Pop.

"What're you guys talking about?"

"Price of tea in China," said Patra, who'd wound out of her seat and was buttoning her pea coat.

"Did it go up?"

"Hey," Gray said to Patra. "We'll talk more later?"

"Sure thing, Graymaker. Oh, and-"

Patra jerked her head at Barbarella.

"-number three?"

Gray's brain spun. Number three on their list was *The World According to Karp*. What did that have to do with Barbarella Destino?

While Gray was pondering what Patra could have meant, Barbarella eased into the seat across from Gray. She examined her fingernails, which were painted alternately in silver and gold.

"I came over to tell you that, well, I'm sorry for the racist thing at the dance."

"The incident at the dance," said Gray, leaning down so he could see into Barbarella's eyes. "The dancident, if you will. The first thing is: it wasn't racist. We're the same *race*, you and me. Just slightly different *ethnicities.*"

Barbarella's face rotated in 15 degrees of confusion.

"OK," said Gray. "We'll stick with 'racist.' So, it was awful of you, and you're sorry, you're never going to do it again, you've taken a vow of chastity and you're going to live out your days in a convent?"

"Yes," said Barbarella. "All of those."

"Really? Even the convent part?"

Gray nodded at Barbarella's blouse, which was as low-cut as her jeans. Barbarella followed Gray's eyes. She pulled at the top edge of the blouse.

"What? My mom wears stuff like this to her hair conventions all the time."

"You think a convent is…nevermind. I appreciate the semi-apology, but I've got things to do."

He glanced at Mr. Edison, who was leaning against the wall next to his closet door, his copy of the *Beaudelaire Bee* unfurled in front of him.

"Before you go," said Barbarella. "I just wanted to tell you that if there's anything I can do, I hope you'll let me know."

That's when it hit Gray: what Patra had been talking about. They needed a way to neutralize Bartholomew Karp. And Barbarella could be the key.

"There might be something," said Gray, rubbing his chin.

Barbarella leaned forward again, squashing her breasts together in a way that tested all of Gray's gaze control. "Tell me," she said.

"You know how, in schools, there are all these backchannels about who likes who, and it's something we all do so we don't have to run the risk of getting our feelings hurt?"

"Um, sure?"

He'd confused her again. Better to keep it straightforward. "Bartholomew. He's thinking about asking Ariel to King of Courts. But you can't tell Ariel."

To complete the charade, Gray reached across the table for Barbarella's hand. The boldness of this move surprised Barbarella. Who *was* this kid, this Gray Taylor, who'd recovered from her public humiliation of him, and who was now grabbing her hand in plain sight?

"Of course I won't," Barbarella said.

Which meant that of course she *would*. Which was exactly what Gray had decided that he wanted her to do. If he could get Ariel thinking Bartholomew was interested in her, Ariel might be able to use her feminine wiles to get Bartholomew actually interested in her, which might get Bartholomew's mind off torturing him and onto more important things. Like getting into Ariel Bickle's pants.

As Barbarella was crossing her heart to confirm her promise, Gray felt impact on his shoulder. It was Coach Rutherford's hand.

"Here's the man I'm looking for."

Rutherford released Gray's shoulder just as the day's first bell rang, warning those assembled in the commons area that they had five minutes before class started.

"Walk with me," said the coach.

Gray grabbed his backpack and glanced at Mr. Edison.

"I need to talk to-"

"Eddie's not going anywhere," said Coach Rutherford. "And this'll just take a second."

Dodging stragglers, they walked into the tunnel that connected the commons with the gym. Coach Rutherford pulled two discs out of the pocket of the blue Beaudelaire windbreaker he was wearing.

He held up the first. "This is Santa Fe playing at DeSoto. We play Santa Fe tomorr-"

Coach Rutherford stopped himself.

"Sorry, you know that. Anyway, Santa Fe has this press they run that's a real sumbitch. And I want you to take a look at it."

"Because you need help breaking it?"

"Don't get ahead of yourself, freshman. I know exactly how to break it. That's what we'll be working on at practice tonight. But I want you to get especially familiar because you're playing tomorrow. A lot."

Gray's chest tightened up. It was like in the video games he'd played with his dad. Just when you'd earned enough doubloons to buy a horse and the life extension to deal with one level, the game sent you on to the next level. And that new level was always harder, meaning you had to find new equipment and new life extensions.

"OK," said Gray, nodding at the second disc. "What about that one?"

"This one is me trusting you. The game I have here shows a team we don't play for two weeks. St. Anthony."

Gray smiled.

"What?" said the coach.

"Oh, nothing. I was just talking about that game with Patra. And I remember what you said about them and their coach, about how he screwed you over."

"Then you get it."

Gray took the discs and peered at them for a moment. He said, in a voice that was more solemn than he'd planned, "I do."

And *then* Gray went to talk to Mr. Edison.

Thirty-six hours and eight minutes after Gray's meeting with the janitor, Bug Biancalana hoisted a poorly conceived jump shot that made Coach Rutherford catch Gray's eye inside the thrum of the Beaudelaire High gymnasium.

Gray nodded, quick and curt.

Rutherford did, too, and Gray took off toward the scorer's table in a half-crouched shuffle so he wouldn't block anyone's view of the game.

At the scorer's table, he went through the necessary details for Mr. Hoffman.

"Taylor, 22. For Biancalana, 11."

"Bravo, Sir Gray," said Mr. Hoffman, making a mark in the scorebook without taking an eye off the game. "Godspeed."

Gray dropped onto the bleacher beneath Mr. Hoffman. The scene in front of him—so much color, so much noise—made him think of when the gym teacher had tried to teach them double-dutch in fourth grade. The ropes were spinning so fast and how were you supposed to find your way in? Especially if you were about to make a fool of yourself on purpose.

Under his warm-ups, Gray was wearing one of the uniforms Mr. Edison had dug out of a footlocker marked *1961-4*. Gray was going to show the town of Beaudelaire that "old" didn't necessarily equal "bad."

Out on the court, the referee blew his whistle after a scrum under the basket. Oskar Haart came out of the tangled mass of bodies with the ball wrapped in his arms. He'd also committed a foul and a referee trotted to a spot at midcourt, where he reported the foul to Mr. Hoffman.

The same referee waved Gray into the game.

Gray pulled one string from around another string. His warm-up pants dropped to his ankles. Then, to make sure the effect was complete, Gray tore off his warm-up top as he stepped out of the warm-up pants. He knew he couldn't break character—couldn't let on that anything was different than anyone else on the court.

He jogged out to Bug Biancalana and held out a hand.

"You'll be defending number 10," said Bug, with a nod behind him at Santa Fe's point guard. Then he waved at Gray's shorts, which had a one-inch inseam. "Don't hemorrhage anything."

The referee blew his whistle and handed the ball to a player from Santa Fe—Gray's man, Number 10.

Gray snapped his rubber band and it began: real basketball, when the game mattered, when the crowd was paying attention, and all of it while wearing the shortest and tightest uniform anyone in the gym had seen.

He shadowed Number 10, sliding left and then right and in the process forgetting about his tiny shorts and the crowd and whether his tiny shorts were affecting that crowd the way he was hoping they would.

The guard—whose dark hair was cropped a half-inch from his head, leaving him looking like an inmate or a Chia pet—had his attention on his team, which was downcourt, awaiting his instructions. Gray could tell number 10 wasn't thinking about him. And if Number 10 wasn't thinking about him-

Gray planted his left foot and lunged for the ball. As he did, he could see what was going to happen next: he'd push the ball toward the sideline, scramble after it, and then, once he'd tracked it down, score a basket—his first ever. And that would be the beginning of a surprisingly effective first full game: maybe twelve points, a few assists, and a big win.

But as is often the case in sports and life, theory and reality did not intersect. What actually happened was that Number 10 pulled the ball away from Gray and, when he noticed that Gray's lunge had left him out of position, accelerated downcourt, leaving Gray stuck like a cat in quicksand.

Gray made a quick recovery and by the time the point guard had gotten to half-court, he was only ten feet behind him. He had a clear view, then, of Elmer helping off the man he was guarding, coming out to meet the point guard. This, though, left Elmer's man unguarded. Number 10 saw this opening and tossed the ball to Elmer's man, at which point Gray saw his (second) chance. He accelerated and, as the ball rose from waist to chest to head, he stuck up his hand and jumped.

There were a couple of things working against Gray. One, the shooter was right-handed and Gray was on his left side, meaning Gray would have to get all the way across his body to get to the ball. And two, the shooter was four inches taller than Gray, which meant Gray had to stretch every available ligament to its limit to have a chance. But those same characteristics also worked *for* Gray. Because the shooter was right-handed, and because Gray was on his left side, Gray had the element of surprise on his side. And because the shooter was four inches taller than Gray, he thought he had time for a slow, easy shot. Gray stretched and, this time, the Fors won out over the Againsts and Gray blocked the shot, launching the ball out of bounds, where it bounced once at the base of the bleachers, and then caromed into the crowd, coming to rest at the feet of Patra Patterson.

Not that Gray noticed whose feet the ball had landed near. He was breathing so hard that his brain wasn't getting any oxygen. This was far more work than he'd expected. How was he going to manage an entire quarter of this? Let alone an entire *game*.

"Gray."

Patra picked up the ball and faked a pass at him.

"Gray!"

Patra threw the ball and this finally got Gray's attention. He caught the ball just as Elmer appeared at his side.

"Take a breath," said Elmer.

Gray's hand went to his wrist and his rubber band. But before he could pull, Elmer clapped his own hand around Gray's wrist. Then Elmer was pulling, hard enough that Gray was starting to worry that the rubber band would take off some skin.

But Elmer wasn't snapping the rubber band. He was yanking the rubber band entirely off Gray's wrist.

He tossed the band to Patra and grabbed the baby blue piping at the edge of Gray's ancient jersey.

"When you're out here," he said. "This is your rubber band. Now, do like I said: take a breath."

Gray sucked in a breath like he'd once taken after being bowled over by a wave at Dockweiler Beach, when he'd feared that he might never get air again.

"Good," said Elmer. "Now let's go have some fun."

"I'll hold onto this," said Patra, twirling the rubber band.

Gray smiled at Patra—the devilish sort of smile that can only come when we've relaxed, when we've realized that the only way to learn how to double-dutch is to get hit by the ropes a few times.

"You'd better," he said.

Then Gray Taylor clapped his hands and started playing basketball.

CHAPTER
23

The Rhoads basement was steamy and smelled of cheap perfume and cheaper cologne. Bodies weaved together, a mass of bright colors and exposed flesh moving in time to music thumping from the corner of a landing made of raw boards. The rig of electronics producing the music sat atop a door supported by two sawhorses, like something from the first Deadmau5 concert.

Mitzy Tundin was standing on the landing above the sweaty, weaving bodies. She turned to Dusty Rhoads, cupping her hands to combat the music coming from speakers hung from the vaulted basement's walls.

"I like what you've done with the place!"

Dusty held up a red plastic cup in salute.

Mitzy held out her arm for Gray. "Let us perambulate," she said.

At the bottom of the wooden stairs, Gray and Mitzy slipped into a pocket formed by half a dozen dancing teenagers. It was quieter here. And less sweaty.

Mitzy stood on her toes, trying to peer into the mass of students. "Do you see her?"

Gray scanned the crowd for Patra. This was how Mitzy had talked him into coming—the promise that Patra would be here. She'd been right to use that particular motivator. Gray wanted to see Patra, and he wanted her to say she'd seen how well he'd played. Because he *had* played well. From the moment Elmer had torn the rubber band off Gray's wrist to the sound of the final buzzer, he'd been all over the court, seeing and doing things before anyone else. And they'd won. By 16. But even with all that, he'd waffled regarding the party Dusty Rhoads and his brother had announced in the shower—this reluctance because Gray was exhausted. There'd been all the dashing up and down the court. But there'd also been all the directing, of Oskar Haart and Devon Rutherford and Elmer Niehaus and-

"Frosh!"

Before Gray knew what was happening, Bartholomew Karp had an arm around him. His red cup was draped over Gray's shoulder.

"Leave him alone," said Mitzy.

Bartholomew withdrew the arm and put both hands to his chest. "Why, Mitzy Tundin, I merely wanted to congratulate the freshman. He looked good out there tonight, didn't he?"

"He did," said Mitzy.

"Can we borrow him for a second?"

Bartholomew nodded at Bobby Murphy, who'd materialized from the crowd holding a red cup of his own.

Mitzy's eyes got narrow.

Gray nodded so only Mitzy could see. Whatever was happening, he needed to face it on his own.

"I'll go find Patra," she said.

"Tell her hello," said Bartholomew. He collared Bobby Murphy, whose face was cold and calculating under the everpresent John Deere hat. "Should we get the frosh a beer, B-Murph?"

Bobby snapped his fingers at someone near the keg. Within seconds, a red cup appeared like a magic trick.

Bartholomew nodded at the cup.

"First brew?"

Gray took the cup and peered over its rippled white edge. Once, he and his dad had been washing his mom's car on a Sunday afternoon. His dad had passed him the tan can of Montejo he was drinking. After Gray's first, reluctant sip, Fausto had watched Gray's expression intently, asking without asking if Gray had liked it. Gray had not liked it. But he'd also not been entirely sure what his father had wanted him to say. So he'd shrugged. "It is OK," Faustino had said. "No one likes it when they're your age."

This felt the same. Was he supposed to sip the beer Bobby had handed him? Toss it back all at once? Refuse to drink? Wasn't it enough that they'd won the game and that he'd played so well and that he'd passed the ball to Bartholomew when he'd been open?

Then, before Gray could decide what to do about the beer, it happened: Ariel Bickle made her entrance.

First down the stairs were the open-toed wedges about which Ariel had debated for ten minutes with Barbarella and Christy. It probably *was* too cold, but also "these shoes are too cute!" Then the rest of Ariel came into view. Ariel had not debated long on the rest of her outfit, because she knew the rest of her outfit worked. As did anyone who watched her finish her stride down the stairs.

The outfit in question was simple enough: a pair of black pants with a pink sweater. What turned heads (including Bartholomew's) was the way Ariel was wearing them. The sweater came down only to her belly button, which showed off a strip of Ariel's flat stomach. The pants came up only to her hipbones, which accentuated the two diagonal muscles at Ariel's hips. But these were only mortar shells compared to the heavy artillery that awaited: Ariel Bickle wasn't wearing a bra. It was a move of considerable genius. Ariel didn't have breasts like Barbarella Destino. But that didn't mean she was without recourse, as anyone watching her walk down the stairs could plainly see.

When she got to the bottom of the stairs, Ariel put up her hands, threw back her head, and screamed out the lyrics to the Kelli Uzi song—a move born of the confidence that had come when Gray's bit of misinformation about Bartholomew's interest in Ariel had been delivered by Barbarella Destino according to the expected channels.

Ariel's scream-singing wrangled the attention of everyone in the party, including Bartholomew Karp, who forgot about potential insults aimed at upstart freshman point guards holding red cups of bad beer.

"Gotta go, bro!"

As the realization of what had just happened calmed a stomach that had continued to flop since Mitzy's departure, Gray held up his cup toward Bobby Murphy, whose head was on a swivel: Gray, Ariel, Bartholomew, back to Gray.

"Thanks for the beer!"

Then Gray swam to safety: Mitzy, who was standing on the bottom-most stair, surveying the crowd with her own red cup held loosely in her off hand.

"How'd it go with Sitting Bull?"

"Are we allowed to say that?"

"Lesbian advantage. I can say whatever I want. Now answer the question."

Gray hopped onto the stair with Mitzy, watching Bartholomew pass Ariel a red cup. She was laughing at something he'd said.

"I think," said Gray. "It went OK!"

Mitzy held up her red cup. Gray tapped her cup with his own and had his first-ever swig of beer. Then, just as the tension was melting down his body and out the bottoms of his feet, Gray felt a looming presence from beside him. It was Elmer, a cup of his own in his hand.

Gray stretched so he could see into Elmer's cup. The only thing left was the dregs. And then Elmer was gone, swimming back into the crowd.

"Should we be worried?" asked Gray.

"Maybe?" said Mitzy. But her eyes weren't on Elmer.

It took Gray half a second to see what was distracting Mitzy. Barbarella Destino had brought her own artillery to the party—skin-tight jeans, a V-neck T-shirt, and a choker whose effect on his penis Gray couldn't explain.

But this wasn't about him and his genitals.

He slugged his beer, stepped off the stairs, and swam back through the party to Barbarella.

She held up a flask. "Gray! Do you like vodka?"

Gray took the flask and a swig. His eyes went wide as the vodka sloshed into the back of his throat like a tsunami made of fire. He forced it down and tried to keep from coughing.

"That's terrible!"

"Sorry," said Barbarella, tossing back a gulp of her own.

"Maybe it's because I don't know vodka that well!"

Barbarella handed him the flask and Gray had his second mouthful of Burnett's vanilla-infused vodka. When he was finished, Gray grabbed Barbarella's hand.

"Ooh la la," she said.

"No," Gray shouted. "It's-"

Then he gave up on explaining. Basement parties were not the place for talking.

Gray dragged Barbarella through the crowd and deposited her in a spot in front of Mitzy. He bowed like a maître d' and withdrew so the two of them could be alone. And so he could make a break for it. He'd seen enough movies about high school parties to know he was in danger of becoming a stereotype—the freshman who can't hold his booze and makes a fool of himself.

He aimed himself up the wooden stairs that would take him back to the hallway, the kitchen, out the door, down the sidewalk, home. In his spin, he saw Bobby Murphy marching up the stairs.

And Patra Patterson, coming down them.

Patra was wearing an oversized N*Sync T-shirt she'd turned into a knee-length dress with the help of a black leather belt. She had on the same boots she'd worn when Gray had first met her—boots that carried her down the stairs just as Gray was dancing up them to meet her.

"You came!" said Gray.

"I had to return this," said Patra, raising her arm.

"My rubber band!"

"The one and only. But don't expect me to be here long. Dad wants me home in-"

Patra checked her other wrist, the silver watch there.

"-twelve minutes."

"We'd better get you a drink! And then I can tell you about Barbarella and Bartholomew. It worked! It was amazing. Anyway, the keg's-"

Gray turned to point at the corner of the basement where the keg was bathing in a slurry of ice and water. But before he could orient Patra, he saw a sight that shot something even colder than the keg's slurry down his spine. Elmer was hoisting a girl like she was his figure-skating partner. There was one problem. The girl did *not* look interested in being hoisted into the air. Her face had the panicked expression of a driver who's just learned the brakes are out.

"So *that*'s what he meant," said Gray.

"What? Who?"

"Elmer. The football game. When he. The deal. Can you?"

"Go take care of Elmer," said Patra.

"OK, but stay here. I need to tell you about Bartkarp."

Patra held up her watch.

"Eleven minutes," she said.

Gray hesitated. He didn't want to leave Patra here. He wanted to *talk* to Patra. But a pledge was a pledge; he'd made that promise to Elmer at the football game.

So he took off, weaving through the bodies on the dance floor. As he zagged past a pair of juniors who had their red cups held high, he couldn't help but think of what Dusty Rhoads had said about help defense on his first day of practice.

Yes, he was focused on Elmer (who was spinning the girl like they were a two-part top), but he was also tracking Patra (still on the stairs), Bartholomew and Ariel (within breathing distance of one another), and Mitzy and Barbarella (not as close, but closer than he might have thought).

The one person he'd lost track of was Bobby Murphy. And that was alarming. There was something strange about the way Bobby Murphy had been looking at him after Ariel Bickle made her entrance. But Gray pushed that thought aside; he had plenty to deal with for now.

When he got to Elmer, he popped him on the shoulder.

"What's up!" said Elmer.

Gray pointed at the girl on Elmer's shoulders.

"Her, for one."

"She likes it! Don't you?"

While Elmer tried to crane his head around the legs of the girl in question, whose name Gray was pretty sure was either Lindsay or Lindy, the girl in question looked down at Gray. She mouthed, "Get me down."

Gray scanned the room, running through the options. Mitzy? No, she was occupied. And anyway, Elmer saw Mitzy every day at school. Christy Tisdale? But if Elmer had wanted to talk to Christy Tisdale, she'd probably be the one on his shoulders. More beer? Nope. Worst idea yet, and now the girl was spinning like a dervish on Elmer's shoulders. He needed to come up with something fast.

"Dude!" Gray was shouting into Elmer's ear. "Dusty needs you, upstairs. Right now!"

"Dusty? Why?"

That was the part Gray hadn't figured out yet.

"I'll explain when we get up there," he said. "For now, you have to put her down."

"I can't bring her with?"

"You can't bring her with."

"Fine."

Elmer leaned over much more quickly than the girl was expecting and one of her legs swung into space, her small dress flapping as it followed. Gray reached out to catch her. But instead of grabbing her leg (his intention), he grabbed her inner thigh.

"Uh," she said. "Thanks?"

The girl—Lindy or Lindsay—disappeared into the dance party.

"She was heavier than I thought," said Elmer, watching her. Then he shook his head. "Now, what's Dusty want?"

"Let's get upstairs. He'll be able to tell you."

Elmer shrugged and Gray began to hack his way through the crowd. He could tell he wouldn't have Elmer's attention for long—not that having Elmer's attention was going to guarantee success.

He hazarded a glance behind him. Elmer was clumping through the crowd with the undue concentration of the moderately intoxicated. Then Gray broke through, into the empty space at the bottom of the stairs. He was expecting to see Patra there. But in this, Gray was disappointed: Patra was nowhere to be found. If this was help defense, he was failing.

"Where's Dusty?"

Elmer's eyes were swimming.

Gray pointed up to the wooden landing. "Kitchen. Let's go."

At the top of the stairs, Gray pulled open the door and ushered Elmer into the hallway. Dusty Rhoads was holding court in the kitchen, his long legs hanging from the countertop.

"So Bug is like, 'But that's not even the damsel I came with!'"

This got a laugh out of the girl against the refrigerator, a clap out of the guy by the stove, and a knowing, mustachioed grin from Bug Biancalana, who was perched on the edge of a tiny kitchen table piled with unopened mail.

Dusty took a long pull from his beer. "Gray Taylor, what's happening?"

What Gray said with his mouth was nothing. What he said with his eyes was that he needed Dusty's help, pronto.

"I got you," Dusty said with a nod. He hopped off the counter and strode past Gray, lassoing Elmer's neck with his free arm. "Bro, I'm glad to see you. I need your help, like, meow."

Elmer looked at Dusty like he'd never seen him before. "Yeah?"

"Yeah, dude. I got-"

Dusty stopped and searched the kitchen for inspiration just as the song that was playing into the basement came to a thunderous close.

Then it hit Gray: the music!

Gray waved his fingers so only Dusty could see. He made the universal sign for "DJ." (Head tipped, record being scratched.)

"-a job for you! This music is Glad bags."

Dusty pulled Elmer through the hallway, and out onto the wooden landing. Meanwhile, Gray got exactly two breaths before it hit him: where was-

"Patra!"

When this came out of Gray's mouth, Bug glanced up from the mini-conversation that had started as soon as Dusty had gotten occupied with Elmer.

Gray clapped a hand over his mouth. This produced a smile from Bug—a smile and a beer-can salute toward the door beside him.

"You rang?"

Patra curtseyed from the tiny hallway by the front door. She had her purse slung tight over her shoulder: the cue that caused Gray to ask, "Leaving already?"

She held up the wrist with the watch. "Four minutes."

Elmer's first selection came in behind Gray. At first, it seemed like an odd choice: a few simple licks on a guitar, followed by someone saying, "Turn it up." But then the natural swing of Lynyrd Skynyrd's biggest hit took over, and the crowd realized that "Sweet Home Alabama" was one heck of a party song.

"Can I walk you out?"

"You can," said Patra.

An ooooooo came from the girl by the stove.

Gray darted toward the front door, past the pile of shoes on the welcome mat. He pushed open the door and saw the edge of a faded porch swing and an idea blasted to the front of his brain: maybe Patra would have time to sit with him on the swing! That would be romantic, the two of them, side by side, swaying to and fro. And who knew what might come of that?

Gray turned to locate Patra.

A voice rose from the porch's darkness.

"Gray Taylor. Just the man I was hoping to see."

With one hand on the doorframe, Gray leaned into the cold night air.

First, he saw a point of orange light. Then, as his eyes caught up, the point of orange light moved up to a face under a green John Deere hat.

Patra slipped through the front door, arriving at Gray's side on the front porch.

"Robert Wayne Murphy," she said. "How the heck are you?"

"Cleopatra," said Bobby. "I did not expect to see you here."

"I'm nothing if not full of surprises," said Patra.

Gray's head whipped between doorway and porch swing.

"Bob and I go way back," said Patra. "In fact, I'd probably sit and share that lung dart if I didn't have to get home."

"Shame," said Bobby Murphy, dragging on his cigarette. "But that'll give me and young Gray a chance to…catch up."

He patted the seat next to him on the swing. The sudden movement caused the chain holding the swing to creak like a gallows and the truth washed over Gray: the encounter with Bartholomew had been a fakeout, a false flag, a red herring. Bartholomew was loud and obnoxious and difficult. But he was just the tip of the spear. And like his dad had always said, you had to worry more about who was holding the spear.

Patra's hand went to her wrist and his rubber band.

"I almost forgot."

Gray grabbed Patra's wrist. "I think you should hold onto it. For safekeeping."

Patra twisted Gray's hand into hers, pulling him toward her and kissing him on the cheek. She scampered down the front stairs and into the darkness.

Gray's stomach was churning at the prospect of dealing with Bobby Murphy. But he couldn't stop the fingers on his right hand from going to the spot on his cheek where Patra had kissed him.

"She's a pistol," said Bobby Murphy. "Now come sit a spell."

Gray could think of several hundred things he'd rather do than sit down next to Bobby Murphy, especially tonight. He'd had such a good night!

Nonetheless, he plopped down in the chair, sending it backward with enough force that Bobby Murphy's legs shot out.

"Easy there, kid."

"Sorry," said Gray.

When the swing had regained its equilibrium, Bobby pulled the pack of cigarettes out of his shirt pocket.

"Want one?"

Gray hesitated. But not for long, because if he didn't miss his guess, the right answer was: "Sure."

Bobby shook two cigarettes out of the pack. He took one for himself, sliding it into the side of his mouth. Then he held out the pack, one cigarette peeking out like the tall kid in a kindergarten picture.

"You're going to cough if you pull too hard. So with your first one, take it easy."

"Got it," Gray said.

Bobby snapped a lighter out of his front pocket.

"Lean down," he said. "And suck when the flame hits the tip."

So that's what Gray did. And even though he knew smoking cigarettes was basically the worst thing in the world, there was something intimate about allowing Bobby Murphy to light his cigarette. Even though—or perhaps especially because—he was terrified of Bobby Murphy.

"Now a little at a time," said Bobby.

Gray inhaled, slowly, trying to follow instructions. But when the smoke hit the back of his throat, he lost track of the instructions. Instead of exhaling, he inhaled more aggressively. He doubled over, coughing and snorting. It was like the vodka, but ten times worse.

Bobby whacked him on the back.

"Try again," he said.

This time it was a little easier, although Gray couldn't help but think the cigarette tasted a lot like what it tasted like when you leaned over a campfire.

After a few puffs, Bobby leaned forward, his arms resting on his knees. "What's your angle here?"

"My angle?"

"I've been watching you," said Bobby. "You're up to something."

Gray took a drag of his cigarette. This time, it was followed by only a mild cough.

"You wouldn't believe me," he said between hacks.

"Try me," said Bobby Murphy, crossing his legs and leaning into the back corner of the swing.

So, because Gray had come to his first-ever high school party and because he'd had vodka for the first time and because he'd had a cigarette for the first time and because he was tired of coming up with tricks and workarounds and because he couldn't think of anything else to do, Gray took a deep breath and told Bobby Murphy the truth—he outlined the plan that, until now, only he and Patra knew about. He explained why he wanted to stay in Beaudelaire, why he wanted to show everyone in Beaudelaire what they had, and how he thought he could accomplish all of it.

When he was finished, Bobby pointed at him with the butt of his cigarette and Gray stiffened, expecting the worst—a curt dismissal of his assessment of Beaudelaire or some remark about how naïve he was being.

But all Bobby Murphy said was, "What's in it for you?"

"I think I'm going to need another cigarette."

This got a dry laugh out of Bobby Murphy. It also got another cigarette out of Bobby Murphy.

While Bobby was lighting this cigarette with the end of his own, Gray thought about the question. He knew the answer; he just hadn't put it into words.

When Bobby handed the cigarette to him, he did.

"I get to feel like a superhero," said Gray.

He expected Bobby to laugh, because who said something like that? But Bobby didn't laugh. He took a drag of his own and said, "I know what you mean."

"You do?"

"Sure. You know what it felt like, being out on that field in Lawrence?"

"And basketball's the same?"

"I'm not built for basketball. But either way, I get what you're saying.

Then Bobby Murphy put his arm on the back of the swing. He fingered the chain at the other end. "You know why my brother never came to practice after he belted you?"

"I always wondered."

"I told him not to. That was a cheap shot."

"And mine wasn't?"

"Bartholomew had that coming. That's why we love football. And basketball. There's rules. Out on the field, or the court, actions have consequences."

They sat in silence for a few seconds, smoke from their cigarettes mingling with the steam of their breaths as Gray pondered this new information.

Bobby was the first to speak. "So you've got two games left to make it all happen."

"Yep," said Gray, his voice still cautious. "Wellsville and then Saint…what's it called?"

"Anthony. You know about Rutherford and that thing with the coach there?"

"He told me a little. He's got me studying some film, to scout them."

"That coach—from Saint Anthony—I guess he kinda screwed our man the Deacon over. Offered him a job, then took it away."

"That sucks," said Gray.

"That's how life works. Sucks, like the wind."

"The wind?"

"You know, the wind: as soon as you try to hold onto it-"

Bobby Murphy feathered his hands through the air. His eyes were lit by the cigarette's ember.

"-it slips away."

When Nicole Taylor had put her head in her hands on their back patio in Reseda, Gray had been surprised by the way he was able to feel two things simultaneously. There was terror. But there was also peace because the thing that had needed to happen was finally happening. Gray felt something similar on the porch swing—

like Bobby Murphy had just said something that made a lot of sense, but also that Bobby Murphy had a handle on something he, Gray, wasn't sure he wanted to have a handle on.

"Can I ask you something?"

Bobby Murphy blew jets of smoke from his nostrils.

"Shoot," he said.

"Why are you being so nice to me?"

"Why wouldn't I?"

"Seriously? Bartholomew and the bullying and-"

Bobby Murphy leaned forward on the swing again. He took one more drag and then looked at Gray, pointing the cigarette at him.

"Think back, Gray Taylor. I'm never an asshole just to be an asshole, like someone we both know. But I'm also not just going to assume that some outsider should be an insider. You know what I'm saying?"

Gray nodded, but only as cover. He was thinking back on all his encounters with Bobby Murphy: the crack about his pants on his first day; the way he'd said "Too late" after stealing the ball during his first practice; when he'd laughed about Gray's condition at Bonerdance. And it was true when he thought about it. Bobby had never gone out of his way to be *mean*. He'd mostly been telling the truth. But then again...

"So why do you keep hanging out with him?

"Bartkarp?"

"Yeah."

"Because we've known each other since we were three. I'm also loyal. As in, a good one to have on your side."

"So are you on my side now?"

"I might be," said Bobby.

Then Gray stood up. He'd gotten very tired, from the matchmaking, from saving Elmer, from dealing with Patra, and now from this revelation that, what, Bobby Murphy wasn't a bad guy?

"I'm going home," said Gray.

"Good talking to you, freshman," said Bobby Murphy. "I'm glad I got to give you your last cigarette."

"You mean my *first* cigarette."

"You're not cigarette people, Gray Taylor. And that's a good thing."

As he walked away, Gray looked back only once. He saw the cigarette's ember move slowly on the porch one last time before it pinwheeled into the street, where it lay glowing for another few seconds before the cold finally put it out.

"We wearing the tighties?"

Devon Rutherford was leaning over the plastic-coated bus seat behind Gray, his chin resting on muscular arms that were crossed atop the vinyl seatback.

"Only if it's unanimous," said Gray. "That's what your dad said."

"Did you think about us being on the road?"

At Gray's feet was a canvas bag that had ridden from Beaudelaire to Wellsville. Inside were ten 1964-edition uniforms.

"Duh," said Gray. "Now, help me get them off the bus?"

"Sorry," said Devon, standing to his full height. "Can't be carrying a white boy's bag."

From behind Devon, Oskar Haart's eyes lit up. He cupped his hand so everyone behind him could hear him.

"Pretty sure they took your black card at Dusty's on Friday." Oskar hunched up his shoulders, once, twice, three times. "You were trying to do the Running Man, but it was more like the Crippled Man."

This got a round of laughs from the back of the bus.

"At least I made it to the end of the night."

"Can't return an empty keg," said Oskar.

By now, Oskar had worked his way up the aisle. Gray looked up at him, hope in his eyes.

"Sorry," said Oskar. "Can't be carrying a freshman's bag."

When the rest of the team had gotten past him, Gray heaved the giant bag out from under the seat and onto his shoulder. At the bottom of the bus's stairs, he eased the bag onto the asphalt parking lot in front of Wellsville High School—a flat, one-story structure built of tan brick. It didn't so much stand on the hill as much as it slouched on that hill.

"Beautiful, isn't it?"

Elmer kicked off the side of the bus, his voice giving Gray a start. Since the party, Elmer hadn't said much to Gray. Or to anyone.

"Looks like a prison," said Gray.

"They had their own bond issue, a few years ago."

"Didn't go so well?"

"Went great," Elmer said, snatching the enormous black bag's handles and pulling the bag onto his shoulders in one swift motion. He nodded toward the windswept high school, where a few spindly trees were staked into the brown grass. "That's a win."

The vista in front of them confirmed what Gray had suspected: these Midwesterners were determined to ruin the good things they had going.

"Elmer," he said.

Elmer tilted his head so he could see Gray past the bag's handles.

"Yeah?"

"We're not going to let that happen."

"What makes you say that?"

As they walked up the sterile sidewalk and as Gray pulled open the door to the sterile commons and as they walked down a sterile hallway that led to a sterile locker room, Gray made Elmer the fourth person to know about the plan.

When Gray was finished explaining, they were in front of the door to the sterile locker room. Elmer still had the bag on his shoulder.

"So we need everyone to wear these uniforms tonight? I don't totally get it, but I'm in. Especially after what you did at Dusty's."

"Oh, you remember that, do you?"

"Barely," said Elmer. "But thanks for holding up your end of the bargain."

Elmer pulled open the door to the visitor's locker room and heaved the bag onto the concrete floor.

"Listen up!"

Elmer's voice froze everyone in the locker room, including Oskar Haart, who was inspecting a locker to see if he could get a sports bra out of it.

"We're wearing these uniforms. Gray, dish them out."

Like St. Nicholas, Gray bent to his work, tossing the uniforms to their intended recipients.

#21 for Elmer.

#25 for Devon.

#55 for Oskar.

#41 for Dusty Rhoads.

And so on.

Gray reserved two uniforms for last: Bobby Murphy (#13) and Bartholomew Karp (#11). Yes, he'd shared a cigarette with Bobby Murphy. And yes, according to all reports, by the end of the party Ariel Bickle and Bartholomew Karp had been seen making out in the corner furthest from the stairs. And yes, Elmer was leading, like he should have been all along. But none of that mattered if the two upperclassmen decided they didn't want to follow.

Gray tossed shorts and jersey to Bobby, who caught them with a jerk of his hand.

Then it was Bartholomew's turn.

When he caught his uniform, Bartholomew looked immediately to Bobby Murphy. Gray looked to Bobby, too. Or rather, Gray tried to build a phone cord out of thin air—a phone cord that stretched between only himself and Bobby Murphy and through which he wanted to draw on the capital they'd built up at the party at the Rhoads house.

Bobby nodded at Gray. Then at Elmer. He hit Bartholomew on the chest with the back of his hand. He jerked his chin at Devon, who'd already put his jersey on.

Devon Rutherford sensed the eyes on him and rose to his full height. He flexed both biceps like a prizefighter from the 1940s.

Gray watched as the wheels in Bartholomew's brain whirled into action. He grinned.

"Good lookin' out, frosh."

And just like that, the uniforms were approved, thanks to the awareness Bobby Murphy had for one of Bartholomew Karp's Achilles heels: vanity.

Gray folded the empty bag and found a home for it underneath a folding table in the back of the locker room. Then he sat down to put on his own uniform.

Two hours later, Gray was sitting again—this time on the bottom-most red bleacher in Wellsville's sprawling but cartoonishly bright gym. The floor was unnaturally shiny. The walls were so white they glowed. Even the rims looked fake—the sort of orange children color their pumpkins in Halloween illustrations.

Gray's teammates had squandered a couple of early gifts from Wellsville: a bad pass that should have led to a fast break lay-up (but didn't) and a silly adjustment by a Wellsville guard that should have resulted in a wide-open shot for Elmer (but didn't).

Otherwise, the game was playing out just as Coach Rutherford had predicted. Wellsville High School, the coach had explained, was one of those maddeningly consistent teams that everyone hates to play. They'd had the same coach for two decades, and this coach didn't care about stars or fads. He cared about routine. In Wellsville's case, routine meant their offense: a continuity offense called the Flex that flowed in and out of itself like a Mobius strip. The problem wasn't the offense itself. Mostly, Wellsville ran it to tire the defense before switching to a new play they used to score. The problem was that you still had to pay attention because there was always the chance that someone would come off the baseline screen and catch the ball for a lay-up.

It was, Gray thought, a little like some of the NBA offenses he'd seen on the discs Coach Rutherford had continued to give him. A team was happy to take an easy basket if the defense gave it to them, but if that didn't work out, they could always give it to Michael Jordan or Allen Iverson or Kobe Bryant or LeBron James or James Harden or any of the isolation specialists he'd watched during Coach Rutherford's education.

Wellsville didn't have Jordan, Kobe, Iverson, James, or James. Nevertheless, they raced out to a 6-0 lead inside Wellsville's new gym—a 6-0 lead that became an 8-0 lead when Dusty Rhoads turned his head at exactly the wrong time and a Wellsville player slipped free for a lay-up.

"Aw, Christ," said Rutherford, rocketing out of his seat at the other end of the bench. He motioned toward the referee for a timeout.

Gray scrambled onto the court, acting like he was going to congratulate his teammates as they came off the court.

Instead, he slid in next to Coach Rutherford. "The 1-3-1. Now's the time."

Coach Rutherford looked up at the shiny scoreboard, which hung above the eight pennants representing the teams in the Kaw Valley conference.

"Might as well. Remember, bait the corner guy into throwing you the ball."

"Are we playing with six?"

"Bug."

Gray pulled off his warm-ups and found a spot inside the huddle, pointing at Bug.

"Yes, I believe my play warrants that decision," said Bug.

When Coach Rutherford got to the huddle, he explained the new plan: the switch to the 1-3-1 trapping defense.

"Only here's the thing," he said. "Don't let them know we're in a zone until they make the first pass. Got it?"

On the court, Gray wiped the bottoms of his Vans with the palms of his hands. He jogged to the referee and asked him if he could have the ball. He dribbled it once, twice, three times. He'd seen a player named Steve Nash, then of the Phoenix Suns, do something similar.

Gray handed the ball back to the referee, who handed the ball to Elmer, who passed the ball to Gray, who dribbled the ball for a fourth time. Only this time, it was in play. Because, before they could do any setting up of any defenses, they needed to do something on offense.

When Gray got the ball to the half-court line, he held two fingers out to the side. On his signal, Oskar Haart and Dusty Rhoads darted up the lane to the junction of the lane line and the free-throw line. Meanwhile, Bobby Murphy and Elmer Niehaus faded to the corners of the court.

Gray faked a pass high and then bounced the ball to Dusty. He took one jab toward the middle of the court, setting up his man like he'd been taught by a Hall of Famer named Scottie Pippen. He slid past Dusty, who faked like he was going to hand the ball to Gray before pivoting, taking one dribble, and handing the ball to Oskar Haart.

Meanwhile, Gray was sprinting to the corner, where he set a screen for Bobby.

As Oskar took the ball from Dusty, Bobby burst toward the top of the key. He took the handoff from Oskar, turned the corner, and rushed toward the basket, where he dropped the ball off the backboard for Beaudelaire's first two points of the night. Because, Gray thought, if anyone was going to score first, it might as well be Bobby Murphy.

Gray sprinted to half-court, sticking out his hands as his teammates went past. This being something he'd seen out of a guy named Chris Paul, who'd played for the Houston Rockets at the time.

When everyone was behind him, Gray held up one finger—their signal for man-to-man defense. Then he settled in to take on the job he'd been sent out here to do.

The Wellsville point guard looked a lot like the team's mascot: a bulldog. There wasn't much between his face and his shoulder blades and his mouth seemed permanently fixed in a scowl.

Gray found the bulldog's belly button, just like Coach Rutherford (and his father) had taught him. And, for a split second, Gray forgot where he was. It was just him and the ugly kid across from him, nothing else in the world to think abou-

"Gray!"

Coach Rutherford was waving from the sideline. He held up one finger, then three fingers, then one finger.

Oh, right, the 1-3-1 defense.

Gray flashed Rutherford a thumbs-up. Then he winked at the bulldog, unknowingly channeling Faustino Torres, who'd done his share of taunting his opponents in his nights in the ring.

The bulldog drove to his right and for a split-second, Gray thought he was bringing the ball at him. But in reality, the bulldog hadn't yet figured out that Beaudelaire was in a zone defense.

When he did, he called out: "Zonebreaker!"

The bulldog dribbled away from Gray, across the top of the defense. He stopped and threw the ball over Gray's head, to a guard who'd helped form a two-guard front. The recipient of the pass took one dribble toward the baseline. Then he bounced the ball to the Wellsville center, who'd slipped into the middle of the 1-3-1. This center had hair long enough to require a headband but he hadn't gotten as far as the actual headband. He dribbled once before he was cut off by Dusty Rhoads. This left the Wellsville center desperate for a way out. He found it in the corner, where a teammate was waiting.

Oskar Haart and Bobby Murphy converged.

Gray's job, as he'd learned on that day way back in November, was not to prevent the ball from coming out of the corner. Instead, he was supposed to bait the player in the corner into throwing the ball out of the corner. But as Gray had *also* learned on that first day, this was easier drawn than done. And if it was done wrong, a Wellsville player would be slipping past him in a tornado of sweat right before he scored two humiliating points.

Gray's first instinct, then, was to hang back a little too far from the man he was guarding. He quickly corrected, moving closer. Then he saw what he was waiting for: the eyes of the kid in the corner.

The player faked low and then jumped so he could find a teammate. And Gray could see what was going to happen next. The ball would come out of the trap high and hard and he wouldn't have much time to get his own arms up.

Gray was right. The ball did come out high. And hard. And he *didn't* have much time to get either (or both) of his arms up. He also needed to jump to get anywhere close to the ball. And the problem with jumping was that once you left the ground, you couldn't change direction.

Then Gray felt three things in rapid succession: a burn on his fingertips, impact on the soles of his Vans, and the sweaty arm of the Wellsville player, slapping his own.

These sensations could be explained by what was happening. Gray had tipped the ball.

Now he was landing, spinning to find where it had gone.

At the same time, the Wellsville player who'd expected the ball to land in his own hands lost his balance sufficiently that the right side of his body smashed into Gray. Meanwhile, the ball was bouncing toward midcourt.

As soon as he spun off the kid from Wellsville, Gray saw the ball. He darted out toward the middle of the court. He gathered the ball, took one dribble, and then saw the sight he'd hoped for on that day they'd put in the 1-3-1 defense: Elmer Niehaus, sprinting ahead, calling for the ball.

Elmer let Gray's pass bounce once. Then he gathered the ball and leapt, a mass of grace and fury, and threw down a smooth and authoritative dunk.

The ball pounded toward the floor.

The Wellsville coach signaled for a timeout.

Gray ran over to Elmer and jumped into his arms.

Wellsville didn't have a chance.

CHAPTER 26

As Gray pushed through the door to the Taylor apartment, he wasn't expecting a hero's welcome. Nicole Taylor hadn't been at the game, and Gray assumed he'd have to tell her what had happened. It wasn't like Beaudelaire's games were on TV.

Gray was thus surprised to find the whole Taylor family waiting for him when he got into the living room. His grandfather's voice boomed from the kitchen as Gray dropped his gym bag onto the wood floor.

"Gray!"

"Grandpa!"

"What happened to your pants?"

"Little mishap with my foot!"

After Gray's entry, the Beaudelaire Bearcats had gone on a 75-56 run that had left them, at the end of the game, bouncing in celebration at half court of Wellsville's bright new gym.

When the celebration was over, the team went into the sterile locker room, where they showered and where Gray, after he was done showering (and after he was done collecting the uniforms and putting them in the bag), accidentally put his foot through the crotch of his jeans.

He'd torn them into jean shorts.

When Gray was finished explaining this series of events to his grandfather, Darby Taylor cocked an eyebrow. "And how'd that go over on the bus?"

"Not as bad as I thought," Gray said. "I guess my teammates like a little inner thigh in their lives."

He stuck out his leg and shook it.

Until now, Darby was the only person in the room who'd said anything to Gray. This hadn't really bothered Gray, who was still wrapped in the game's afterglow. He'd felt this way for the entirety of the bus ride home—an unexpected warmth that was somehow better than how he'd felt after the game against Santa Fe because during that game he'd been able to surprise everyone. This time, he'd had to live up to expectations.

Nicole Taylor looked up from the kitchen table. Her arms were crossed and her body was folded in on itself.

"Tell me all about the game," she said.

"In a little bit," said Gray. "First, tell me what's going on here."

"She quit," said Gayle Taylor, easing off the kitchen cabinet she was leaning against.

Darby Taylor caught Gray's eye, expressing male solidarity in the way of a man who's spent most of his life being baffled by the women around him.

"Why?" asked Gray.

"She didn't like her boss," said Gayle Taylor.

"What'd he do?"

Nicole Taylor patted the chair next to her.

"I'll explain later. Tell us how the game went."

"Yeah," said Darby. "How'd y'all do against Smellsville?"

He winked at Gray, who banished the domestic whirlwind that was brewing long enough to affect a modest shrug. "We won. Elmer was amazing."

"And how'd you play?"

"Not bad," said Gray. "I mean, I didn't score a ton of points, but it's weird, things just seem to go well when I'm in."

Darby nodded in approval.

"I remember someone else like that."

"I wasn't that good," said Nicole.

"Of course you were, honey," said Gayle. "If you'd stuck with it-"

Gayle caught herself. "We should go," she said.

"Really?" said Darby. "I was just getting into this recap."

"It's late," said Gayle. "We can talk more tomorrow."

"Speaking of tomorrow," said Darby Taylor, with a look at Gray. "Come by and tell me more, eh?"

"Will do, Grandpa."

After the appropriate hugs and kisses, the eldest Taylors left Gray and his mother alone in their apartment. And like all environments whose populations have just been halved, this one needed a few seconds before it could be returned to normalcy.

"I'm going to get some water," said Gray. "You want some?"

Nicole Taylor collapsed into the couch. The back of her hand went to her forehead.

"I should be getting *you* water," she said.

"Your day was probably just as long as mine."

"You might be right about that," she said, closing her eyes.

As Gray poured himself water from the clear jug in the refrigerator, he was thinking of his first day and when he'd raced out of the gym. If not for Coach Rutherford, he would have come here and begged his mother to take him back to Reseda. And now he wanted the exact opposite.

Gray stowed the plastic jug in the refrigerator. He closed the refrigerator door, allowed himself a deep breath, and took the glasses of water back into the living room. He set one of them on the coffee table in front of his mother.

"Sit next to me," she said, coiling into a corner of the couch.

"What happened?" Gray asked after he'd plopped onto the couch.

"At work, there was this guy—a guy I went to high school with. He sells, like, seed now, and he was in picking up something for his wife. Just this cream for eczema. It's worse in the winter sometimes. You know, the dry air-"

"Mom. Back to the point."

"Sorry. He says, 'Why, Nicole Taylor! I never thought I'd see the day.' And there was so much *satisfaction* in his voice."

"Maybe he's just glad you're back."

"That's the point! He's glad because I had to come back."

"He sells, what, seed?"

"Yeah, for corn."

"It doesn't sound like he's the next Elon Musk," said Gray.

"That's not the point! The point is that I swore I'd never come back here. And I just don't know if I can do it. All these memories, and all these people. They're so boring. You know?"

Here Nicole Taylor swiveled her eyes back to Gray's, hoping for—no, *expecting*—confirmation. Since they'd arrived in Beaudelaire, Nicole Taylor had been proud of her son for soldiering through: a new school, new people, new friends. But she'd assumed that Gray wanted to go home. Which was why she was surprised by what happened next, which was that Gray's eyes got bright blue, right before he slammed the glass on the table.

"Boring? They're not any more boring than those people in LA. They're probably *less* boring. They at least have real jobs. I haven't met an actor yet. Plus: they actually like each other. You know how everyone in LA talks like they're looking past you to see if there's someone else more important in the room? That hasn't happened once since I've been here. Well-"

Gray stopped himself. Because that wasn't *totally* true.

"-except with the ABC."

"The ABC? Another Bad Creation?"

"What?"

"ABC. BBD. The East Coast Family. It's from a song."

"Whatever, Mom. It's not the point. The point is that it's *nice* here. And I'm just starting to fit in and I can see where you're headed with this—you're going to say that now that you've quit, we can go back. But I don't want to go back."

Nicole tilted her head in a way that many men had found charming over the years.

"Don't you want there to be a chance?"

"A chance of what?"

"A chance of seeing your dad again."

"Of course I'd *like* to see Dad again. I'd *like* it if everything was perfect in our little family. But I'd also *like* to be six-foot-five and weigh two hundred pounds. What I'd *like* to have happen and what *will* happen are two things. Us being a happy little family unit: that's not going to happen."

This hit Nicole Taylor like a slap.

"It's not?"

And *this* hit *Gray* like a slap. How did his mother not see this?

"No, Mom. It's not."

Nicole Taylor knew her son was right. But she was also the parent in this conversation. And parents do not like to be told what they need.

"Maybe you're right. But none of it matters if I can't get a job here."

Gray picked up his water and took a sip as one thought shot through his brain:

Do I have to take care of everything?

Patra Patterson was leaning against the locker next to Gray's. She was wearing a teal Hypercolor T-shirt that had first hit shelves sometime during her father's childhood. She'd found it at a thrift store in North Topeka.

"G.T.," she said.

Gray's head was inside his locker, where it was dark and cool and calm, like a miniature version of the basement locker room. A part of him wanted to keep his head in this locker for the rest of the day, an ostrich with its head underground. Which was a real thing, he'd learned back in middle school.

"G.T.," Patra said again. "That's what I'm thinking, for your nickname."

"It'll never take. Too boring," said Gray.

"Fiddlesticks," said Patra. "You're right. But we'll get there. Now what's got your attention in there?"

Gray took a breath inside his locker. The truth was that he'd been daydreaming. Well, not daydreaming, exactly. More like going over the options. Since his mother's announcement about the lost job, Gray had been doing that a lot—going over and over and over the plan, while also going over and over and over how he didn't want to get dragged back to Southern California. Especially not now that they were so close to executing that plan—the St. Anthony game was only a day away.

He reached into his locker and grabbed a book: the one Patra had given him on his first day in Beaudelaire. He waggled it at her.

"Big happenings in Western Civ these days."

"At least they got the 'Western' in there, right?"

Patra slung her backpack onto her shoulder, the strap pulling the sleeve of the Hypercolor shirt up just enough that Gray glimpsed the curve of her upper arm. It was enough to get him moving.

He traded Western Civilization for Algebra and bopped his locker closed, roping his own backpack onto his shoulder and joining Patra in the colorful current of students moving between fourth and fifth period.

"So," said Patra. "Are we good for tomorrow?"

"Depends," said Gray, "on which part of tomorrow you mean."

As they passed the principal's office, Patra nodded at the door. "What about that guy?"

"Free admission for everyone," said Gray, a dose of satisfaction in his voice.

"How'd you pull that off?"

"We want as many people to hear the presentation about the bond issue, don't we?"

"Clever," said Patra. "And the uniforms?"

"Wore them against Wellsville. Speaking of Wellsville: where were you?"

"I was there in spirit."

"You were in Lawrence?"

"I was in Lawrence."

This was disheartening enough to Gray that his shoulders slumped. The movement dipped his backpack into his sacrum as they passed the school's front office. Inside, Mrs. Rutherford was listening with her arms crossed to an excuse about a misplaced lunch card.

"With my sister," said Patra. "And we listened on the radio."

"Our games are on the radio?"

"They are. And it sounded like you were good."

"I was OK," said Gray. The backpack was headed back up.

"I think you're being modest," said Patra. "But anyway, back to the plan. What about the ice cream at Tundin's?"

"Mitzy says if we're ready, they're ready."

"Staying open late?"

"Til midnight," said Gray.

Patra whacked Gray's backpack. "So that's it!"

When Gray didn't react, she said, "Is that not it?"

"No, yeah, it is."

"Gray," said Patra. "What's going on?"

"It's my mom. She quit her job."

"And you're afraid she's going to take you back to California."

"I am."

"That'd be a shame," said Patra, her voice smaller than usual—small enough that Gray wasn't entirely sure he'd heard her inside the scrum that was the hallway. Then her voice returned to its normal level. "Sounds like you need a little insurance."

This was confusing to Gray until he heard a familiar voice.

"Taylor. It's quiz time."

Harris Bickle was standing outside his doorway, like he did every passing period.

Gray pointed a thumb at his chest—a thumb meant to indicate Mr. Bickle.

"It can't hurt," said Patra.

Then she spun on her heels, the teal T-shirt whipping with her.

"You ready, Taylor?"

That's when it hit Gray: he had an algebra quiz to take. In all his machinations over the team and the school and his own family, his attention to his academic success had been shuffled to a portion of his brain that was just as dark as his locker. But Mr. Bickle didn't necessarily need to know that.

"So ready!"

Gray sped through the door, up the aisle, and into one of the few left-handed desks he'd found at Beaudelaire High School. He draped his backpack on the back of the chair, pulled out his Algebra book, and flipped to the section they were on: quadratic equations. He ran a finger over the page, hoping this would magically transfer some of the details from paper to brain. Then the bell was ringing and Mr. Bickle was wasting no time. "Alright gang, quiz time!"

He began distributing quizzes like they were birdseed and he was an old man in the park.

"Remember," he said. "Don't let me fool you."

Mr. Bickle was famous—or infamous—for his "bonus" questions:

Which weighs more, a pound of fat or a pound of muscle?
What's the capital of Kentucky, Louisville or Lexington?
And everyone's favorite:
Where IS Waldo?

Like *that* had an answer.

Gray spent the entire period on the quiz, missing more than he should have, in part because he hadn't been paying attention in class for two weeks and in part because his mind was on what Patra had suggested.

It wasn't like it was a stretch—he'd already set up his mother and Mr. Bickle once. Maybe they just needed a little boost.

"Two-minute warning! If you're not already, you should probably be on my super-duper bonus question by now."

Gray looked to the bottom of the page.

Which weighs more, the moon or the sun?

He scribbled an answer just as Mr. Bickle called time.

Gray gathered his quiz and his backpack, taking his time. He needed to be last in line.

Bickle took in a bundle of papers from each person, calling them by their last names like he did. When Gray got to him, Mr. Bickle asked him how he'd done.

Gray dropped his quiz on the pile.

"I don't know about the quadratics, but I think I got the bonus question."

"Go on."

"The answer is: it depends on where you are. Because weight is based on gravity, so you could only measure that weight relative to the planet you were on."

"Someone's got his brain turned on."

Mr. Bickle picked up the papers and slapped them, bottom first, on the desk. When Gray didn't leave, he looked up at him. "Anything else?"

Gray took a deep breath. He had a game to win. And a town to save. And a girl to get.

"Here's the thing, sir. The game tomorrow night. We're doing this promotion with Tundin's where, if we score 80 points, everyone gets a free milkshake."

"That's a good idea. Yours?"

"Yes, sir."

Bickle laced his hands behind his head.

"Might have to try something like that in the fall. Probably hard to get to 80 in football, though."

"Maybe make it, like, 40."

"Yes of course. Anyway, what's on your mind about Tundin's? You want me to come down and scoop ice cream? Maybe mention it when I give my half-time talk about the bond issue?"

"Not exactly. The thing is, my mom's going to come to the game and I'm wondering if, afterward, you might be able to take her down to Tundin's. You know, help her find-"

"I've got to stop you right there, son. I'm actually in the process of seeing Ariel's mom, er, my ex-wife, and I don't know if that'd be appropriate."

"Oh," said Gray. "You guys are trying again?"

"We are, son. We are."

"Well," said Gray. "That's great. Just great."

"It's nothing against your mom," said Mr. Bickle. "It's just that it's time for me to, you know-"

He punched one hand with the other.

"-do the right thing."

"Sure," said Gray.

Mr. Bickle stood, abruptly. He stacked the tests again. "Good luck tomorrow," he said.

Gray heard Mr. Bickle's voice, but he wasn't really listening. He was thinking of another option. He flashed back to the library and the way Peter Patterson had looked at his mother. It would be an innocent enough request.

I was wondering.

My mom said she'd feel better if.

She asked me to ask you.

"I said, good luck."

Mr. Bickle's voice was more insistent this time. It shook Gray out of his trance. And out of the crazy place he'd gone: he couldn't ask Patra's own *married* father to escort his mother to the game. That was the behavior of an insane person—a desperate person. And he wasn't desperate. He had a plan.

"Thank you, sir. But we won't need it."

As Gray walked down the stairs to the locker room before the most important game of his brief basketball career, he ran his hand along the pitted concrete wall, tracing from one circular imperfection to the next, using them to connect the history that had led up to this moment.

His mother and the back patio.

New states and their welcome signs.

Truck stops and their snacks.

Mr. Patterson and his blazer.

Coach Bickle and his blue windbreaker.

Mrs. Patterson's dress.

Mitzy's haircut.

Bobby's hat.

Elmer's kindness.

Bartholomew's meanness.

The ABC.

Patra.

And Coach Rutherford, who was watching Gray through his office door.

"Yo, Gray Taylor. What's the word?"

"Bird!"

Coach Rutherford leaned back on the physioball so Gray could see the big poster behind him: Larry Bird, life-sized.

"The word," he said. "The truth, the gospel!"

"Isn't that, like, sacrilegious?"

"Not at all," said Coach Rutherford. "You're in church right now. And that one is your Jesus. Whatever you do, remember that tonight."

Gray flashed the sign of the cross on his chest as Coach Rutherford rapped on the door jamb.

"I'll let you get dressed," he said.

"Coach? What happened with this guy? From St. Anthony?"

Coach Rutherford blinked once, twice. Then he walked over to Gray. He put his hands behind his back and leaned against a locker. "You saw the film I gave you, right?"

"I did."

"We ain't ever got them. Not even close. But it's not just that he's whooped my ass all four times we've ever played them. It was something he said after the second time. 'You'd better leave this to the big boys.' With a smile, like it always is with these guys."

"Yeah, it has to be tough for you-"

Coach Rutherford's chin lifted. "Don't get it twisted," he said. "You can get it from a brother just as easily. It has less to do with black or white than with being part of, I don't know, The Establishment, like it always was."

Then the coach popped off the locker. "We're going to win tonight, Gray Taylor."

"I think so, too."

"No, I don't mean 'I think' we're going to win. We *are* going to win. Also: you're starting."

"I am?"

"Of course. You're ready. Now get dressed."

Coach Rutherford withdrew and Gray walked to his locker. He clicked it open and traced the etching there.

HB

+

NT

Gray put a palm to his face.

The answer had come to him like the one on Mr. Bickle's test.

HB + NT = Harris Bickle + Nicole Taylor.

And on one hand: gross. But on the other, it was fitting, wasn't it? Then Gray shook his head—he was getting distracted. He was going to *start?* It wasn't like he didn't *want* to start. Or even that he didn't think he *deserved* to start. The truth was that he was already a better basketball player than Bug. He wasn't even surprised. No, the problem was that Coach Rutherford's proclamation had taken him out of the conceptual and into the practical. There was no more preparation to be done—no more arranging and negotiating. Now, he had to play. And they had to win. And score 80 points. All against a team that Coach Rutherford hadn't ever beaten-

Gray's hand went to his wrist. Then he remembered: his rubber band was different now.

Out of the locker came his shoes, which smelled like a sponge that's been left wet for too long. Then his throwback jersey,

which smelled better than it might have thanks to Katherine Niehaus, who'd volunteered for laundry duty when she'd found out the
jerseys were 50 years old.

When Gray was done, he went to the mirror over the sink
in the back of the locker room, where it was darker. He brushed
his hair out of his eyes, considering how miraculous it was that
his mother hadn't forced him into a haircut. Then he puffed up his
chest, stretching the jersey to its maximum capacity.

"You can do this," Gray mouthed to his reflection.

Then he set about trying to make himself right.

The national anthem ended with a flourish provided by
the drummer—a full solo he'd worked on over Christmas break to
much displeasure from his neighbors.

The crowd roared its approval—a true roar because the
gym was packed. Word had gone out on the appropriate small-town
channels. There'd been a story in the *Beaudelaire Bee* about the
half-time presentation. (Headline: BOND. SCHOOL BOND.) The
news of the special promotion at Tundin's had gone up on the
school's social media. The Casey's by the highway had even gotten
into the act, changing the letters on its sign to:

CATS N CONES
FRI, 8 PM
BHS

Thanks to the extra bustle in the stands, it took Gray two
revolutions of the court to find Patra. She was in one of the cor-

ners, on an aisle, with Darby and Gayle and Gray's mom only five rows up. They were all in blue and white. A thought arced across Gray's brain:

Replica throwback jerseys!

They could sell them at the concession stand, get the crowd just as involved as the players, use the proceeds to fund postgame meals on the road. Maybe even make it so people could get their own names embroidered on the-

"You ready, son?"

The head referee was looking at Gray.

Gray nodded.

The referee nodded, too, and squeezed in among the players lined up for the opening tip-off. He lofted the ball into the air between Dusty Rhoads and the St. Anthony center and for a split-second the ball hung there in the yellowish light, motionless in front of the 1,252 people who'd shown up for free basketball (and maybe free ice cream). Then Dusty Rhoads was scooping the ball out of the air and back to Gray, who quickly flushed his concerns about starting his first game by flipping the ball ahead to Devon Rutherford, who laid it into the basket.

Mr. Hoffman's voice boomed across the gym.

"Rutherford for two! Just 78 to go for freeeeeeeee ice cream!"

As Devon ran back on defense, Gray held out his hand for the requisite five. His attention, though, was on the point guard from St. Anthony.

One thing Gray had learned from all the game tape he'd watched was the following: any time you allowed the other team's guards space, they were able to see the court. And when they were able to see the court, bad things happened for *your* team. The other thing he'd noticed was that people usually made mistakes at two points in the game: at the beginning, and at the end. This happened in the former case because they weren't yet in the flow of the game. And in the latter case because of things that had happened while they *were* in the flow.

Specifically, that someone had worn them out.

Gray met the other team's point guard at half court, shadowing him and unconsciously learning his tendencies. In this case, the St. Anthony point guard was bigger than Gray, and Gray knew he'd have to be careful about the way he positioned himself in order to avoid having to rely on his own subpar musculature. But Gray also knew that with size usually comes a measure of sluggishness, like when the point guard raised an arm to call a play and Gray slapped the ball away and toward the Beaudelaire basket.

He slipped past the point guard and chased down the ball just in time to catch sight of Devon Rutherford, who was once again streaking toward the basket.

4 – 0 Beaudelaire.

The St. Anthony coach, his round face the color of a heart attack, stalked to the free-throw line and called timeout with chops of both hands.

This gave Beaudelaire's head cheerleader the opening she'd been waiting for. Megan Haart bounced onto the court, her big Oskar-shaped head bobbing in time with her fist as she mustered her squad into an impromptu, "Let's go! Beau-dee!"

Despite the commotion around them, the Beaudelaire players found their way to the huddle in the same way that a river finds its way to a waterfall. Devon Rutherford was beaming as he said, "Just like you drew it up, huh, *Coach*?"

"That's a good start," said Coach Rutherford. "But don't get all fat and happy. You know as well as I do that this team is good. Real good."

The players nodded, their cheeks and chins shiny with the beginnings of sweat.

"Anybody got anything?"

Devon checked the group and then said, "No, sir!"

"Alright, hands in."

When the fivesome was finished with 1-2-3-Beau-dee, they replaced Megan Haart and the rest of the cheerleaders on the court. Around them, the crowd was standing, stomping, shouting through cupped hands, thrilled with this start and turning to one another to say things like, "I'd forgotten how much fun this could be!"

Inspired by their enthusiasm, Gray took up position near his man's hip, hoping to add pressure to the out-of-bounds pass. The guard caught the ball and brought it up the court, more cautious this time. But Gray knew enough to know that he'd gotten away with his one attempt at a straight-up steal. He concentrated instead on what the guard was going to call so he could file it away for later, hoping that by the end of the game he'd have an entire catalog of possible plays at the ready.

But the guard didn't call a play.

Instead, after arriving past the half-court line, he moved to a corner and waved his partner—the team's other guard—up from the wing where he'd been. Then, with his teammates in their positions, the guard changed his tack and drove toward the middle of the court. He didn't blow past Gray but he was able to get a shoulder past Gray, thanks to that other trait of his: his size. This caused Bobby Murphy to help from *his* corner. The point guard tossed the ball to that man. When Bobby recovered, he drove past him, toward the middle, which warranted help from Devon.

And so on and so on for the next 45 seconds.

Gray shouted to the bench: "They're not trying to score!"

Coach Rutherford looked down at the St. Anthony coach, then at the court. Like everyone in the gym, he was trying to figure out what was going on.

Then his eyes regained focus.

He waved at Gray.

"They're running Four Corners. Killing time. Back off!"

So that's what Gray did. He was soon joined by Devon and Bobby and the three of them formed a wall at the top of the key. This, though, was exactly what the St. Anthony coach was hoping for.

He hopped up and down, shouting at his point guard.

"Just hold it!"

The point guard tucked the ball on his hip and stood near half court, staring at the clock just like Dean Smith would've liked, back when he'd created the Four Corners offense at the University of North Carolina.

Soon came the boos.

First, from the student section, where some of Gray's classmates were wearing tight white tank tops with blue numbers painted on them. The rest of the crowd picked up the chant. But this only served to embolden the St. Anthony coach. His arms were crossed, a gleeful smile on his boyish face.

Gray looked to Coach Rutherford, pleading for permission to pressure the St. Anthony point guard. He was already doing the calculations. They had four points, which meant they had 76 to go. And with each second that ticked off the clock, that job was going to get harder and harder. But even that wasn't at the crux of the problem. They had a gym full of people—a gym full of people who could very well be attending their first basketball game. And if their first experience with high school basketball was a game that ended with six total points scored, well, it would probably also be their last experience with high school basketball.

While keeping an eye on the St. Anthony guards, Gray called Devon and Bobby toward him.

"What do you think?"

"Pussies," said Bobby.

"Think the Deacon would get mad if we put some pressure on them?"

Devon Rutherford glanced over at the bench, where his father was staring down at the St. Anthony coach, his own arms crossed.

"Oh for sure," he said.

"Then he's about to get mad," said Gray.

A grin spread across Bobby Murphy's face.

"Hell yeah," he said with a clap.

"I'm in," said Devon.

Gray led the advance, trotting toward the St. Anthony point guard with a smile.

"You sure about that?"

Gray nodded and bent to the floor, which he slapped with open palms.

All of this caused several other reactions. One from the crowd, which gurgled with relief as they returned to their feet. Another from Coach Rutherford, whose eyes blazed as he glared out at Gray Taylor. And one more from the St. Anthony coach, who calmly stirred an invisible pot held in his opposite hand.

The oversized guard swung the ball past Gray's waiting arms and started left. After a hitch, he slipped past Gray, causing Elmer to help off his man. The guard threw the ball to that man, who took advantage of Elmer's position to fake and drive to *his* left. This forced help from Dusty Rhoads, whose man was in the corner.

The second St. Anthony player threw the ball to Dusty's man, who calmly shot the three-pointer that was available to him. It tore straight through the basket.

4 – 3 Beaudelaire.

Gray didn't dare look to the bench. Instead, he clapped for the ball Dusty Rhoads was gathering behind the out-of-bounds line. If he could get upcourt, he could fix this: call the right play, make the right pass, make Coach Rutherford forget about his insolence.

Dusty found Gray and started to pass him the ball. But, at the last second, he stopped. And Gray knew why. He'd sensed that a St. Anthony player—the same one who'd made the three-pointer—had snuck up beside him.

Gray juked one way and then spun, hoping Dusty would see where he was going.

And Dusty did.

There was a problem, though. Dusty threw the ball too hard. It wasn't much, this too-hardness. But it was enough. The ball sped past Gray's outstretched hand and directly into hands of an entirely different St. Anthony player, who then did some speeding of his own: right by Gray and Dusty and to the basket.

Just like that, it was 5 – 4, St. Anthony.

Gray winced when he heard Coach Rutherford's voice Dopplering toward him.

"Timeouttimeouttimeout."

Gray didn't need to see it to know what was happening; Coach Rutherford was walking onto the court, just like the St. Anthony coach had done.

"Sorry about that, yo," said Dusty, breezing past Gray on his way to the bench.

Gray kicked the floor in front of him, not wanting to face Rutherford.

"Gray!"

Behind the coach, the rest of the team watched the coming confrontation while Megan Haart and the rest of the cheerleading squad pranced onto the court.

"Beau-de-laire, strong and fair! Beau-de-laire, everywhere!"

Coach Rutherford crossed his arms.

"What. Thehellwasthat?"

"I was just trying to push-"

Gray stopped short when he noticed the way Coach Rutherford's chest was expanding underneath his black sweater. He looked like a volcano, preparing to erupt. And then, erupt he did. With his eyebrows pinned inward, the words exploded out of the coach.

"I think we've all had about enough of your pushing, with the kicking people in the nuts and these tight-ass uniforms and the cotton-pickin' ice cream. Why don't you push a little less, for a change?"

Gray's head snapped back at this. Not so much because of the content of Coach Rutherford's tirade. It was more the tone. He'd never heard him like this.

Coach Rutherford waved at Bug.

"Get Gray."

Bug Biancalana pointed at his own chest.

"Yeah! You!"

Bug started on the process of taking off his warm-up as Coach Rutherford whirled back to Gray, his dark eyes far darker than usual.

"Take a load off."

Then Coach Rutherford left Gray on the court, a few yards away from the last cheerleader in line, a bespectacled girl with thin lips and bright orange hair who Gray had only seen haunting the Home Ec. department during the school day.

She caught Gray's eye out of the corner of her own as she finished the cheer. Then, she moved her gaze back to the crowd, as if she could sense that Gray had just become *persona non grata*.

The buzzer sounded, marking the end of the timeout, and Gray walked to the end of the bench, where he plopped down next to Rocky Rhoads.

Rocky patted Gray's knee.

"Sorry, dude."

A minute on a game clock never goes fast. There are always interruptions: fouls, substitutions, injuries. And all these interruptions make it easy to think that if the clock would just run, the game would move more quickly.

The next minute of the game between the Beaudelaire Bearcats and the St. Anthony Saints put the lie to that theory. As the clock ticked down, the St. Anthony point guard stood at half court with the ball on his hip, and time slowed to a crawl. In the crowd, phones got checked, conversations got started, Beaudelairians got bored.

It was all going just like St. Anthony coach Jack Woodman wanted. The Four Corners offense was neutralizing the home crowd and making Beaudelaire play on St. Anthony terms—a fact that dawned on Coach Rutherford at the end of that excruciatingly long minute. If he let the clock continue to tick away, his nemesis would get his way.

Rutherford waved Bug toward the St. Anthony point guard. The crowd responded with a burst of semi-sarcastic applause. But this applause had a brief half-life. Just like had happened before: because the Beaudelaire players had been standing around for the previous 60 seconds, they were on their heels (both proverbially and literally) and three passes later, it was 7 – 4, St. Anthony.

The rest of the first quarter played out in a similar fashion. Coach Rutherford waffled between letting St. Anthony kill the clock and trying at half-hearted attacks. None of this was anything like the crowd wanted to see. At first, the trickle toward the tunnel was a slow one. Then, it became a stream. Even those who were left were checking the surrounding bleachers for old friends, the paper programs in their hands for some tidbit of interesting information about the opposition, the popcorn box at their feet for remaining kernels they could chew on.

When the first quarter came to a merciful end, Gray stood from the bench to help congratulate the players coming off the court. He held out his hand for Dusty Rhoads. Then Devon. Then his replacement, Bug. Then Elmer, who slapped that hand a little harder than the rest, which made Gray pinwheel right into Bartholomew Karp and Bobby Murphy.

Bartholomew looked to Bobby.

Then to the scoreboard.

Then back at Gray.

"Got any ideas?"

Gray hesitated for half a second. Even though he'd made all that progress with Bobby, he couldn't help but be suspicious. Then Gray's fingers went to the edge of his uniform and he remembered: that was the old Gray at work.

Gray nodded, which was something of a body-language lie—he didn't actually have any ideas. But he figured he could come up with something.

"Whatever it is," said Bartholomew. "We got your back. Don't we, B?"

Bobby Murphy nodded.

Then, as Bartholomew headed for the bench, content in his assumption that *he* was Batman, Bobby leaned toward Gray.

"It's the Deacon," he said. "He's scared all a sudden. That's what you've got to do something about."

Bobby patted Gray on the chest as Megan Haart led the cheerleaders into a line on the court, exhorting the thinning crowd, this time with pom-poms in their hands.

You can do it, you know where!
You can do it, Beaudelaire!

Gray watched the huddle form around Coach Rutherford, who was screaming at his team in a way Gray had never seen. Then, Gray noticed movement at the far edge of his vision: Patra, coming down the stairs, her book under her arm, headed for the tight turn into the tunnel.

Gray glanced once more into the huddle. And then he took off, down the sideline, across the baseline, and into that same tunnel.

———————

When Gray caught up with Patra, the brick tunnel was deserted. He grabbed Patra by the hand. Or, to be specific, by the wrist—the wrist that was still occupied by his rubber band.

"You ready to do something crazy?"

Patra tapped her teeth. "Are we talking get-nachos-at-the-concessions-stand crazy? Or drive-to-Vegas-and-get-married crazy?"

"Somewhere in between."

"Good. Those nachos are garbage. It's like they insert the poison directly into the chee-"

Gray yanked Patra out of the tunnel and into the commons and then across that commons, toward the Coke machine. They trotted in the way that two people who are holding hands will trot, which is awkwardly.

"Where are we going?" asked Patra.

"You'll see," said Gray, pulling open the door to the basement.

At the bottom of the stairs, Gray put on his tour guide's voice and said, "So this is the boys' locker room. I'd give you a tour, but we don't have much time."

"It's OK, I've been down here before."

"Oh yeah, I guess, principal's daughter and all."

"Actually," said Patra. "I've only been here once. When you guys were done practicing. You were the only one in here-"

Gray's eyelids split open like pistachio shells.

"I knew I heard something!"

"You did?"

"Yeah, it was the day I finally did something right. I thought maybe it was Mr. Edison. Wait. Does this mean-"

Patra was already nodding and if this had happened in a classroom, or at a party, or even at Tundin's, Gray's face would have gone bright red. But thanks to the uniform he was wearing and the confidence it generated, Gray's face did not go bright red.

Instead, he took a step away from Patra and put his hands to his mouth like she was a piece of art.

"Sounds like you owe me."

Patra lifted her shirt an inch, baring a thin strip of her midriff. "You want me to-"

Gray's eyes went wide. Had it worked?

"I'm kidding," said Patra, dropping the edge of her shirt. "But maybe someday."

Then Gray went back into action, grabbing Patra's hand and pulling her off the stairs, across the locker room, and into Coach Rutherford's office.

He stopped in front of the Larry Bird poster.

"Who's that?" asked Patra.

"Coach Rutherford's spiritual guide."

"A white guy?"

"That's what I said!"

"So what are you going to do?"

"I'm going to give him a reminder."

"With the poster?"

"With the poster."

For half a second, Patra looked at Gray like he'd escaped from a mental hospital. Then she shrugged, moved over to the poster, and pulled up a corner. Gray moved to help her and they got the poster off the wall without damaging it.

"You sure about this?" asked Patra.

"Nope. But we're going to do it anyway."

Gray took hold of one end of the poster and together he and Patra carried it up the stairs. They marched it through the commons area, which was even busier now.

They attracted a few eyes, including those of Harris Bickle, who was standing next to the Coke machine, going over the note cards he'd prepared for his half-time speech about the bond issue. But Mr. Bickle didn't say anything. He was lost in thought, worrying about the crowd's exodus in his own way—if no one was there to watch his pitch for the bond issue, he might not get the football stadium he knew he deserved.

Gray gave Mr. Bickle a nod, dodged a bored cluster of parents, and then it was upon them: the entrance to the tunnel.

He felt the poster go taut.

Patra was shaking her head.

"You have to take it from here," she said.

Gray crouched so he could see into the gym behind him. At half court, the St. Anthony point guard was standing with the ball tucked against his hip, just like before.

Patra was right. She'd helped get him this far, but the rest was his job.

He walked to her. The poster fell slack between them, its white backside touching the floor. The tips of their fingers touched. Gray leaned down so his face was three inches from Patra's.

She smiled.

"You're going to kiss me now, aren't you?"

"I was, until you ruined it."

Patra's eyes danced, sparkling in the dark tunnel.

"We'll save it 'til later then. Anyway, we wouldn't want you to get distracted. You've got a basketball game to win."

If the game between the Beaudelaire Bearcats and the St. Anthony Saints had been a normal one, the crowd wouldn't have noticed Larry Bird for several minutes. But this game was not a normal one. The crowd was well and truly bored, and so it took only a few seconds for a murmur to start in the stands opposite the tunnel where Gray was standing, his arms outstretched, holding the life-sized poster as high as he could.

When the murmur began, Coach Rutherford looked first to his left, toward the cheerleaders, wondering if Megan Haart had led them into some new cheer. Then he looked to his right, at his bench, wondering if Bartholomew Karp was up to something. And then, when neither of those locations told him the story he was expecting, he looked across the court, at Larry Bird.

His chin rotated as his brain calculated exactly what had gone on: Gray Taylor had left the game, gone downstairs, taken his beloved Larry Bird poster off the wall, and was now standing across the court, holding it out like it was the boombox from *Say Anything*.

The poster shimmered, its glossy face catching the gym's lights. Larry Legend looked a little like he was ready to check in.

"Jesus Christ," said Coach Rutherford, right before he bent and put his hands on his knees, a snort firing its way out of his nose. "What an idiot."

He wasn't talking about Gray.

Rutherford called out to Bug Biancalana, who was at the top of the key watching the St. Anthony point guard.

"Bug."

"Bug!"

"BUG!"

Bug's head jerked to the sideline.

Coach Rutherford pointed at the guard and mouthed, "Foul him," as he chopped his left forearm with his right hand.

Bug advanced on the point guard and hacked his arm. As soon as the referee blew the whistle, Coach Rutherford walked onto the court, signaling for time out. Then Coach Rutherford kept striding across the court to Gray Taylor and Larry Bird.

"Gray."

Gray peeked from behind the poster, one bright blue eye making its way around the edge.

"You can put the poster down."

Gray allowed his arms to drop, which happened significantly faster than he'd expected. The poster had been heavier than he'd thought. It crumpled between player and coach.

"Sorry," said Gray.

"Don't be," said Coach Rutherford. "You ready to help me put on a show?"

"I am. But-"

Gray pointed at the poster.

Coach Rutherford said, "I think I see someone who might be able to help with that."

Patra was at the near edge of the tunnel.

"Not me," she said. "I've got a show to watch, apparently."

"Fine," said Rutherford. "Grab that end."

Which was the beginning of a process that led to the crowd being treated to the sight of a life-sized picture of Larry Bird floating across the court, suspended between their basketball coach and their favorite point guard.

When they got to the bench, they settled the poster in the well behind the first row of the bleachers.

"He can watch over us, keep me in line," said Rutherford. "Now get Bug."

"Thank the good Lord," said Bug.

Gray reported to Mr. Hoffman and checked into the game. He returned to the timeout huddle in time for the buzzer and in time to hear the end of Coach Rutherford's instructions.

"…and we're not going to let up until we're up 30."

The five players in the huddle—Dusty, Devon, Elmer, Bartholomew, and Gray—put their hands into the middle.

Elmer said, "1, 2-"

"Hold on."

Bartholomew Karp was staring at Gray, whose stomach had just done a swan dive into his hip bones. What he didn't need was Bartholomew Karp gumming up the works.

"Gray says it," said Bartholomew.

Elmer nudged Gray and with a smile, Gray shouted, "1, 2, 3!"

"Team together!"

Then the rest of the team dispersed onto the court, leaving Gray in front of Coach Rutherford, who was absently rubbing the blank dry-erase board with a towel.

"Coach."

Rutherford looked up.

"Thank you."

"No, California," said the coach. "Thank *you*."

Then Gray joined his teammates on the court. He found his man—the point guard from St. Anthony—waiting to get the ball. He crouched down so he was under the kid's elbow.

The point guard said, "We both know you're backing off as soon as I get this."

Gray smiled.

"Wanna bet?"

Beaudelaire's progress toward Coach Rutherford's goal of "not letting off the pedal 'til we're up 30" started the right way: with an 8-0 run that was facilitated by one of the negative side effects of running the Four Corners offense, which is that it can lead to a sense of complacency on the part of those who are using it. This was the case for the St. Anthony Saints, who'd become so accustomed to taking time off the clock that they'd forgotten how to score. The pressure applied by Gray and the rest of the Beaudelaire backcourt felt smothering, and in those first two minutes, the Saints turned the ball over more often than they took a shot.

This run had a side effect: a buzz in the gym that made it out to the commons area, where all those bored Beaudelaireians stopped talking about the weather, looked at each other, shrugged, and then marched through the tunnel to see what was going on.

By half-time, the gym was full again. But now, those people were like revelers at a party that's been resurrected late. They weren't going to let go of this new lease on the night. After the horn that marked the end of the first half, the crowd rose with a collective roar as Gray and his teammates jogged into the tunnel and, for a few seconds, Gray was able to soak up their enthusiasm. Until he saw Harris Bickle at the far end of the tunnel, high-fiving the Beaudelaire players as they slid past him.

"Crap," Gray said out of the corner of his mouth. Harris Bickle was going to have a much bigger audience.

Devon Rutherford looked over inside the darkened space of the tunnel.

"What's that?"

"Oh, just thinking about that pass I screwed up in the second quarter."

Devon clapped him on the back and, beaming, said, "C'mon, Taylor! We're up 18! Cool out!"

"Yeah, Taylor," said Harris Bickle, who had his right hand up. "Cool out!"

Gray slapped Bickle's hand and then waited for Devon Rutherford to catch up.

"Nice job," he said. "You gave Bickle a new catchphrase."

"Man could use a little soul in his life," said Devon.

They jogged to the door behind the Coke machine, which Gray pulled open for Devon and the rest of his teammates.

When they'd all passed him, thundering down the stairs and into the basement locker room, Gray heard Principal Patterson's voice from the gym.

Ladies and gentlemen, if I could please have your attention.

Like any experienced administrator, Patterson waited for the crowd's buzz to settle. A few people—those who'd already started toward the tunnel—turned back, their attention captured by the authority figure with the microphone.

This doubling-back served to form a clot in the tunnel—a clot Patra emerged from by ducking under the outstretched arm of a man wearing a tan parka.

Patra caught Gray's eye, and for a second, Gray wondered if maybe she was going to come over and they were going to have that kiss. But instead of walking across the commons to Gray, Patra walked along the wall, toward the vending machines in the corner.

She arrived just as her father's voice picked up again.

We've got a special guest for y'all tonight. A man who needs no introduction—although I'll give him one, anyway. If that's OK with you, Harris, er, Coach Bickle.

Gray imagined Bickle hamming it up for the crowd, his palms upturned in mock modesty.

He looked back at Patra.

She held up a set of keys.

She shook them and turned to the wall behind the vending machines.

Inside the gym, Mr. Patterson started back up.

Harris Bickle has been a math teacher here at Beaudelaire High School for eleven years. And, as some of you may know, he's coached a little football. He's got a career record of 74 and 28, good for the top winning percentage in school history.

This set off a round of applause in the gym—a round of applause that almost masked the shout Gray heard from the bottom of the stairs.

"Gray! We're about to start down here!"

He's also the coach of the reigning football state champions: your Beaudelaire High Bearcats! Ladies and gentlemen, Coach Harris Bickle!

This round of applause wasn't like normal rounds of applause: it didn't have the crescendo that those do. Instead, it started loud, and stayed loud, until it stopped all at once.

For half a second, Gray wondered if this was on purpose. Maybe it was a part of the presentation; maybe Harris Bickle had done something like the first entrance Gray had seen—his ill-fated trip to half court on his motorcycle.

But then he heard Bickle's voice, not on the microphone, but unamplified.

Stay calm, folks! Stay calm!

"Gray! Let's go!"

It was Bartholomew's voice, shouting from the bottom of the stairs. And Gray might have hustled down, except for something that was happening over by the vending machines.

Like the blonde woman from *Wheel of Fortune*, Patra presented her handiwork: the bank of switches that controlled the electricity to the gym, whose box she'd opened with the keys she'd shown Gray. And which were all now in the down position.

"So then Bickle looked over at Patterson and, well, you should have seen Patterson move! He looked like he'd been shot out of a gun!"

Mitzy Tundin wasn't shouting, but her words had the kind of intensity that usually only comes when words *are* shouted. It had been that kind of night at Tundin's.

Elmer licked his fork clean of the banana cream pie that was remaining on its tines.

"The man knows who pays the bills around there," he said.

"I guess," said Mitzy. "It was crazy. Anyway, it didn't take him long to figure it out—someone had turned off the electricity to the gym. You know how there's that box in the commons area?"

"Yeah," said Elmer, his eyes getting narrow. "I know the ones you mean."

Gray opened his mouth in an O of disbelief, touching his chest in mock outrage that Mitzy didn't notice.

She kept talking.

"The good thing was that it didn't take long to get it figured out. And then Mr. Bickle was like, 'I guess that's another sign of why we need to pass the bond issue.'"

Gray saw Patra wince. He also saw Elmer pick up on this wince. He kept his eyes on Mitzy and asked, "So how was the rest of his speech?"

"Oh, you know. Bad jokes. But he knows how to hold an audience. The thing is, though-"

Mitzy waved a hand between Gray and Elmer.

"-I think the show y'all put on in the second half made most people forget about the speech."

The second half to which Mitzy was referring had been consistent with the theme established at the end of the first. In the process, the Beaudelaire Bearcats had made a liar out of Coach Rutherford. They hadn't let up when they'd gotten up by 30. They'd kept their "foot on the gas" (as Rutherford put it) until the four-minute mark in the fourth quarter, at which point the score had been 79 – 37, guaranteeing a healthy win, but not yet guaranteeing everyone in the gym a free milkshake at Tundin's. That had only come with Elmer's last shot of the game—an unlikely three-pointer just before Coach Rutherford called timeout to get the bench players (led by Rocky Rhoads) into the game, once and for all.

Gray held out his hand for Elmer to high-five.

"Let's not get ahead of ourselves," said Elmer, slapping Gray's hand like he had to, not like he wanted to.

"Dude," said Elmer. "You scored 27 points!"

Elmer dropped his hand with a shrug.

"I'm a good athlete," he said.

From the stool next to Elmer, Patra rolled her eyes for Gray's benefit.

Gray swiveled to Mitzy.

"So, would you call it a success?"

Mitzy put her hands on her hips. The restaurant was still three-quarters full, even though it was 10:30.

"Yes, Gray. Yes, I would."

"So would I!"

Theresa Tundin was wiping her hands on her unmarked apron. When she was finished, she pulled open the drawbridge in the bar and ducked through it so she could get to Gray.

"I have to hand it to you, Gray Taylor," she said. "You've got some balls, boy."

Gray didn't know how to respond.

"Dude," said Elmer. "You got a hundred people here!"

Then Gray recognized the symmetry. It had been annoying when Elmer wasn't willing to take credit for what he'd accomplished. Now he was doing the same thing.

"I'm glad I could help," he said.

Theresa Tundin leaned in for a hug. "Now where's this mother of yours? I want to meet her."

"I think she might be at my grandparents' store," said Gray. "Speaking of, I should probably go find her."

"You know," said Theresa Tundin. "We should think about doing something together. Like a joint discount plan."

Yeah, Gray wanted to say. *Duh.*

But what he said instead was, "That's a good idea! I'll ask!"

"Mind if I tag along?" asked Patra.

"I think I could be convinced," said Gray.

"Yeah, get out of here, the lot of you," said Mitzy. She whacked Elmer with her washcloth.

"So soon?" said Elmer, rubbing his shoulder in fake concern.

"We're not used to this kind of traffic," said Mitzy. "It's going to take me a while to clean up. Plus, I've got someone I need to see."

The threesome followed Mitzy's eyeline to the back corner of Tundin's, where Barbarella Destino was staring into the parking lot, one hand absently pushing her straw in and out of the milkshake in front of her.

Gray thrust an arm into his coat.

"Any progress on that front?"

"Yeah, she says if no one asks her to the dance, she'll go with me as a protest. It's not exactly love, but it's a start."

Elmer held up a finger.

"Wait," he said.

There were three sets of blinks, while Gray, Patra, and Mitzy waited for the light to go on.

Then it did and Elmer said, "That makes so much sense."

———————————

Outside Tundin's, the night air had that crisp feeling that is only possible when all the moisture has been frozen out of the atmosphere.

Gray shivered and pulled his coat tight around his neck.

Patra grinned.

"Not quite like California?"

Gray shook his head. Now that they were alone, he felt some of the shyness that had always plagued him in Reseda.

"By the way, I figured it out," said Patra.

"You figured what out?"

"Your nickname. Mrs. Tundin just gave it to you."

"She did?"

Patra moved close enough to Gray that she could tap him on the chest.

"She said you have some balls, boy. That's you. Ball Boy. Because of basketball, obviously, but also because she's right."

Gray looked up at the stars, which were brighter than he'd ever seen in LA.

"Does it matter if I hate it?"

"Nope!"

Patra turned for the street, but Gray didn't move. In fact, he hadn't moved from the spot on the sidewalk since he'd come out of Tundin's. There was something comforting about the lights shining through the windows, especially on this frigid winter night.

In the nearest window, a family was finishing a late-night meal of burgers and fries (and milkshakes). Behind them, a group of middle-schoolers was tossing ketchup packets at each other. Mitzy wouldn't be pleased by the ketchup packets. But she'd be happy about the group.

"You know," said Gray. "Someone ought to get a picture of this, from out here. Put it on an ad or something."

Patra grabbed his coat and pulled him toward her.

"Seriously, Gray. You don't have to do everything. Let's go."

So Gray Taylor and Patra Patterson set off through Tundin's eight-car parking lot and across a snowbank that Patra hurdled in one bound. Then down First Street, past the abandoned grocery store, the post office, and the gray Masonic lodge that was used, most of the time, for wedding receptions. Then the library, an accountant's office, and then, finally, shining almost as brightly as Tundin's: Taylor's.

Inside, Gray could see his grandfather taking someone through the photo-printing options they offered. His grandmother was manning the cash register, ringing up a round of purchases, her glasses on her nose.

"Where's your mom?" said Patra, peering in through the windows.

"Maybe she went upstairs?"

Then Patra pointed.

"Nope!"

Gray followed her finger. Sure enough, his mother was coming from the back room, holding a set of hand-cut greeting cards. When Gray caught sight of her, she was talking to someone behind her—someone who was still in the back room, following her back into the store.

Gray's stomach lurched. He hadn't seen Peter Patterson since the game. What if the person behind his mother was Patra's dad? Would that ruin the night? If they were, like, flirting?

He put his arms around Patra, spinning her from the storefront.

Patra wormed her way out of the hug as her eyes went squinty. "Is that-"

Out of the back room came Trina Patterson.

"Oh thank god," said Gray.

"What?"

"I'm just, um, glad your mom and my mom are getting along. I mean, remember what I said—or *you* said—about her needing someone to hang out with?"

"You about done?"

"Sorry, just, you know, hyped up from the game!"

"Yeah you are, Ball Boy."

Patra winked and pushed through the door to Taylor's, ringing the tiny bell overhead.

Nicole Taylor forgot about the stack of greeting cards in her hands. She rushed to her son and smothered him in a hug.

"Oh my gosh, Gray! You're so good!"

"It *was* quite a game," said Dr. Trina Patterson, nodding in the way teachers will.

Nicole Taylor let go of Gray and stepped away.

"But what was the thing with the poster?"

"Kind of an inside joke," said Gray.

"Well, whatever it was, it worked like a charm. It was like there were two different teams out there. Before Poster and After Poster. BP and AP."

Trina Patterson put her hand on Nicole Taylor's arm.

"Oh, that's good!" she said.

"Speaking of posters-"

Peter Patterson emerged from the back room holding two pieces of poster board. He held up one, then the other.

"Which of these, do you think?"

Patra looked up from a tower racked with postcards.

"For what, Dad?"

"For more bond issue posters, of course. I figure we might as well shop local, right?"

Gray closed his eyes so hard that a reverse negative of the interior of Taylor's was projected on the back of his eyelids. How were these people not getting it?

Patra saw Gray's blue eyes squeeze shut. She also saw the air go out of him. And so she thought, for half a second, about saying something to her father. But she quickly cast that thought aside. Patra knew her dad wasn't going to listen to her. So Patra went to her next option: her mother, flashing her a glance that Trina Patterson intuited in a heartbeat because it couldn't have been more clear.

The answer wasn't a new school. It was to embrace what they had. But Trina Patterson knew her husband wasn't going to listen to her, either. Her position was too predictable, so consistent after all these years that it had become like the color scheme in a living room, no longer noticeable to the people closest to it.

So both Patterson women appealed to the one unknown quantity in the room—the one person capable of surprising their father, their husband—and asked a favor with their eyes. They both did this with some measure of regret. Patra, because she wanted to believe that her father had eyes only for her mother. Trina, because she knew he didn't.

It took Nicole Taylor another half a second to get it.

Which meant that by the time she spoke up, Gray had opened his eyes again.

He watched his mother's head tilt as something clicked into place like a key in a lock. Her eyes squinted, briefly, as she put it together: everything her son had done, and what she needed to do now, which was to give up on going back to Los Angeles and commit to the town that was her real home.

Her face got soft and her green eyes got bright. She put a hand on Peter Patterson's arm.

"You know," she said. "Maybe a new school isn't the answer."

Peter Patterson looked down at Nicole Taylor's hand and then up at her face, still not comprehending but enjoying the feeling of having her full radiance on him.

She went on.

"All these people came here tonight, on a Friday. Maybe the answer isn't in building something new. Maybe the answer is in, I don't know, embracing what you...I mean...*we* have."

When she was finished speaking, her words hung in the air like they were a bubble. They were a little too earnest, perhaps, and thus ripe for bursting. Nicole knew this, which was why she flashed Peter Patterson the tiniest of smiles, constructed to make her words less prone to falling meaninglessly to the ground.

Peter Patterson put a hand to his chin.

"Interesting," he said. "I'm going to have to think about this."

And here Gray was tempted to say something—to double down on what his mother was saying. But he didn't, because at that moment Patra grabbed his arm and said, "Show me the parking meters you were telling me about, Gray."

Gray looked at Patra like she'd just announced an alien invasion. But when she jerked her head toward the door, Gray realized he didn't care why she wanted him outside.

———————————

"Parking meters?"

This is what Gray said after Patra had pushed them through the door and back into the cold. Patra nodded at the inside of Taylor's, where Peter Patterson was still lost in contemplation.

"My dad is like most of you males. He needs to feel like he came up with an idea himself."

"You mean, like if a certain male came to a certain female for help on a master plan to save the school, and then that male started to think he did all of it himself?"

"Yeah," said Patra. "Something like that."

Gray took Patra's hand, which was soft and cool.

"Thank you," he said.

"You're welcome," she said, folding herself into Gray's chest.

And so it might seem that what happened then was that the hero of the basketball game and the prettiest girl in school (at least, according to that hero's way of thinking) would finally have their first kiss.

But that is not what happened.

Not yet, anyway.

What happened is that Gray and Patra turned to face the window. Where, with their fingers intertwined, they watched their parents talk themselves into a decision—a decision that had already made for them by the two people standing outside, together.

Thanks largely to the turnaround by Peter Patterson, Beaudelaire High School's bond issue failed by a wide margin. Harris Bickle wasn't happy about this and threatened to "take his football talents" elsewhere. But Peter Patterson, while prone to certain weaknesses when it came to having crushes on the mothers of certain of his students, knew too much about Harris Bickle to be intimidated by that threat. Specifically, that Harris Bickle didn't want his marriage, version 2.0, to go south, and that his former ex-wife did not want to leave Beaudelaire.

As for the Beaudelaire High School's basketball team: the game against St. Anthony proved to be the high point of the season, which didn't fit with the storybook progression that Desmond "Deacon" Rutherford wanted. But the thing about storybooks is that they usually don't have much applicability in real life. And anyway, Coach Rutherford's turnaround was a storybook ending in its own right. The team lost in the Sub-state semifinals but finished with 14 wins and 8 losses. His contract was renewed for the following year.

Nicole Taylor went to work at Taylor's and helped engineer a Shop Local campaign that was aided by her photo's presence on the billboards around town. That summer, she and Gray moved into a house on Third Street, within walking distance of Tundin's, Taylor's, and the school.

So, what about the big question?

That's right, the dance.

Did Gray take Patra to the King of Courts Dance?

He did, and he didn't.

But that is a story for another time.

This story is about Gray Taylor, a boy from California who came with his mother to a town in Kansas, never expecting to like that town as much as he did, and never expecting that he'd work so hard to save it.

But he did.

And he did.

THE END

19381080R00182